The Naked Angels

Anthony Grey is a former foreign correspondent in Eastern Europe and China. His enduring epic, *Saigon*, has won international critical acclaim in the Far East, Australasia, Europe and America. His first book, *Hostage in Peking*, was an autobiographical account of two years' solitary confinement in China during the Cultural Revolution.

Also by Anthony Grey

AUTOBIOGRAPHY
Hostage in Peking (1970)

SHORT STORIES
A Man Alone (1972)

NON FICTION
The Prime Minister Was a Spy (1983)

NOVELS
Some Put Their Trust in Chariots (1973)
The Bulgarian Exclusive (1976)
The Chinese Assassin (1979)
Saigon (1982)
Peking (1988)
The Bangkok Secret (1990)

Anthony Grey

The Naked Angels

PAN BOOKS
in association with
Macmillan London Limited

*Dedicated with much gratitude
to all my angels, past, present and future*

First published 1990 by Macmillan London Limited

This edition published 1991 by Pan Books Ltd,
Cavaye Place, London SW10 9PG
in association with Macmillan London Limited

1 3 5 7 9 8 6 4 2

© James Murray Literary Enterprises Ltd 1990

ISBN 0 330 31192 1

Printed in England by Clays Ltd, St Ives plc

This book is sold subject to the condition that it shall not,
by way of trade or otherwise, be lent, re-sold, hired out,
or otherwise circulated without the publisher's prior consent
in any form of binding or cover other than that in which
it is published and without a similar condition including this
condition being imposed on the subsequent purchaser

Author's Note

The Cold War ended with an unbelievable suddenness, didn't it? Almost overnight, against all the odds, the two most powerful men in the world, who had been sworn enemies for decades, became friends. It seemed too good to be true, at first. Now it's an everyday reality.

But what was it really that made them change their minds? Have you never wondered? Newspapers and television don't always get all the facts, you know. Who, for example, was the mysterious, shapely go-between, who entirely escaped the attention of the world's media? Was this shadowy, curvaceous figure really the most sexually alluring woman ever seen in human history? And where did her mysterious band of spectacularly beautiful helpers come from?

These are questions which, fortunately, I am now in a position to answer exclusively, for the first time, in the following pages.

To tame the Superpowers one after the other and avert World War III, this remarkable woman called on *superhuman* powers of seduction and feminine guile. She was prepared to do anything to succeed in her mission. But was she working for the CIA or the KGB – or just the human race? Did the world truly hover at the brink of total destruction while she worked patiently to defuse the explosively moribund libidos of two desperate, ageing males in Washington and Moscow?

More importantly, what was the crucial secret role played by the English gossip-column journalist who — fortunately for the future of mankind — had the erotic stamina of a whole herd of sex-crazed stallions? But for him, the final holocaust may still have consumed our entire planet, anyway.

These earth-shaking happenings, I'm afraid, are still too recent to be described with unvarnished truthfulness. This is why I am forced to present facts as fable. I have changed the locations, altered dates and even the names and positions of the world leaders concerned... There's no other way really... But this account of the mysterious deeds of those modern, naked-headed angels of mercy remains nevertheless, I submit, a momentous parable of our times.

Chapter One

A smooth, white, rounded knee jutted out tantalisingly from beneath the folds of smoked grey mink. She wore the coat as mink should be worn, with a brazen carelessness, with nothing underneath, the belt knotted loosely, the front falling open to reveal that jutting alabaster knee but no more. The glistening fur hung softly round her loins making a warm, shadowy tepee which denied entry to his eyes.

She stared with disdain into the space above his head. Her round, heavily lashed eyes were unblinkingly unaware of him. Despite his nearness and his fixed gaze she stood absolutely immobile, contemptuously unattainable behind the glass.

His hand flew involuntarily to the window and pressed itself there, leaving a warm imprint that faded only slowly in the cold air. He rubbed it off quickly, looked nervously up and down the deserted street, then hurried on.

She continued to stare at the empty space above where his head had been. To her he had never existed.

But as he walked on he continued to see others like her from the corner of his eye. He was never sure whether it was Fifth Avenue, Bond Street or the Champs Élysées. But they were always there, always haughty, always totally impregnable.

The bright lights poured tantalisingly through the glass onto the pavement in front of him but he strode on looking determinedly ahead, resisting. Then he saw them. A group of three with no hair. They caught the very corner of his eye because of their naked heads. He'd almost got past.

He stopped and gazed helplessly up at them, a little whimpering, two-tone groan gurgling in his throat. Beautiful but bald! Two of them had their backs to him, frozen in a moment of swinging on slender, pivotal ankles to hold their arms in graceful supplication to the third. The dark brown fur of their coats brushed the back of bare, floodlit legs.

But the third, adorned in mink of snowy white, was ignoring their fealty. She looked boldly and unwaveringly down at *him*. Round blue eyes, dark curling lashes, arched brows, pouting, parted lips – and no hair! His lower lip fluttered wetly as he stared up into her blue gaze. The lip began to tremble uncontrollably as his eyes shifted over the smooth roundness of her bald head.

Now he couldn't help himself!

The thin, high-pitched cry that escaped his lips was only briefly audible before the clamour of breaking glass rang in the empty street. Blood appeared on his face and hands as he went through.

He stumbled forward in a snowstorm of glass fragments and fell upon the three of them, his arms flung wide. They collapsed in a brittle, fractured heap. Blood from his face and hands shone among the broken glass.

But *she* was whole in her white fur! He had clasped *her* to him as they fell together.

The glass crunched beneath them as they rolled in frenzy. His moans were lower, more musical, now. At first he clutched her in the snug smoothness of her fur. Then he stopped and thrust his hands inside the belted coat, first relishing the cool smoothness of her back. He clutched briefly at the plaster of her small, pointed, dummy breasts. Then with the cry of a drowning man he dived his hands down over the burgeoning curve of her dummy belly to clasp in relief at the cool, featureless, undemanding and sexless arch.

His taut body relaxed suddenly with a contented sigh. Glass stopped splintering as his rolling ceased. After a moment his left hand came free and climbed to caress the shining dome of her head. Her wide blue eyes, with their dark lashes still curling saucily, stared sightlessly up over his shoulder into the blinding glare of the lights.

He lay still, clutching the dummy to him.

When he opened his eyes briefly and saw the crowd of people gathered outside the window of the fur shop, he screamed abruptly and woke himself up.

What, in God's name, would people say if they knew the President of the United States had dreams like that? And here in Berlin, too, on an official visit. Suppose his hosts had bugged the bedroom, suppose he had talked in his sleep, giving a running commentary of his dream? He shuddered, got out of bed, sweating slightly, and went to the shower to get ready for the day's ceremonies.

Once he was dressed in a neat, single-breasted thoroughly American business suit, the President tiptoed to the door of the bedroom suite to see if any of his aides were waiting outside within earshot. When he was satisfied he was not overheard he placed an urgent international call to Berkshire, England. As he waited for a response he glanced furtively over his shoulder and brushed a suggestion of perspiration from his forehead.

A white telephone rang on the leather-topped antique desk in the empty study of the Director of the Uncommon Cold Research Station in Berkshire, England. Engraved notepaper in neatly arranged piles on the desk top proclaimed its occupant as Dr Dagmar Froggerty, MD PhD, President of the American Institute of Psychiatric Sexology, Founding Fellow of the American Society of Medical Sexiatric Hypnosis, and Nobel Peace Prize winner for Research into Chronically Contagious Diseases.

In his West Berlin bedroom the President glanced nervously at his watch. Time was running short. If he didn't answer in thirty seconds ...

The door of the study in Berkshire burst open abruptly

and a badly overweight man with a large bald head shot into the room with a rapidity surprising for an individual of his bulk. He grabbed the telephone in a fist like a bunch of fat white bananas.

As he heard the answering click an expression of relief passed over the President's face. 'Dr Froggerty?' His voice was conspiratorially low. 'It's the President. I've had one of those damned dreams again.'

'I'm sorry to hear that, Mr President.' The doctor's deep American voice had an echoing, resonant quality even across a continent's telephone wires.

'What can I do, for God's sake?' asked the President desperately.

'Well, Mr President, although I have resigned as your personal psychiatric and sexiatric adviser, of course I still share your concern—'

'Look, cut that out, Dagmar,' said the President petulantly. 'You resigned in a silly huff, but let's not go over that again. I gotta kick this dream. A man in my position needs to keep a clear head and steely nerves for important decisions. It's getting worse. I can't think of anything else now.'

'I've told you, Mr President,' said the resonant voice, 'yours is a problem confronting many men of your age. The diminution of the ... ahem ... natural physical powers in a man ... ahem ... in the same way as it plays havoc after middle age with the metabolism and mental stability of the female—'

'Yeah, yeah, cut all that couchside-manner stuff, Dagmar,' said the President testily. 'I'm desperate now, that's why I'm calling you ...'

The President could not see the large, oyster-shaped eyes of the scientist narrowing into an expression of vindictive hostility. And it did not show in the voice coming down the line from Berkshire.

'Relax, Mr President. I can tell you that this very day I'm expecting to demonstrate some startling new therapeutic developments in the field of psychiatric sexology that might be a particular help to you and people like you. I can't say more now.'

'Really? You really mean that?' The President almost shouted and a grin of eager, boyish delight lit up his face. 'That's great news.'

'I only wish I could be in Berlin to tell you about it personally, Mr President,' said Froggerty, 'but, of course, my work now necessarily keeps me here.'

'Of course,' said the President. 'But you've cheered me up a lot. Thanks a million. Bye, Dagmar.'

Dr Dagmar Froggerty replaced the telephone and picked up a British Excelsior Airlines ticket from the desk. He flicked it open, checked the time of his flight to West Berlin, then looked at his watch. Hurriedly he pulled open a drawer and drew out a large plastic carton of cream cheese. He scooped out several dollops of the moist fatty food with his fingers and stuffed them quickly in his mouth. As he ate he mentally congratulated himself once more on having had the good sense to undergo the operation for removal of twelve feet of his small intestine to speed up the digestive process. He licked his fingers, put away the half-emptied carton and wiped his greasy lips and finger-tips with an enormous handkerchief. He looked round, picked up his briefcase, put his air ticket in his pocket and quickly left the room.

He hurried down into the research station, passing through a large echoing chamber where white-gowned, hygienically masked researchers of both sexes bent over microscopes set up on benches between cavernous draught-simulator tunnels, walk-in refrigerators and man-sized dehydrating drums with glass fronts that looked like spin-driers from some mammoth launderette. Shivering, sneezing volunteers in various stages of undress stumbled in and out of the tunnels and refrigeration vaults with thermometers sticking out of their mouths.

Froggerty nodded and waved to several of his assistants as he waddled fast through the plant. But he reserved his friendliest greetings for the white-aproned female staff.

Without exception all of them were distinguished by one striking characteristic – their bald heads gleamed dully in the overhead neon strip-lighting, having been shaved clean of the crowning female glory of their hair.

The President's five-ton Ford Lincoln Continental saloon with its quarter-inch-thick armour plating, bullet-proof tyres and windscreen, hydraulic bubble roof, fold-down running boards for the Secret Service and a trunk full of electronic gadgetry rushed at high speed through the gates of Schloss Belle Vue at precisely nine-fifteen with a phalanx of shiny official cars in close pursuit heading for the Berlin Wall. The anonymous men responsible for the President's safety had at last decided to take a leaf out of Stalin's security notebook. He had always made it his habit to emerge through the hastily opened gates of the Kremlin in a column of six cars going at ninety miles per hour. Would-be assassins, even if the speed didn't defeat them, never knew which car he was in. And Stalin died in his bed.

In the flying wedge of vehicles heading through the Tiergarten behind the President's half-a-million-dollar limousine, rode many important men whose entire lives were devoted to remaining within a few feet of the President of the United States with certain kinds of equipment. A Communications Man carried a red telephone which in seconds could connect his chief with the hot lines of any one of fifteen commanders of fifteen different Armed Forces throughout the world; a Heart Man carried an electric portable defibrillator in case the presidential heart suffered an attack; a Blood Man carried a supply of Group A positive; a Refreshments Man carried bottles of Mountain Vale spring water untouched by pollution and a Pentagon brigadier-general carried a black business case with the destiny of the world inside.

They and many others rode stolidly in the fast-moving cars behind their President – who came close to needing the defibrillator when he caught sight of a bald-headed woman staring at him among the crowds lining the Strasse des 17 Juni. He hoisted the fixed smile hurriedly back into position and tried to forget the dream and the reasons why he kept dreaming it almost every night at the age of fifty-nine.

A swift look over the Wall into the bizarre front garden of Communism was scheduled at Potsdamer Platz – part of a quick visit to Europe to reaffirm support for NATO and publicly relate to the Common Market. He'd worked out the plan himself with his special foreign policy adviser: pop into West Berlin, low posture, faint symbolic pat on the back for the West Berliners, try not to offend the Russians. No 'Ich bin ein Berliner' speech, just shake some official German hands, peek over the Wall from a viewing stand, and on to Brussels.

The cars drew up in the grey-brown cobbled area by the Wall. Red and white barriers held back the applauding, flag-waving crowd a hundred yards away.

As he mounted the steps to the wooden platform overlooking the Wall, the President glanced nervously at the press stand where about two hundred newsmen and photographers huddled together watching the scene intently. Irrationally he felt they suspected what sort of dream he'd had in the night and he could not meet their gaze. From their stand the journalists could already see across the bleak concrete barrier into the East. The presidential carriers of telephones, black bags and plasma grouped around the foot of the viewing stand. The crowd hushed as the eyes of the Most Powerful Man in the World fell upon alien soil.

Only one of the two hundred journalists on the nearby press tribune, a fair-haired Englishman with spectacles, didn't seem surprised when the floor of the stand gave way and the President plunged through it and out of sight.

The man with the defibrillator was among the first to rush forward. Then total chaos and confusion descended as rapidly as had the President.

'Aaieiiigh!' said the President noisily as he plunged downward into total darkness. He bounced to rest on one of those sorbo beds employed to provide happy landings for pole-vault competitors in the Olympic Games. As he rebounded into a sitting position, an earnest, fresh-faced, crew-cut young man switched on a powerful flashlight, stepped towards him and caught him by the arm. He hauled him quickly to his feet and to one side, away from the faint shaft of light that fell from above as the President had done. He reached quickly upwards and drew a heavy lead trapdoor into place on well-oiled runners. Then he thrust home four bolts. This cut off both the faint light and the tumult of shouting and running above.

'Badezimmer, Mr President, sir. Harvey Badezimmer, Secret Service Agent 1978421, civil service, grade four.' The young man pushed a plastic-covered card bearing his photograph and the details he'd just proclaimed under the President's nose. 'An attempt on your life has been uncovered, sir,' he went on urgently, 'and we're into Evasive Action, Stage One. Will you follow me, please, sir, without argument. It's vital to the preservation of your person, sir.'

The shocked President began to breathe more easily after the shaking of the sudden tumble. It was a great relief to know he was in the hands of one of the 880 special agents employed solely to preserve his person.

'Where are we going, Badezimmer?' he asked in a shrill voice. The President could still hear the faint sounds of tumult and confusion coming from above the leaden door.

'No time to explain, Mr President, sir,' said Badezimmer quickly. 'Please just follow our instructions.'

The President became aware of other men moving in the shadow of the tunnel just beyond the beam of Badezimmer's flashlight. One of them stepped forward on a silent signal from Badezimmer and held a battered hat and cheap nylon raincoat towards the President.

'Secret Service Agent 1978422 Patrick Kafferty, Mr President. Evasive Action, Stage Two. Put on this apparel please, sir.'

When he had helped the President into the raincoat, Kafferty produced a pair of scuffed shoes – 'Just your size, Mr President, don't worry' – and a worn, imitation-leather brief-case with a broken brass lock and a carrying handle. 'Your passport to safety, Mr President,' he said with a smile, as he took the Chief Executive's highly polished shoes and flung them into the darkness.

The President wondered vaguely for a moment at the slight foreign throatiness that marred Kafferty's Irish-American accent. But he had no time to ponder on this. They urged him into the tunnel and as they ran he noticed that Badezimmer, Kafferty and the third man were struggling into cheap macs and similar trilby hats. They also carried worn brief-cases similar to his own.

'How much further, Badezimmer?' the President gasped irritably as he stumbled along in the darkness of the tunnel.

With a start he realised that for the first time in six years he had been separated from the red telephone, the black bag, the defibrillator, the spring water untouched by pollution, his protocol aides, his speech-writer, his national security adviser, the chief of his White House staff, his press secretary.

He suddenly felt very lonely.

The running group rounded a corner in the tunnel and saw light at the end. There was a loud roar, a clatter and a swooshing sound.

'Where are we coming—' the President started to ask again, his chest heaving from the unfamiliar running. He didn't run much in the White House.

Badezimmer stopped, ushered the President past him, then reached upwards to pull down another heavy lead door sealing off the tunnel along which they had come. Their side of it was painted yellow and bore a legend in German which said, 'U-Bahn N.9 Arbeitsmittel. Kein Eintritt.'

'It will be better if we say nothing at all from here on in, Mr President,' said Badezimmer, as he urged the President forward again. 'We're coming to a public place.'

A few steps more and they were standing outside a men's lavatory. The President staggered, out of breath, and stumbled into a clump of brushes and cleaning pails stored in an alcove. Badezimmer extracted him deftly and pushed all three of them quickly through a swing door. Inside, he motioned his two companions and the President towards the urinals.

'Evasive Action, Stage Three. Just follow suit, please, Mr President,' Badezimmer hissed out of the corner of his mouth. All four men postured towards the wall, still fighting to control their heavy breathing after the run.

The three Secret Service men eventually succeeded, as far as the President could see, in making their presence at the urinals appear convincing. But the President himself, his face flushing pink, stood inactive among them. His nerves always got the better of him in this particular situation. He had to be alone. Were the Secret Service men hiding grins at his expense? He glanced sideways but couldn't tell.

Badezimmer finally nodded his head. His companions shook themselves, zippd up and turned round. They grouped themselves close around the President and walked out onto the platform of a U-Bahn station.

The platform was almost empty. The whoosh, rattle and roar they had heard coming up the tunnel had obviously been a departing train. Badezimmer, using only motions of his head, directed his men to cluster even closer round the President. They edged towards the lip of the platform and stood staring out over the track at the blank, dirty-cream wall.

Funny that there were no advertisements in capitalist West Berlin stations, the President thought – and would have said so to Badezimmer if the Secret Service man had not warned him into silence with a meaningful narrowing of his eyes. Other passengers were coming down onto the platform now.

The President glanced sideways. Badezimmer was impassive on his right, Kafferty impassive on his left. Both were unnaturally close, both staring fixedly ahead. The third man was just visible next to Kafferty.

The President felt suddenly unreal. He felt as if he were one of those four giant, inanimate presidential rock-heads carved out of the mountainside in South Dakota. To his left and right, immobile granite brows and jowls hemmed him in. Kafferty, Badezimmer and the third man did not really resemble Lincoln, Washington or Roosevelt but their features seemed set in an unnatural cast. He looked down and saw they all wore the same scuffed, grey, imitation-leather shoes. Their thin nylon raincoats were identical; their styleless grey trilbies gave them a puppet-like similarity. They all held their worn imitation leather brief-case by the handle in their right hand.

A little man in a brown nylon raincoat, grey trilby and carrying an imitation leather brief-case exactly like theirs sidled up and addressed the President.

'Fährt der nächste Zug nach Karlshorst?' he asked in a nasal whine.

The President looked bewildered. He turned beseechingly to Badezimmer.

'A giraffe has sneezed in his brain,' Badezimmer cut in smoothly in surprisingly good German. He rolled his eyes at the little man and nodded with the back of his head towards the President in a manner that indicated he was more than marginally insane. The little man went away nodding understandingly.

At that moment the yellow underground train rumbled into the station and Badezimmer ushered his group in, still cautioning silence with what the President thought was an undue flickering and narrowing of his eyes. The Secret Service knew best in these situations, the President reminded himself, you mustn't forget that. As the train slid out he saw from a sign on the wall that they had been waiting in Thälman Platz.

The South Dakota rock formation reassembled itself on a seat along one side of the carriage. In this rigid position the President watched several stations flick by – Stadtmitte, Spittelmarkt, Märkische Museum. Then they alighted and, still unspeaking, went up the steps and out into Alexanderplatz.

The President's mouth fell open.

Hurrying all around him in Alexanderplatz were men in uniform – the same uniform that he and the Secret

Service men wore! Styleless trilby hats, thin nylon raincoats, grey, pointed, imitation-leather shoes and brown leather-substitute brief-cases with tarnished brass locks.

The President promptly became convinced he was dreaming again and waited uneasily for the bald women to appear. But nobody looked at him, nobody stared, nobody cheered, nobody offered their hand. The Secret Service cover was obviously perfect. Even in a dream, it seemed, they had made him anonymous.

Badezimmer stepped up to a dun-coloured taxi standing at a kerbside rank. A black-and-white chequered strip was painted along both sides of the car under its windows. The President didn't know it then but it was a Volga automobile built on a Moscow production line.

Badezimmer winked at the driver without the President seeing him, then said in a voice loud enough for the President to hear, '1600 Pennsylvania Avenue, please.'

He grinned at the President as he held the rear door open for him and the President grinned back at him, sharing the joke of giving the taxi-driver the official postal address of the White House as a password in Berlin.

On the small back seat the four men resumed their rock-formation even more closely as the Volga carried them off eastwards through the drab streets of East Berlin towards the outskirts.

The shoppers on Karl-Marx-Allee didn't give a second glance to the Volga taxi moving at an unremarkable speed through the light traffic. The President, though puzzled and uneasy, remained trustingly unaware of his true plight. He settled himself between what he thought were his Secret Service agents in the back of the Russian-built car and waited to be delivered safely to his entourage.

He didn't know then it was all over, for ever.

A three-year-old East Berlin child played on the pavement with a wooden duck unaware that the car stopped beside him at the traffic lights contained the kidnapped President of the United States, history's greatest hostage. A green-uniformed People's Policeman on point duty waved the Volga through courteously, wishing that all comrades drove with such care and consideration.

On the western side of the wall at Potsdamer Platz a seething commotion of people ran hither and thither like agitated ants after boiling water has been poured on their citadel. They lacked direction and all sense of purpose. One particularly dejected man sat apart on the kerb, his head in his hands, taking no part in the turmoil. Beside him, a portable defibrillator machine lay unnoticed in the gutter. He was inconsolable and his shoulders were hunched in the resigned attitude of a man who no longer had any heart for his job.

Chapter Two

A dome of silence descended over the hurriedly convened meeting of the Special Actions Group of the National Security Council for the Repatriation of the American President. Six pale, strained faces looked at each other at close range round a cramped, circular table deep within the bowels of the White House. From outside the sound-proof glass their mouths were immediately seen to start opening and closing like those of goldfish in a bowl. Some mouths made slow, regular, pouting shapes, others snapped open and shut more quickly, forming circles of varying and erratic circumference. All the men were puffy-eyed, having been dragged from their beds at four o'clock in the morning. At least half wore their suits with enough unscheduled lumps to excite a justifiable suspicion among their colleagues that they had their pyjamas underneath. Some of them turned, even as they fish-pouted, to stare at a younger man who stood beside the table with cheeks bulging from the effort of blowing into a thin, aluminium tube.

Inside the dome the Vice-President could be heard speaking: 'Genitalmen,' he intoned, his voice weighted with what he thought was appropriately sonorous emotion, 'I declare this first convening of the Special Actions Group of the National Security Council for the Repatriation of the American President to be in session . . .'

The men around the table winced inwardly at his

fractured pronunciation of the world 'gentlemen'. Nobody knew whether the word invariably emerged from his lips as it did because of a mysterious impediment of speech or some more deeply rooted impediment in his physical and psychological make-up. His pronunciation, however, had never been known to vary and his colleagues had long ago given up the unequal struggle to understand why.

'We're all under enormous strain, genitalmen, so let's try to keep our heads. We're not here to indulge in petty squabbles and if the Director of the CIA considers it necessary to have one of his men standing by blowing on a silent dog-whistle to ensure total security, I think in this hour of unprecedented crisis for our nation, we should respect that...'

'Not a silent dog-whistle. Just *like* a silent dog-whistle, I said.' Gerrard K. Conroy, Director of the Central Intelligence Agency, scowled his correction gracelessly. 'Something I dreamed up myself to provide final scrambling interference inside technologically unimpeachable maximum security sound-proofing such as this. Remember the Ray Bradbury story where one spaceman kills another with a rusty stiletto three thousand years old? Remember that. That's what I tell my technical men.' He turned proudly to his puffing agent. 'This whistle kills all known bugs.'

Conroy's eyes, permanently narrowed by years of mistrust and suspicion, dilated to emphasise his final words. He looked round pop-eyed for a moment until all other eyes were cast down. 'Yeah, sure kills all known bugs,' he said again quietly and lapsed into a brooding silence.

The florid face of the Vice-President, that had grown more florid as he drank his way through the empty years as powerless deputy to the Most Powerful Man in the World, twitched nervously as he remembered he was close to having a meaningful role in life at last. He cleared his throat impressively. 'We're here, genitalmen, to review the range of our response in all possible contingencies. Let's get all our ducks in a row on this – but quick! I call on the Secretary of Defense to report on the deployment of the Armed Forces in the hours since the disappearance of the President.'

The Defense Secretary, a thin, ascetic man with two first names, Stanley George, stood up. He reported that Sherman tanks were deployed for a distance of three miles along the Berlin Wall in the American Sector with their cannons pointing eastwards. Three parachute groups at bases in West Germany had been brought to full alert in the presence of invited American newspapermen and television crews reporting to the world by satellite. The nation's two largest aircraft carriers from the Sixth Fleet were at the moment steaming up the Skagerrak to take up station in the Baltic off the East German coast. Forty-eight helicopters were sweeping the airspace directly above the Wall and would continue to do so around the clock. Three missions of B-1 strategic bombers were flying to fail-safe limits at twenty-minute intervals. Land-based defensive and offensive missile-launching sites at home and abroad had been locked into action patterns and the entire nuclear submarine fleet, including those vessels armed with the latest long-range Trident missiles, had been raised to 'blue' pre-strike readiness.

Having reported this Stanley George sat down. He began to bite his fingernails when he thought nobody was any longer watching him.

'Thank you, Stan,' said the Vice-President solemnly. He glanced round briefly at the inflated cheeks, reddening neck and bulging eyes of the CIA agent standing beside him blowing on the instrument like a silent dog-whistle. He listened for a moment to see if he could hear its high-pitched note, failed and returned his attention to the meeting.

'Gordon, would you tell us what your department has turned up.'

Gordon Garstenmeyer, stocky, corpulent chief of the 880 men of the Secret Service charged with protecting the President's person, rose to his feet.

The obvious embarrassment of the head of a bodyguard of nearly a thousand men, who had lost without trace the body they were supposed to be guarding, was suffocating to the other five men in the sound-proof glass dome. Embarrassed in their turn at his embarrassment they stared out through the glass at the khaki uniforms of the four army colonels on guard outside with pistols in their belts.

'At 0914 hours local Berlin time today two of my operatives Smith and Clancy were one step behind the President of the United States as he walked to the viewing stand overlooking the Wall and the Eastern Sector of Berlin at Potsdamer Platz.' Garstenmeyer was reading from elaborate, typed notes. There were those among the members of the meeting who cursed the pedantic nature of the Secret Service chief, while others simply called up their reserves of patience.

'They waited at the foot of the viewing stand as the President mounted the steps to observe the view across the Wall,' Garstenmeyer continued doggedly. 'At 0915 precisely, local time, they noticed the President absent himself from their view through the floor of the stand. They drew their weapons, rushed the steps and found a trapdoor had been cut in the floor of the platform. But it had been jammed closed from below and it defied the assault of their feet and the butts of their pistols.'

Garstenmeyer paused and wiped his brow with a white handkerchief. Then he continued, his embarrassed eyes staring fixedly at his brief.

'Several minutes elapsed before axes were brought and the trapdoor was destroyed. When Smith and Clancy dropped through into the interior of the stand they found the trapdoor had been wedged closed with an iron scaffolding pole. This pole was embedded in a second, leaden trapdoor which had been drawn into place over the entrance to an underground tunnel. The two operatives concluded that the President had been abducted through the leaden trapdoor into an underground passage.'

Conroy let out an exaggerated gasp of admiration for the quick-thinking astuteness of the two Secret Service agents.

'The leaden door would not yield to their efforts without tools,' Garstenmeyer continued, ignoring Conroy with an effort, 'and a considerable space of time elapsed before the heavy viewing-stand could be removed and laser-beam equipment obtained to cut through the leaden door.'

'What did you find in the tunnel?' the Vice-President put in impatiently.

'I'm just coming to that, Mr Vice-President,' said Garstenmeyer stolidly. 'When the leaden door was finally penetrated, Smith and Clancy led seven other operatives into the tunnel with weapons drawn—'

'How long was this after the President disappeared unexpectedly from your view?' interrupted Conroy, on the CIA's behalf.

Garstenmeyer made a great show of looking further on in his notes, although the fact was probably burned deeply into his memory for the rest of his life. He tried to bring out the answer casually like an announcer with a time check on an early morning radio show. 'Approximately twenty-seven minutes—'

His entire audience gasped, including the Secretary of State, who had not been known to make a noise of any kind at a major meeting for two and a half years.

'But as I was saying,' continued Garstenmeyer, clinging desperately to his dubious initiative, 'my operatives were able to penetrate some twenty yards along a well-constructed, lined and adequately propped tunnel—'

'Leading in which direction?' interrupted Conroy, laconically.

'Eastward,' replied Garstenmeyer without looking up.

'Yeah, I kind of expected that,' said Conroy, softly.

'But after twenty yards they were halted by the presence of armed East German and Russian troops standing behind a sign saying in German, "You are now entering Berlin, capital of the German Democratic Republic". After a moment's hesitation my operatives decided not to open fire but stood their ground with weapons drawn while they sent up to ground level for political advice.'

Garstenmeyer hesitated, then went on with heavy emphasis, implying that what followed had prevented his men from recouping the situation. 'The political decision was that no further pursuit was to be allowed at this time in view of the danger to world peace.'

'Were no other precautions taken to safeguard the person of the President?' asked Stanley George diffidently.

Tears of frustration welled in Garstenmeyer's eyes. 'We had twenty operatives on surrounding rooftops and eight more in helicopters a hundred and fifty feet above the scene,' said Garstenmeyer defiantly.

'What did they report, if anything?' asked Conroy.

Garstenmeyer shuffled his papers and drew out the relevant one. 'That the President absented himself from their view at precisely 0915,' blurted Garstenmeyer. He stared out of the glass dome over their heads.

'No additional surveillance underground, huh?' asked the burly Chairman of the Joint Chiefs of Staff.

'None, sir,' replied Garstenmeyer regaining his composure. 'We don't work underground. We're security men, not miners.'

'What is the present situation in the tunnel?' asked the Vice-President.

'Soldiers of the United States Armed Forces have taken up guard in the tunnel five feet from the German and Russian troops. A sign in English saying "You Are Now Entering the American Sector" has been erected.'

Garstenmeyer sat down. Then he jumped up again immediately to say, 'All my operatives except two liaison men have now been withdrawn from the area and are being held in reserve pending the return of the President.'

Then he sat down again.

'Had your operatives not inspected the stand and the area beneath it before the President arrived?' asked the Secretary for Defense.

Garstenmeyer, who had hoped they wouldn't ask that, stood up again. 'The stand was inspected last night along with the surface of the road. Both were found to be in a "nominal" state. At present we are assuming the stand was tampered with during the hours of darkness. The cobblestones of the road concealing the leaden trapdoor were apparently removed from below once the stand was in place.'

'So no provision had been made to deal with attacks on the President from below ground-level?' asked Conroy, a triumphant grin illuminating his heavy features.

Garstenmeyer drew himself up to his full height – five feet four inches. 'No specific provision had been made against the ground opening and swallowing up the President, no, sir,' he replied belligerently.

The two men stared balefully at each other. Just at the moment when the tension between them appeared to have reached lapel-grabbing level, the CIA man operating the silent dog-whistle to kill all known bugs pitched forward across the table between them in a dead faint from all the blowing.

Chapter Three

'Genitalmen, I'm sure you're all waiting to hear what we've had on the hot line from the Kremlin.' The Vice-President was moving the meeting smoothly on with what he was sure was a display of good chairmanship after the two minutes' adjournment. The dome had been raised and the unconscious agent had been carried out and replaced by a fresh man. The Vice-President had waited properly until the dome sighed hydraulically back into its foundation grooves before resuming.

Now he was trying hard not to show how much he was enjoying his new-found authority. 'I'm sure, genitalmen, that like me you wish to know why this dastardly and blatant act of aggression against the President has been committed by the Communist powers. I am sure that, like me, you are waiting apprehensively to hear what they are demanding in this, the most outrageous act of blackmail that world history has ever seen. In short, what terms they are demanding for the safe return of our greatly respected Chief Executive.'

The Vice-President noticed the meeting was becoming restive. With a start he realised he had launched unconsciously into the remarks he had prepared mentally for the television address he was due to make to the nation from the White House following the meeting.

In the short silence that this reflection caused, Conroy's voice was heard. It was little more than a murmur, as though he were talking to himself, thinking out loud. 'Nobody can hostage the President of the United States with impunity,' he mumbled quietly.

The Vice-President opened his mouth to point out to Conroy that the word 'hostage' could not be used as a verb. But he realised quickly that a man of his executive stature ignored such things. What he himself had to say was paramount. He must remember that.

'I regret to report,' the Vice-President continued, glancing at his watch, 'that nearly two hours after my first message to Moscow on the hot-line teleprinter, we have yet to receive any meaningful message from the Soviet leaders.'

He looked in turn at each of the five faces grouped around the table, giving each man the frank, serious glance he fancied was appropriate to a born leader during great crisis. Moisture was beginning to gather on the inside of the glass dome just above their heads. Rivulets of sweat ran down the face of the silent CIA piper.

The Vice-President picked up a sheet of paper torn from a teleprinter and read from it. 'My message to Moscow was as follows: "The United States Government demands the immediate return of the President of the United States from territory under your control and instant confirmation that he is unharmed and in sound health. This government wishes to register a protest of the utmost and most extreme seriousness and reminds your government that the Free World will not submit to blackmail of any kind even though the fragile membranes of world peace be put at risk by your rapaciousness." '

'Exactly what replies have we received, Mr Vice-President?' asked Conroy.

The Vice-President picked up a small sheaf of teleprinter flimsies and leafed through them one by one, reading them aloud. 'One: We are carrying out monthly overhaul of our teleprinter, please repeat your message. Two: We are continuing to check our equipment, kindly repeat your message. Three: Stand by for test signal – the quick red fox jumps over the lazy imperialist hyena. Four: Equipment now confirmed in order; please repeat any traffic during the last three hours.' The Vice-President glanced up. 'Since that time no message has been received. That is if you exclude the message that came in half an hour ago.' He paused then went on sheepishly, 'A Happy Christmas to all the hot-line operators and their families in Washington from all the hot-line operators and their families in Moscow.'

'What, in God's name, does that mean?' exploded the Chairman of the Joint Chiefs of Staff. 'Is that some kind of code?'

'No, I guess not,' said the Vice-President. 'The operators have finally owned up that since they have to man this machine twenty-four hours a day all year round and it's almost never used, they do break the monotony of running tests by inserting tapes wishing each other seasonal compliments on occasions like Christmas and May First. This tape, the operators think, was inserted erroneously in Moscow.'

In the aghast silence Conroy was again heard murmuring menacingly to himself that nobody could hostage the President of the United States with impunity and it reminded the Vice-President that the meeting had not yet heard the CIA director's report. 'Genitalmen, I'm sure we're all interested to hear from Mr Conroy? So, please give him your full attention.'

Conroy rose warily to his feet. He never delivered a report from a sitting position. He liked to look down on people. He was a man of large proportions and, from the back, the shape of his shoulders left the impression that he wore quarter-back shoulder pads inside his jacket.

'All agents in the East and West Sectors of Berlin,' he said gruffly, 'have been switched to full-beam alert. But as of this moment I am not in a position to report the location of the President.'

Garstenmeyer saw his chance and leapt at the rival who had buffeted him mercilessly during his own threadbare report. 'You don't know, Conroy. So why not just say you don't know, fellah?'

Conroy glowered. But instead of replying he pushed a

map of Berlin into the middle of the table. 'I do have some information on the tunnel through which the President was abducted,' he said smugly. 'It is one of a network of several tunnels under the Wall, here, here and here.' He pointed with a spatulate finger. 'These tunnels exist with the knowledge of our own and the enemy's intelligence services. We both use them to insert and recover agents in both directions, under a gentleman's agreement. The tunnel is known to lead ultimately to a men's room on the subway station at Thälman Platz.'

Little gasps of vicarious humiliation at the President's probable destination escaped from his listeners.

'If you knew about these tunnels, Conroy, why didn't you tell me?' demanded Garstenmeyer angrily. He looked round expectantly to see if the others agreed he'd scored.

'Because you didn't ask,' said Conroy, continuing as if the interruption hadn't happened. 'From that railway station in those twenty-seven blank minutes, the President could have been removed to almost anywhere in East Berlin or its environs.' Conroy paused significantly. 'I have nothing further to state until fresh reports arrive.' He covered the lameness of his final statement with an intimidating glare at his colleagues. Then he hunched his shoulders twice in the reflex action of a punch-drunk prize-fighter, morosely withdrew his head and neck into them like a turtle and sat down.

'Genitalmen, let's be calm.'

The Vice-President's face puckered as he prepared in his mind a crisp resolution that would bring the meeting to a quick conclusion. But his ambitions were marred by a little pearl of spit that flew from his excitedly wet lips. To his horror, it landed on the front of the bemedalled tunic of the Chairman of the Joint Chiefs of Staff and shimmered there for all to see. 'Genitalmen, in view of . . .' his gaze fell sideways and he flushed slightly at the sight of the little bead of spit glistening in the strong light. Everybody studiously ignored it. Only a lifetime of soldier's discipline prevented the general's face displaying his disgust. '. . . in view of the obfuscated nature of the current situation I suggest that despite the extreme provocation and a great sense of national distress, our scale of responses for the present at least should be limited.'

The Vice-President looked quickly round the table. He began speaking again hurriedly when his glance came back to the general's despoiled tunic beside him. 'I propose, therefore, that we continue to make manifest and intimidating preparations for military retaliation while pressing Moscow for information through our emergency communications channel. But in fact I believe we should refrain from any precipitate action in view of the danger to the President's life.' He looked round the table again, pretended to shuffle his papers and managed to brush one of them quickly and surreptitiously down the General's chest to remove his latest government decoration. 'Agreed, genitalmen?' He smiled with unnecessary broadness in his relief.

They all agreed. Except Conroy.

'I take the view that nobody should be allowed to hostage the President of the United States with impunity—' he began belligerently.

At that moment the attention of the meeting was suddenly drawn to a gesticulating figure mouthing words and waving a sealed paper outside the glass dome.

The Vice-President gave a signal for the dome to be raised, Conroy signalled his man to stop blowing and the meeting fell silent as the sealed paper was allowed to enter.

The Vice-President opened it and read the message with a worried frown. The others waited on the edges of their tubular aluminium chairs. It was clearly hot-line news from the Kremlin.

The Vice-President opened his mouth to speak, then realised the dome was still raised and the guards were within earshot. He closed his mouth again and waved for the dome to be lowered. Two silent minutes ticked by as the dome was secured and the hydraulics settled it to the floor with a sigh. As the signal was given from outside that maximum security had again been achieved, all five members of the Special Actions Group, including the taciturn Secretary of State, shouted involuntarily in the concerted voice of one man: 'What do the bastards say!'

Even the CIA man on the dog-whistle joined in the yell for information. Conroy rounded on him and punched the shame-faced man roughly in the solar plexus before gesturing peremptorily towards the pipe dangling unblown in the agent's hand. When the whistle was again emitting its silent signal, the Vice-President read the message in a small, puzzled voice.

'They say: "The Soviet Government does not have the President of the United States in its possession, and has no knowledge of his whereabouts. The President was last seen by our observers on a viewing-stand in the American Sector of West Berlin. Regret we are unable to help further."'

Everybody began talking at once. Outside in Pennsylvania Avenue at ground level, newspaper vans roared by flinging bundles of the special morning editions out at street corners. The first pages bore black headlines still damp from the presses that proclaimed, 'Reds Snatch President – World at War Brink.'

The Vice-President looked up at the glass dome above his head. It was becoming heavily misted with condensation. He glanced at the CIA agent on the bellows. Holding his solar plexus area with one hand, the agent was clearly showing signs of whistle fatigue.

'Genitalmen, our resolution holds. Meeting adjourned,' he said crisply and after the dome was raised, hurried upstairs to the Oval Office to tell the waiting nation via the miracle of television that the enemy had denied kidnapping their President.

Chapter Four

As the world trembled on the brink of war, a long-legged, heavy-breasted air hostess of British Excelsior Airways trembled on the brink of her third induced orgasm at the hands of Gilbert Groot, a widely disrespected Fleet Street purveyor of gossip-column half-truths who had flown into West Berlin on her flight the day before.

A cold grey early-afternoon dusk was falling outside the hotel window but for shapely air hostess Moira the inside of the room was suffused with a hotly flaring glow of sensual frenzy. Her breath moaned through her lips mixed with low, unintelligible vocal sounds, exploding in regularly ascending cadences that the Dutch businessman behind the thin partition wall in the next room thought was somebody revving the engine of a Porsche 911 in the hotel's basement garage.

'You're so gentle, Gil,' moaned Moira. Her head was flung back and her eyes were closed in close-to-ecstasy oblivion.

'I practise – milking a mouse,' Groot breathed in her ear.

This dubious endearment unaccountably moved Moira into an unprecedented paroxysm of wildly threshing limbs, and Groot had to ease back his delicate acceleration to bring the moaning revs down to their former steady, long-drawn rhythm.

But soon Moira was clenching her fists and arching her back as Groot drove the Porsche of the Dutch businessman's imagination tantalisingly close to the brow of the hill. He slipped the clutch deftly until the engine note rose to a roar. Every time the burning rubber of Moira's front radials started to impinge on the summit, he let her slip back a few wheel lengths before rocking back almost to the top again.

From where he lay alongside the squirming Moira, Groot could see through the window the clock on the Gedächtniskirche tower at the end of the Kurfürstendamm. It showed five minutes to four. Whoever it was that had sent him mysteriously and anonymously to Berlin would be telephoning any minute.

Meanwhile he would return his attention to the matter in hand. It wasn't every day that he could enjoy an all-expenses-paid trip abroad. It made a change from the tedious round of keeping tabs on the decadent aristocracy at home and chronicling the doings of their spoiled offspring.

'Please! Please! Oh, please,' groaned Moira without being more specific.

'I always aim to please, darlin',' said Groot, exaggerating his Cockney accent and leering as he brought his face close to hers. To prove his sincerity he brushed his lips quickly and repeatedly over the pink peaks of her copious breasts then returned to linger on her squashy mouth.

Moira tried to chew his lips in the frenzy of her razor's edge frustration. But he withdrew his face for safety reasons and sat well back as he accelerated Moira sharply away again and held her rocking convulsively just short of the hilltop.

Long, loud vrooms of engine noise emanating from the sensation-crazed Moira filled the room and the Dutchman next door, fearing that the Porsche was about to burst through the partition, began banging loudly on the wall. At this moment the telephone began ringing and a dog barked loudly in the street outside. The barking turned to howling as a passing bus struck the dog. With brakes screaming the bus mounted the pavement and smashed through seven successive plate-glass windows of a department store before coming to a halt.

With a final plunge of acceleration Groot sent the desperate Moira rocketing ecstatically over the hill to the accompaniment of an anguished, long-drawn scream of exhaust.

With his free hand Groot banged loudly on the wall at the Dutchman and shouted, 'Shard Aarp!' Then he covered his left ear with the same hand and freed the other from Moira to lift the telephone receiver and jam it into his right ear. The smashing, tearing and screaming sounds then reached him only faintly from the accident in the street outside.

'Hello, yeah, Groot,' he said into the mouthpiece.

Moira, recoiling from the spread-eagled position into which she had momentarily subsided, snapped back like a pent spring and clamped herself around Groot's naked torso in a blind spasm of post-orgasmic affection. One arm constricted his windpipe, knocking his wire-rimmed spectacles askew and cutting off his breath. His eyes bulged for a second, then he managed to loosen the arm and thrust Moira roughly back into the pillows.

'Groot, I want you to listen carefully,' said a resonant American voice. 'I want you to meet me at the sauna bath on Heersstrasse in half an hour. Take the lower bunk in the fourth steam cabin on the right. I will be in the bunk above and will give you further details then. Goodbye.'

'Hey, wait a minute,' shouted Groot. 'What's this all about? Why all the mystery? I want to know a bit more before—'

The smooth tones at the other end of the line were patient and controlled. 'You're not a rich man, Groot, are you? You're a rather squalid, poorly paid hack. You won't pass up a golden opportunity or make conditions. Goodbye.' The caller hung up.

Groot unwound the clinging, protesting Moira, and started to climb out of bed.

'Don't go yet, Gilbert,' the air hostess pouted petulantly. 'Stay and put your arms around me.'

'Sorry luv,' said Groot disengaging himself and walking

towards the bathroom, scratching. 'I've got to go to have a sauna bath in the Heerstrasse.'

Moira propped herself up against the pillows and her eyes widened. 'You brute. Who are you meeting there? It's a mixed sauna bath where men and women can go together.'

'Is it now?' said Groot, poking his head out of the bathroom. He removed his spectacles and squinted at her myopically. 'I promise I'll take my glasses off and I won't see a thing. Anyway it's strictly business. I'm meeting a fellah there.'

'Oh, I wouldn't have guessed you were like that too,' said Moira, flapping her wrist vigorously in a masculine-effeminate gesture that made her massive breasts bounce around alarmingly.

Groot withdrew his head and laughed echoingly from the cavern of the bathroom. 'Didn't you know? I'm totally insatiable.'

'You're disgusting,' said Moira, grinning happily and snuggling down under the sheets, her eyes contentedly closed.

Twenty minutes later Groot paused fully dressed and combed at the door. 'Bye then, Moira. I'll be in touch.' He laughed lewdly and went out.

As he went through the hotel foyer he saw the television set in the lounge was carrying a satellite transmission of the Vice-President's address to the American nation. He stopped in the doorway to watch.

'. . . in this moment of great national trial, neither our courage nor our resources will be found wanting,' the Vice-President was saying. His florid complexion came over as a healthy sun-tan in colour. 'We shall flinch from no conflict in our iron determination to restore the President of the United States to the bosom of the nation . . .'

He paused and treated the viewers to a long, satellite-borne stare that seemed to have a bottomless significance. In fact he'd forgotten his words and lost his place on the moving prompt beside the camera. 'Unfortunately,' he said at last, when he had found his way again, 'at this moment we still have no firm information on the whereabouts or the state of health of the President. But I can assure you that in this dark hour you, the people, will be kept constantly informed of anything we learn . . .'

Groot walked out through the front door of the hotel and climbed into a black Mercedes taxi. On the way to the Heerstrasse he pulled out the letter that had arrived at his London flat two days before in an envelope that also contained an air ticket to Berlin, the hotel reservation and fifty £20 notes. He read it over again.

'Take the enclosed air ticket and advance of expenses and go to West Berlin,' the letter said. 'Accredit yourself to cover the visit there of the President of the United States. Watch with particular care the moment when the President looks over the Wall into East Berlin from a viewing-stand.

'From the surveillance that I have carried out on you over the past month I know that you exercise your squalid talent as a freelance supplier of tasteless material to Fleet Street gossip columns and that you have ghosted the memoirs of several prominent British criminals. This would seem to indicate that yours is a character which allows itself to be exploited if the money is right.

'In this assignment the money will be more right than you ever dreamed it could be. You may become famous too. You will have to do nothing illegal, just exercise your "profession". Not enough personal risk is involved to alarm the cowardly side of your nature.

'Expect a telephone call at your hotel at exactly four p.m. on the day of the President's disappearance. You will then be given further instructions.'

Groot folded the letter, which had no signature, and returned it to his pocket. Every time he read the sentence about the President's disappearance, the short hairs on the nape of his neck prickled upright. The letter had been written three days before it happened!

The phrase about the money being more right than ever before had hooked him, as the writer knew it would, and the reference saying he would have to do nothing illegal was the barb that kept him on the hook.

The possibility that he might go to the police, never a very great one, had been eclipsed completely by the appearance of Moira in his hotel room. She arrived soon after he returned there from covering the disappearance of the President. He had chatted her up on the British Excelsior flight from London the day before, after admiring her generous bosoms as she served lunch up and down the aisle. He had given her the number of his hotel room and had not been surprised that she'd called. The rough charm of Gilbert Groot that was alleged to affect duchesses and shop girls equally was legendary in Fleet Street.

The Berlin taxi-driver put him down outside the mixed sauna bath with an incomprehensible German wisecrack followed by a dirty German laugh. Groot bought a ticket for a 'Russisch-Römisch' bath and walked to the changing cubicles ahead of two teenage German girls who giggled in his direction and unbeknown to him had placed bets with one another that they would only resolve when they confronted him in the steamy interior.

Groot undressed quickly in a changing cubicle that smelled of sweat and dry wood. Then, draping a towel around his mid-section and carrying the sorbo mat they had given him at the pay desk, he stepped out gingerly towards the steam cabins.

Peering through the glass port-holes in the doors his gaze fell on rows of slack, lolling bodies slumped on slatted wooden bunks. Pendulous bags and rolls of sweating flesh hung from the frontal areas of both male and female frames. Stick-like legs jutted from them at conflicting angles. The comatose abandon of the bodies in the humid heat gave them the appearance of glistening cadavers.

Groot tried not to look at the virulent growths of dark fungus that seemed to be devouring the inmates of the cell-like cabins at armpit and groin. He tried to stop himself categorising the motionless forms according to the presence or lack of pelvic protrusion. But he found himself doing it with a fascinated horror in spite of himself.

After peering through half a dozen successive port-holes he concluded that German mixed sauna bathing was the closest thing to hell on earth he'd seen. It reminded him of those agonised, nineteenth-century line-drawings of naked unfortunates being sucked into raging seas from rugged crosses or being devoured in dark, burning pits infested with the snakes and slime of eternal damnation.

He began to walk with his eyes closed, opening only one occasionally as an early-warning system against collision. Eventually he located the fourth cabin on the right. Through the billowing steam he could see that the lower bunk was empty. He pushed open the door and gasped when the hot steam hit the back of his throat.

As he walked nearer through the fog he was able to see that the bunk above was occupied by a bulging, whale-like form. What appeared to be its head was entirely swathed in a towel except for a hole which had been left, presumably for a mouth. After a moment of hesitation, Groot assumed a prone position on the wooden slats of the lower bunk, placing the sorbo mat under himself and draping the towel modestly over his mid-section. Looking up he noticed that the ceiling of his immediate world, two feet above his head was formed by the bunk above and puffy strips of flesh that oozed down between its slats. The fat man used no mat and obviously saw no need for the modesty of a waist towel. After studying the undulations of the white flesh for a moment Groot closed his eyes tight to blot out the sight.

A couple of minutes passed before he noticed that regular plops of moisture were raining gently on him from above. When he realised what it was, he got up quickly and rushed to the corner of the cabin to hose himself down with the jet of water provided for that purpose. Then, gritting his teeth and thinking hard of the money being 'more right than ever before', he resumed his position on the lower bunk and waited under the steady downpour of the fat man's perspiration. As he lay there, he noticed from the corner of his eye that another towel-swathed face was appearing from time to time outside the door, peering in through the port-hole, then moving on. Only the eyes were visible through the towelling but Groot fancied they had lingered deliberately on him.

'Groot.'

His name, uttered by a resonant American voice, brought Groot's attention back to the bunk above.

'I apologise for sweating on you during this talk but there was no alternative.' The voice came muffled through the towel but was unmistakably the voice that had spoken to him earlier by telephone.

'You could have taken this bunk and let me sweat on you,' said Groot.

The fat between the slats above him quivered in apparent distaste but the voice ignored the suggestion. 'Groot, I will be brief. I can provide you with the opportunity to obtain an exclusive interview with the kidnapped President of the United States at the place where he is held hostage. This will enable you to report the story of his plight and its reason to an astounded and waiting world. I take it you are interested? Answer simply yes or no to save time.'

Groot's eyes flicked shiftily around the steam room. He licked his lips nervously then said, 'Yeah, what if I am interested?'

'Then go, Groot,' the voice continued softly from above, 'into East Berlin tonight in the routine manner as if bound for the Komische Oper. Wait outside the theatre at six o'clock carrying a folded copy of *Neues Deutschland*. A car will pick you up. Prepare to be blindfolded during the journey. On your return to West Berlin, write your story and dictate it by telephone to the London number which I will give you.'

'Who will that be?' asked Groot.

'Your story will be received by one of London's leading literary agents who will syndicate it to newspapers throughout the world. I have written them a letter in your name asking them to act for you from today. They know nothing of me.' The whole whale-like bulk on the bunk above shifted to a different position shaking down a new flurry of sweat-drops. 'It will be one of the greatest scoops in the history of journalism.'

'Why are you offering *me* this?' asked Groot suspiciously.

'Because, Groot, you are sufficiently unscrupulous and immoral, yet at the same time something of a weakling who would not dare cross the Law. I have an interest in this job being done. You serve that interest ideally.'

'What do I get out of it?' asked Groot, staring up at the fat back and fleshy buttocks two feet above him.

'That remains to be seen. But you hardly need much imagination to realise that an exclusive interview with the kidnapped President at this time will be worth a lot of money. A series of exclusive interviews, even more.'

'Series?' echoed Groot. 'You mean there will be others?'

'Quite possibly.'

The steam swirled around in clouds, and the heat and humidity were stifling. Groot went and hosed himself down again. Before resuming his recumbent position he stared at the anonymous towel-covered head and the swollen corpulence of the body on the shelf level with his eyes. Its enormous, overhanging belly, he found, made visual, cast-iron sexual definition impossible.

'Lie down, Groot!'

He did as he was told. 'I want a guarantee, a percentage,' Groot told the buttocks above him in his most recalcitrant voice.

'You'll have another thousand pounds in cash when you leave here tonight and the rest you will receive in due course. I am not a swindler or a cheat, Groot. My interest is in your doing the job well. You're in no position to bargain. I know you will do this. And you know you will get a fair percentage of the deal back in London.'

Groot started to protest but the bulk above him heaved a tired sigh. 'Russisch-Römisch, Groot, is steam bath followed by dry heat followed by an icy plunge. Go next door to the dry-heat cabin for three minutes then plunge into the pool and return here.'

Groot obeyed, glad of the relief from the fat man's precipitation. He pushed open the door behind the bunks and stepped into a room in which every breath seared his tonsils. The dry heat smelled strongly of singeing wood and the moment he sat down on a bench, he understood why. While he was leaping around screaming and holding himself, it became clear what the sorbo mats were for and when the pain of the burns subsided he returned to the steam room to fetch his. He paused again to stare at the still heap of sweating white flesh on the second bunk – but it remained inert and unspeaking so he returned reluctantly to the dry-heat room.

While he sat gasping in the parched air he eyed the room's two doors. If someone wedged them closed, he realised, he'd bake alive. The heat was squeezing sweat-beads the size of marbles from every pore and he stiffened as the figure shrouded in white towels, that he had noticed outside the steam room, paused again before the glass window. Still only the eyes were visible through a gap in the towelling – and this time they settled steadily on him for several seconds before moving on.

Suddenly Groot couldn't stand the heat any longer. He lunged towards the door, hauled it open and emerged into a tiled area in the middle of which was a sunken pool of water about twelve feet square. He moved towards it, then stopped. Blocks of ice the size of the *Concise Oxford Dictionary* floated on its surface! Although his body burned and steamed, he baulked at entering the water. Then out of the corner of his eye he saw the towel-draped figure moving in his direction and he took a deep breath before stepping onto the air above the plunge pool.

The breath left his body again in a sibilant rush as he descended into the icy water. His skin became desensitised with the shock of the cold on top of the roasting. He opened his eyes in the green-yellow depths of the pool, and rose quickly to the surface feeling light-headed and dizzy. He clambered out in a daze and staggered quickly back along the corridor to the steam cabin.

The upper bunk was still occupied by the now familiar white-whale figure. Groot sank onto the lower bunk and closed his eyes. His body had begun tingling from the cold plunge.

'We can't go on meeting like this,' said Groot gasping for breath.

Slowly the man above him hauled himself upright, descended the little wooden ladder and waddled to the door with a surprisingly nimble stride. The towel turban still covered his entire head. In the doorway the hole in the towel turned to him and said, 'Look on the upper bunk before you leave. And meet me here again at one o'clock tomorrow.'

Then he opened the door and was gone.

Groot got up and felt around on the bunk above. He found a large metal cigar cylinder. Unscrewing the end, he pulled out another fifty tightly rolled £20 notes and a slip of paper with a London telephone number on it. He stretched out again on the bunk below and closed his eyes to think, relieved that it had at last stopped raining.

A moment later he became conscious of another movement in the cabin. He opened his eyes to see the figure swathed from head to foot in towels bending down by the door. Several seconds passed before Groot realised that the little triangles of wood being pushed into the gap under the door were wedging it closed. By the time he found his voice, the figure had crossed the room and was kneeling by the other door, wedging that shut too.

'What's your game, then?' demanded Groot propping himself up on one elbow on the bunk.

No reply came from the white-shrouded figure as it advanced slowly towards him through the swirling steam.

Groot watched speechless as one hand emerged from the enveloping folds. The figure stopped, towering above the low bunk on which he lay.

Another hand emerged.

Groot's eyes widened in alarm as the two hands fumbled

with the fastenings of the towels. He watched them drop down to the floor followed by the other towels that had covered the figure's head.

'Moira, for Christ's sake,' he gasped as she flung her naked body down on his.

Chapter Five

'I have been taken hostage in the name of humanity, peace and freedom,' said the President crisply, 'and I am enjoying it very much.'

Groot's pencil flew across his note-pad. He looked up at the President who sat several feet in front of him, illuminated beneath a narrowly focused spotlight in an otherwise darkened cellar. He wore an open-necked white shirt, a blue pullover and comfortable slacks. He looked surprisingly relaxed and at ease.

'Er, humanity, peace and freedom, you say, Mr President,' said Groot writing laboriously. 'Can I quote you on that?'

The President nodded. 'Sure you can.'

Groot glanced round the cellar again. Three figures dressed in close-fitting black clothes were ranged behind the President's chair in the shadows. Wearing black hoods with slits cut for their eyes, they stood watching and listening silently with arms folded. Although he could see little in the shadows, there was a good-quality carpet beneath his feet and a sense of discreet luxury pervaded the cellar.

'And you're enjoying it . . . very much,' murmured Groot, his lips forming the words as he wrote. Desperately he searched his mind for what he should ask next. He wasn't used to interviewing kidnapped American presidents in darkened cellars. 'What did you have for dinner?' he blurted at last, drawing heavily on his experience of interviewing visiting American film-stars in the Dorchester Hotel.

'Caviare, vodka and goulash,' replied the President promptly.

'Who are the hosts that are treating you so well, Mr President?' asked Groot, nodding his head hesitantly towards the shadows.

'They call themselves the Organisation for Peace and Harmony under Communism and Capitalism and they maintain they are in no way connected with the government of the Soviet Union or any of its satellite states,' replied the President. 'They represent a group of dissident, freedom-loving Russian intellectuals dedicated to the fight for peace and freedom both under their own system and for the whole world.'

Groot scribbled on without enthusiasm. He hated politics. He didn't understand the complexities. He preferred the simple snobbish glamour of people he normally wrote about. You knew where you were with them. They fought for simple understandable everyday things like alimony and inheritances. Nothing much in the way of ideology entered their lives – or his, come to that.

'I don't quite understand...' said Groot, 'how they're fighting the government in Moscow by kidnapping you, sir.'

The President smiled indulgently. 'Through you, Mr Groot, their ultimatum will be delivered simultaneously to the Kremlin and to the whole Western World.'

'What ultimatum?' asked Groot.

One of the men in black stepped forward and placed a sheet of paper in the President's hand then retired again. The Most Powerful Man in the World read it aloud in a steady voice.

'We, the Organisation for Peace and Harmony under Communism and Capitalism believe world peace and freedom is endangered most acutely by ageing political leaders who threaten to plunge the world into war in compensation for their unsatisfactory sex lives.

'In return for the freedom of the President of the

United States we demand more enlightened and aware sexual policies from the Soviet Government and its allies which will bring about a climate in which leaders can develop in an atmosphere of well-adjusted sexual happiness.

'We require public guarantees before the people of the world that these demands will be met and we insist also on two immediate tangible gestures of good faith in this new freedom.' The President paused and cleared his throat:

'One: That the First Secretary of the Communist Party of the Union of Soviet Socialist Republics lay in Red Square the foundation stone for a Moscow Playbaby Club.

'Two: *Playbaby* Magazine must go on sale immediately in the streets of all major Soviet cities.

'The President will not be released until these conditions have been fulfilled. If they are not met the President will not be freed alive. World peace will consequently be endangered by the oppressive governments of the Socialist countries.'

Groot looked up and, to his amazement, found that the man whose life was threatened in the communiqué was unaccountably smiling.

Bending over his pad again, Groot wrote furiously, attempting to get the ultimatum verbatim while it was fresh in his mind.

'We shall make a copy of that available to you.'

The low, throaty female voice brought Groot's head up a second time with a jerk. One of the President's captors had moved out of the shadows and crossed through the pool of light. Although a hood made identification impossible, Groot gaped open-mouthed. He had assumed the three shadowy figures were all men. But the black leather matador pants stretched tight over slender, rounded hips, the extraordinarily long legs, the black silk shirt thrust dramatically into contours no male chest could achieve, showed him the error of his assumption.

She held a copy of the ultimatum towards him, released it and let it float down onto his pad. Then moving with an eerie, somnambulistic grace she returned to her place.

She paused momentarily by the President and looked down at him, before passing on into the shadows.

Groot's face creased into a genuine grin of salacious envy. 'I think perhaps I begin to understand, Mr President,' he said. 'If I was you I'd be tempted to stay as long as they'd have me.'

The President smiled a curiously smug little smile but said nothing.

A hand appeared over Groot's shoulder holding a small Polaroid camera. 'Take a picture of the President in case the world doubts your veracity,' said Badezimmer's voice.

Groot held it to his eye, focused, and took two snaps of the President in the circle of light. The hand reached out again and took the camera from him.

'Have you any message for your White House colleagues handling the crisis?' asked Groot, beginning to be pleased by the astuteness of his questions.

'I would counsel them to be cautious in the use of force and not plunge the world into war unadvisedly. I don't find it difficult to sympathise with the aims of those who have kidnapped me. I am confident the Kremlin will see sense.'

'But aren't you concerned about your own safety? Don't you worry that these desperate, well-organised criminals will kill you?' asked Groot in a puzzled voice.

'To be perfectly honest I find it delightful not to be surrounded for the first time in six and a half years by memorandum filers, speech-writers, black-box carriers, heart-machine operators, drafters of option-papers, and that Pentagon general with the black attaché case. I feel a new sense of freedom. From here I can't get my finger anywhere near that button to blow up the world. The relief is indescribable.'

Badezimmer stepped forward and held up his hand.

'I think they feel that's enough questions now, Mr Groot,' said the President. 'The world awaits your message. I think they're ready to take you back.'

The long-legged figure in the dramatically contoured

silk shirt stepped forward, took the President by the arm and guided him away into the darkness. He went eagerly.

As she passed through the shaft of light in which the President had sat she seemed to Groot to float with the wraith-like insubstantiality of a shadow.

And the tightly stretched hood left him with the uncanny impression that, abnormally, the head it covered was roundly and sensually naked of all cranial hair.

Chapter Six

'Heh, heh, heh, heh,' said Groot in a fair imitation of a miser's mad chuckle as he let the international editions of a dozen or so newspapers trickle through his fingers onto the bed covers.

He picked up the French one. '*Par* Gilbert Groot,' he announced shrugging Gallic shoulders and pursing his lips with the accent. He giggled. '*Von* Gilbert Groot,' he rasped in a guttural German voice, holding up *Die Welt*, 'By Gil Groot,' he said through his nose gazing at the *Herald Tribune* headline which announced, 'Reds Demand Moscow Playbaby Club for President's Life.'

He held up a Danish front page for Moira to admire. 'How do you like "*Af* Gilbert Groot"?'

'I would very moch like to "Af" 'im,' said Moira in a Scandinavian voice and moved in predatorily to press herself against the now world-famous British journalist.

'Get off, Moira,' complained Groot, edging to the side of the bed. 'I know I'm irresistible but at least let me read my newspapers in my moment of triumph.'

The Polaroid photograph of the President smiling inanely in the spotlight accompanied all the stories. A smaller one of the straw-haired, bespectacled gossip-writer who had interviewed him in his secret dungeon was printed alongside. Of the two Groot looked the more bewildered, as if in fact he was the hostage. His picture had been taken at a press conference in the early hours of the morning that several hundred furiously jealous newsmen had forced him to give. Although flustered he had stoutly refused to divulge how he managed to get the interview, implying coyly that his scoop was attributable to a mixture of journalistic flair and peculiarly British initiative.

The world's leading journals had taken the liberty of rewriting Groot's ingrained gossip-column prose. His opening paragraph – 'I can tonight reveal that the President of the United States dined enthusiastically on vodka and caviare during his first evening in captivity' – had been refashioned and replaced with hard-fact statements of the kidnappers' demands and the seemingly unbelievable impression that the President was enjoying a new-found 'freedom'. The gustatory details were tacked on the end.

Moira moved round behind Groot and rested her chin on his bare shoulder to read with him. They saw that the front pages also quoted the simple explanation of the crisis from the Soviet news agency, Tass. The CIA had kidnapped their own President in an attempt to effect cultural rape of the USSR, it said. This vile trick to blackmail the Soviet leadership into opening a degenerate Playbaby club at the hub of the Workers and Peasants' universe, and so poison the minds of the proletariat with pornography and gambling, would not succeed.

Groot's eye fell on an item quoting Western news agency reports from Moscow. 'Listen to this, Moira,' he said, excitedly. 'Demolition work began suddenly during the night on a small museum on the west side of Red Square. The only explanation obtainable was that the site was urgently required for a block of workers' flats—'

Groot's newsreading was interrupted by a sharp knock at the door. Moira leapt up and dashed across the room to lock herself in the bathroom two seconds before the door burst open to admit six men wearing black trilbies and black overcoats that reached to their ankles. One of them remained on guard by the door while the other five sat down on the bed around Groot.

'It's suddenly gone dark, hasn't it?' said Groot peering nervously round at what was visible of the grim white faces under the brims of the black hats. 'Whadya want?'

'Information,' said the man nearest him. 'Information about how you found the President.'

The accent was heavily Slavonic, the eyes merciless.

'I can't reveal my sources, can I? It's a journalist's code of honour,' said Groot trying his best to look honourable.

The man nearest him, who was obviously their leader, slowly lit a cigarette. He held the burning match between his fingers and reached out towards Groot's bare chest. Groot recoiled as far as he could against the headboard but the fuzz on his chest sizzled and snapped as the man ran the match quickly through an imaginary hammer and sickle design.

'Hey, leave it out!' shouted Groot. He crinkled his nose at the unpleasant smell of singed hair.

The leader held the match up to Groot's face. 'That is just the beginning,' he said.

Groot puffed quickly and blew out the flame. He grinned sheepishly round at the faces but found no sign of amusement.

At a nod from the leader three men rose suddenly. Two took Groot by each arm while the third took a fist of Groot's hair and held his head back. The man smoking reached out his cigarette and with an efficiency born of years of practice burned all the eyelashes off Groot's left eyelid.

Groot let out a shout of pain. He was convinced his eye had been put out by the tiny red ball of fire that had zoomed towards his retina with the swiftness of Halley's Comet.

After a moment he opened the eye and was surprised that he could still see the five black-coated men through a watery curtain of tears.

'I zhink ve keel 'im,' said one of the men in an accent that reeked of the onion domes of the Kremlin.

'*Niet*,' said the man with the cigarette. 'At least, not yet.'

'If you think this kind of sadistic torture and intimidation can make me talk,' said Groot shakily, 'you're absolutely right.' He proceeded to tell them almost everything that had happened to him, and showed them the letter that accompanied the air tickets to Berlin.

When he had finished, the man with the cigarette stared at him speculatively. 'Say nothing of this to anybody ... otherwise—' he brought the glowing tip of the cigarette up again and ran it quickly along the line of Groot's left eyebrow.

Groot tried to pull away but the man holding his head made it impossible. The acrid smell of burnt eyebrow filled the room. '—otherwise we shall not stop with singeing your hair.'

He gestured briefly with his other hand, tucked Groot's letter away inside his coat and got up and walked to the door. The others followed him and went out without looking round.

A minute passed in which Groot remained motionless against the headboard in a state of shock.

'Have they gone?' said Moira, poking her head round the bathroom door.

'Yeah,' said Groot, tentatively fingering his singed eyebrow. 'And so has a large part of my devastating good looks.'

'What did they do to you?' said Moira in a voice pitched high with concern. She ran over, and took his face solicitously in her hands.

'Russian bastards!' said Groot viciously.

Moira laughed. 'Russian? They weren't Russian, my innocent.'

'What do yer mean, they weren't Russian?' said Groot, outraged. 'Long black coats, black trilbies, Slav accents, one even said "*Niet*". It was the bloody KGB.'

'The CIA,' corrected Moira, her voice quiet and infuriatingly offhand. 'Only the CIA could look as Russian as that.'

Groot looked at her open-mouthed.

'Hey, Gil, you there, buddy?' called a voice from the

corridor outside the bedroom door. The nasal Texan twang had a friendly, all-guys-together note of familiarity.

'This is your KGB, my love,' hissed Moira, hurling herself off the bed and back into the bathroom.

The corridor door flew open and six fresh-faced guys with blond crew-cuts, grey pebble-dash sports jackets, hand-knitted ties, button-down collars and spatulate, custom-made shoes rushed in. Five sat down around him on the bed, the sixth stayed on guard at the door.

'Great to see you, Gil, guy,' said their leader, crinkling the corners of pale blue eyes in a friendly smile as he lit a Lucky Strike. 'Wondered if you might tell us a bit more about how you've gotten to see our gosh-darned President.'

He slapped Groot violently on the right shoulder. As he did so three of his men got up, grabbed Groot by both arms and the hair and held him back against the headboard of the bed.

'Like to tell us, Gil, baby?' asked the blue-eyed Russian moving the hand containing the Lucky Strike with lightning speed towards Groot's face.

The eyelashes of Groot's right eye went up in smoke and immediately after the watering stopped he launched straight into a recitation of what he'd told his previous visitors.

'Sorry I can't actually show you the letter, comrades,' said Groot, 'but I just gave the only copy I have to your colleagues in the CIA. Maybe you've got some arrangement for exchanging important information like that?'

The Russian looked startled for point nought five of a second, then his practised eye noticed that the eyelashes and eyebrow on the other side of Groot's face had already been destroyed by fire. In just under point nine five of a second a practised grin broke out over his face, carving simian bowlines into his cheeks just like his veteran KGB instructor had taught him. 'You're a great joker, Gil, baby,' he shouted, slapping Groot on the shoulder again. 'What's with this comrades crap?'

Groot, still held fast in the muscle-numbing grip of the

three other Russians, winced and decided to be valorously discreet for the better part and say nothing. He just looked back at them apprehensively through watery eyes.

'Okay, Grooty, we'll leave ya now. But you'd betta be on the level with what you've told us baby . . . or else.' Their leader raised the glowing end of the Lucky Strike and deftly turned Groot's one remaining blond eyebrow into a charred gash of comic make-up above his right eye.

'. . . or else we won't stop at singeing your hair,' chorused Groot with the Russian.

For point nought five of another second his tormentor once more looked abashed before his training trip-switch cut in a blank expression. 'See you in the steam bath, buddy boy,' he said, doing the grin again and signalling his men to leave.

When the door had closed Moira unlocked the bathroom door and rushed over to take his head in her hands again.

'My poor, poor love,' she consoled, surveying the further destruction of his facial hair.

'Russian bastards,' said Groot.

'Right,' said Moira approvingly.

He relaxed wet-eyed into the motherly embrace of her bosoms.

Two minutes later he raised his head, a look of suspicion clouding his charred features. 'Hey, how come a mere air hostess for British Excelsior is such a cute number at identifying members of the world's intelligence services?'

'It's my hobby,' said Moira airily. 'You know, little boys spot trains, I spot spies.' In an effort to stifle further conversation, she lowered the twin globes of her magnificent bosoms provocatively towards Groot's face.

He stared back and forth for a moment at the nipples directing themselves pointedly at him through the thin chiffon of her nightdress. They had come so near that he was unable to encompass them both in one glance and his head snapped from side to side like a spectator during a short, tense rally at the Wimbledon Tennis Championships. With an effort he gathered himself and pushed her away.

'How come you know so much, Moira? I want to know,' he repeated.

Moira looked at him fondly. 'I can't lie to you, Gilbert,' she said. 'It's really very simple. I work for British Intelligence. My orders are "Stay close to Groot!"'

Even before she had finished speaking she was lowering and shifting the yielding areas of herself squarely onto the length and breadth of her assignment. Groot struggled and tried to talk but she strangulated all his further questions with a warm, wet, wide-open mouth and a tongue that darted like a viper.

Chapter Seven

The sauna bath was crowded. The traffic in naked human bodies through the steam clouds was heavy. Not only were there more than the usual number of fat Germans but around Groot twelve tall, lean, gimlet-eyed men of evident whipcord fitness stalked the misty boardwalks like watchful tigers in some primeval swamp.

Their strange gait distinguished them among the swarm of nude bodies. They strutted without towels, hips thrust forward in the manner of parading female fashion models, leaning back from the waist with hands hanging straight down in the space behind their hips. The condensation in the large steam room, however, was so thick that casual sauna bathers noticed nothing remarkable.

If the mists had suddenly lifted, the reasons for their strangely taut manner of perambulation would have become clear – each man without exception was holding his buttocks clenched like a fist. It was this determined and unceasing muscular contraction that forced them to strut like perspiring, catatonic ballet dancers in search of choreographic release.

Nothing but the closest examination, however, would have revealed that intelligence agents were using their intelligence, as only they could, to achieve what seemed to be the impossible – concealment though unclothed, armed preparedness though apparently unarmed and in a state of nudity.

In gabbling out his confessions to both the KGB and the CIA, Groot had altered slightly only two pieces of information. First he had said he had talked to a thin man instead of a fat man and second he had said he was due to meet him at the Heerstrasse steambath again at twelve o'clock and not one o'clock. He had practised this deception in the hope it might give him some room for manoeuvre but already ten minutes had flown by without inspiration of any kind arriving.

The slow, mist-shrouded ballet continued to wheel round him. Occasionally a corner of a mouth would twitch and a whispered word would be exchanged between compatriots as the intelligence operatives brushed past each other in the steam.

From time to time Groot passed a figure swathed from head to foot in towels and received a wink through the slit where the eyes were visible. But he wished Moira would go away: it was very difficult to think clearly with her around.

For their part the six Russian and American agents were all utterly oblivious of one another. Each side had noticed that there were other fit, youthful men strutting in similar fashion to themselves but this caused them only to congratulate themselves wordlessly on their ability to merge anonymously into unfamiliar settings.

Groot grinned weakly at his persecutors from both East and West whenever he passed them at close range. Occasionally he would venture the query, 'You all right, then?' But he never received any response.

In an attempt to shock his mind into some kind of clarity, he pushed through the door into the plunge area. After steeling himself, he dropped in among the breath-taking dictionary-sized ice-cubes. When he surfaced trembling and gasping with the shock of cold, he opened his eyes to see the twelve strutting with exaggerated and casual slowness among the men and women in the clear daylight of the plunge room. All were still watching him intently.

Further unnerved, Groot climbed out and hurried back to the steam bath. The only partial visibility there gave him a greater sense of security and protection. But again all twelve followed him.

After a few more tense minutes had passed, the Russian Lucky Strike smoker strolled casually by and hissed in his ear. 'Where is your friend, buddy boy? You see him yet?'

Groot shook his head hurriedly. 'No, I can't.'

'He'd better put in an appearance, buddy boy, or you're in big trouble. We may have to fry you in the steam-maker.'

Groot grinned weakly and moved on, edging to the side of the room furthest from the grille where the steam emerged from the heating machinery.

'Vere is your contact?' said the senior CIA man, coming up suddenly behind him. 'Eef 'e don't show up soon ve may have to freeze you to death in the ice-maker.'

The man's eyes bored into Groot's and his jaw muscles tensed, perhaps as a result of his tightening his grip elsewhere on a miniature, silenced Derringer pistol.

'He'll show up all right,' said Groot, swallowing hard. 'Just relax.'

The man glowered for a moment then strutted away, anything but relaxed.

Groot had admitted under torture by cigarette that he did not know his contact's face because at their first meeting his head had been covered by a towel. He had quickly invented an identity mark – a mole high up on the left side of the pelvic girdle – by which he said he would recognise him again. Groot presumed it was this piece of misleading information that was causing all of the twelve strutting agents to approach from time to time the thin figures filed away on the wooden slatted racks and either stare at their mid-sections, if they were uncovered, or lift the corners of their modest towels. Occasionally these puzzled sauna-bathers raised their heads and stared after a young, slender man gliding silently away into the mist.

By twelve-thirty Groot was perspiring with monsoon intensity through a potent mixture of heat and fear.

If he didn't do something soon, he realised, the mysterious white-whale figure who had moved him unexpectedly to the brink of fame and fortune might walk unknowingly into the arms of the strutting twelve and be torn down the middle in an East–West tug-of-war.

The thought moved him close to panic and he suddenly saw what he must do. Rushing headlong through the steam, he approached the leader of the Slavonic-looking men, the men posing as KGB agents whom he really knew to be of the CIA.

'Look,' he said tugging the man's arm urgently and pointing through the mist to a crew-cut man posing as a CIA agent whom he really knew to be from the KGB, 'that man is a CIA agent, threatening to kill me so that the KGB never discovers the CIA have kidnapped their own President.'

The Slav who was really an American looked startled. His mind raced through the convolutions. He stared at Groot, then through the steam at the man Groot had described as a CIA man. Groot didn't wait for comprehension to dawn but dashed over to the crew-cut CIA man who was really a KGB man and gabbled fast words. 'Look at that man over there,' he said pointing back to the Slav who he knew to be American. 'That Russian KGB man has threatened to shoot me to prevent you discovering that they have kidnapped the President on behalf of their inhuman Communist government.'

The apparent American who was really Russian stared at Groot, *his* mind racing through the convolutions too.

Without waiting until he had worked it out Groot dashed bent double through the steam to the next crew-cut KGB man. 'Look,' he gasped, pointing to the nearest Slavonic-looking bather, 'that man is a KGB agent trying to kill me because—' The steam steamed and Groot rushed sweating from man to man, his lungs heaving, his words jerking out in scalded gasps.

As he completed each pairing and ran on, empty hands flashed behind bare backs and emerged with trigger fingers curled round tiny deadly triggers. The flat, quiet 'phut' of silenced Derringers spitting out tiny deadly bullets was heard dully in the mists.

The regular bathers noticed vaguely that a lot of men were sinking to the floor of the communal steam room to stretch themselves out in loose, relaxed postures. The little red holes didn't show immediately from above because the men mostly sank down with the side with the hole in next to the floor. When the number of reclining men reached double figures, Groot staggered exhausted into the plunge room, and collapsed into the pool's icy depths. After surfacing he climbed out and walked shakily along the corridor towards the row of smaller steam cabins. He stopped by the window of the communal steam room to count the number of men relaxing on the floor. When he reached twelve he knew it was safe to enter the fourth cabin on the right.

Inside, the pale whale-like body with a towel round its head was stretched out on the upper bunk, seemingly unaware that anything unusual had happened. It neither moved nor spoke as Groot entered and the journalist flung himself down on the lower bunk, breathing heavily.

'You seem over-excited, Groot,' said the calm American voice at last. 'You should try to relax more in this bath. That's what it's for.'

Moisture pattered down from between the slats above Groot. 'I'll try to remember that,' said Groot, struggling to control his breathing. 'What's your message? I'd like to go soon.'

'You did well, Groot, on your first interview. Even if your style was a little naîve.'

'How much did I make flogging the story?' asked Groot.

'I'll ignore the vulgarity of that question,' said the voice from within the towel. 'Meanwhile, go again to the Opera in East Berlin tonight. As before you will be picked up and taken to the President. This time you will be granted an even more sensational interview than before.'

'What—?' began Groot interrogatively.

'No more questions now,' said the voice firmly. 'I want to relax in the steam.'

'I shouldn't hang around too long,' said Groot, in a casual tone. 'There are twelve secret agents lying dead on the floor of the big steam room next door – six Americans and six Russians. They were all looking for you... But I managed to persuade them to shoot one another so we could have our word in private.'

At first there was no reaction at all from the bunk above. Because of the stillness and the silence Groot thought perhaps his contact had fallen asleep. Then in a sudden flurry of movement the fat man shot down the ladder, hurtled across the cabin and disappeared along the corridor in a veritable blur of pumping arms and legs.

This hasty departure galvanised Groot in his turn and he raced off, too, in the direction of the changing rooms. Three minutes later, fully dressed but still sweating profusely, the now world-famous gossip columnist flagged down a taxi in the Heerstrasse, climbed in and roared away towards his hotel.

Chapter Eight

At that instant a quiet smile of pleasure was spreading slowly across the face of the President of the United States. Seated alone and at ease on the PVC sofa in his luxury cellar prison, he was beginning to review and relive, minute by minute, the most momentous twenty-four hours of his entire life. Occasionally as he mused and relished the details of his fantastic experience, he took a sip from a frosted, thin-stemmed glass of vodka that stood on a silver tray at his elbow. He had never liked vodka much before. But now its tangy sharpness seemed to symbolise the new awakening that had suddenly transformed his life.

In that comfortable Communist cellar the President felt more consciously at ease than he had done at any time since his early childhood. He felt totally changed, body and soul, and in an effort to understand better what had happened he went back yet again to the extraordinary sequence of events that had begun on the viewing-stand at Potsdamer Platz. The downward plunge into the tunnel and the rescue operation apparently mounted by three of his own secret servicemen had been strange enough. But the most startling moment had occurred in the Volga taxi that carried him away from Alexanderplatz towards his fateful destination.

It came after about twenty minutes of quiet and careful driving through the Communistic suburbs of East Berlin. He had begun to relax on the back seat, confident he was safe in the hands of his three secret servicemen, when a startling sex change occurred before his eyes. It had been the man he knew as Badezimmer who had started it.

After checking through the rear window for signs of pursuit and finding none, Badezimmer had removed his hat and lifted both hands to his face to peel away a mask that had concealed his real features. The new face beneath was obviously Slav and not American and the President had jerked round in his seat as he realised the other two men at his side were peeling off their faces too.

Then he relaxed. His earlier suspicion that he might have been dreaming seemed to be confirmed. One of the men on his left had removed his trilby and his mask to let a tumble of long, black hair fall shining to shoulder length around a pale, high-cheekboned female face.

These dreams get more bizarre by the minute, the President had told himself, settling back to enjoy the rest of it until he woke up. Neither Badezimmer nor his two companions said anything as the Volga ran on inconspicuously through the brown cobblestone suburbs of Karlshorst and into Oberschöneweide. The President sneaked another look to his left at the face of the raven-haired girl-woman in his dream. But she stared straight ahead ignoring him.

Her right profile revealed one dark determined eye, one high cheekbone set in half a pale and powerful face, half of two wide fulsome lips held closed in a determined straight line, half a strongly delicate chin and the suggestion of one ear peeping through half a head of luxuriant black hair. In her lap she held the plastic-rubber mask she had just removed.

'You're not dreaming this time, mister President,' said the new Badezimmer, leaning over from his right and lifting the President's sagging jaw closed with his left index finger. 'Welcome to bondage.'

At that moment everything went black.

The President had half turned as the new Kafferty lifted a rubber-and-plastic mask towards him stretched taut between his two hands. In one fluid movement he let it snap into contraction over the Presidential face. From outside, the artificial blue eyes stared like those of a blind man. From inside all was blackness. Badezimmer perched dark glasses on the President's face to hide the blocked eye-slits.

The last image to record itself on the President's retina as the mask clamped itself round his head was the face of the girl-woman who at that instant turned her full gaze upon him, revealing that the other side of her profile balanced and matched perfectly the half he had already seen.

The broad, pale face had a strange quality of power and its image continued to burn in the darkness of his mind's eye long after his face was covered.

'Who are you? Where are we? What are you doing with me?'

The President's voice came muffled through the restricting mask. It was the imperious voice of the Chief Executive, the voice of a man who had spent six years having 'Hail to the Chief' played to him by brass bands as he descended White House and other staircases, a voice accustomed to having its orders and its whims obeyed. But through a rubber mask it sounded nasal and petulant.

'Relax, Mister President,' said Badezimmer. 'The answers to your questions, in reverse of the order you asked them, are: taking you hostage, East Berlin and lovers of humanity and freedom.'

Badezimmer had abandoned his Secret Service agent Bostonese and enunciated his English with a faint trace of his native Russian vowels.

The President, blind behind his mask, suddenly realised why he'd felt like one of the South Dakota presidential rock faces. The masks had stiffened his companions' features. Now he alone sat rock-faced among three other pink, fleshy heads jogging gently in the rear of the Volga.

Only then had realisation finally dawned that he, the President of the United States, had been kidnapped and was in the hands of Communists in Communist territory. *Kataclysmos* was at hand!

He strained his ears to see if he could notice the drone

of NATO's nuclear strike force winging eastward overhead, or the whine of Inter-Continental Ballistic Missiles homing to their distant targets or Multiple Independently Targetable Re-entry Vehicle warheads screaming in from a launch in space.

But to his surprise, as far as he could tell, the day outside was redolent only of light traffic and the shriek of Communist children playing.

'You are endangering world peace,' said the President sonorously through his mask. 'In kidnapping me you are putting at risk the lives of three hundred thousand million people of all races and several thousand years of history.'

'On the contrary. We are attempting to ensure a lasting world peace in an unprecedented fashion.'

A nerve thrummed somewhere deep inside the Presidential viscera. It was a female voice that had replied.

The pause that followed had that quality of enriched silence that is left after a bow has been drawn lightly over the bass strings of a cello. The accented inflexion on the last two words made the President sure in his blackness that the finely tapered eyebrow crowning that determined dark eye nearest to him had arched in added emphasis.

He sat silent, breath held, waiting for the voice to speak again. It had recalled for him the low vibrancy of Marlene Dietrich, and the faint huskiness of June Allyson to which he had secretly thrilled in younger, more virile days gone by.

'Goddammit, I demand to know what the hell goes on,' said the President in exasperation after waiting for several minutes in which nobody spoke.

'Relax, Mister President,' said Badezimmer, 'we could put a blanket over your head and push you on the floor for the rest of the journey. If you keep quiet you can sit comfortably with your mask on.'

'I demand . . .' the President began in a muffled tone.

'You can demand nothing,' interrupted Badezimmer. 'Be kind enough to remain silent until we finish the journey.'

The tyres of the Volga suddenly ceased to judder over cobbles and tram tracks and instead began humming smoothly over an even tarmac surface. The three kidnappers and their hostage stopped bouncing against each other and settled into a flatter ride. The car stopped and turned at junctions frequently. Always it was driven carefully.

Two hours passed without a word being spoken. The car, without the President knowing, was circling the same area of Köpenick constantly, giving him the impression of covering distance. In the early afternoon it drove quietly down a tree-lined street paved with smooth, cobbled blocks and turned off along a path through thinly spaced trees.

The sun the President couldn't see glinted on distant water that was also invisible to him. But when the car pulled up outside a single-storey house that had been built solidly near the edge of the lake for the enjoyment of Prussian weekends long past, the President could hear the slap of water against the piles of a wooden jetty.

As he was led from the car into the house, he could smell the cool freshness of the Müggelsee, although he didn't know that was what it was called.

Inside he was guided down a flight of steps into the carpeted cellar, and led to a comfortable sofa covered with black PVC plastic. It squeaked suddenly when he was placed on it in a sitting position.

'No doubt you're hungry, Mister President,' said Badezimmer. 'We shall bring you some food. But let me warn you, although we hate violence we are prepared to employ it if you don't behave sensibly. Remain quiet and do as we tell you. You can take off your mask now.'

By the time the President had freed his face of the clinging mask, a door had closed behind Badezimmer and he was left alone in the cellar. A key on the other side of the door turned in the lock. He blinked, rubbed his sweating cheeks and forehead, and stared round through squinting eyes at his prison.

Although it was below ground level, it was no ordinary dark cellar. By dim overhead lighting concealed in circular pots in the ceiling he could see that the floor was carpeted in white mohair. Three narrowly focused lights dropped circular puddles of light on three fat, U-shaped armchairs covered, like the sofa, in shiny black PVC plastic. The seats were arranged in a semi-circle facing him. Above his head another pot let into the ceiling cast its dim spotlight directly on the President.

The walls of the cellar were left in shadow but he could see the outlines of pictures on two sides. The other two walls were covered floor-to-ceiling with what looked like black corrugated plastic screens.

Mesmerised, he stared around him. Idly, without looking at it, he picked up a silver ornament from the low table in front of him. He guessed he was suffering from what he'd once heard psychiatrists refer to as 'cross cultural shock'. His brow crinkled. The thumb of his right hand worked absent-mindedly back and forth over the smooth, cool surface of the silver figure. His eyes gazed without seeing.

Then the Presidential jaw fell open and a tiny hiccup of sound escaped his lips. His right thumb ceased its unconscious caress. The head of the slender nymph cast in silver was a tiny, rounded hairless dome!

'Oh, my God,' exclaimed the President and replaced the statuette hastily on the table as if its metal were white hot. He sat staring wild-eyed at the tiny naked head, his breathing shallow and fast.

'Can they possibly know?' he asked aloud, surprising himself with the sound of his voice in the soundproofed cellar. The almost imperceptible waft of cool fresh air told his air-conditioning-conscious American skin that he was in civilised surroundings. Nevertheless beads of sweat swelled on his forehead.

The key turned in the lock, and Badezimmer came in carrying a tray. He put it down on the table, then stopped halfway through straightening up, staring fixedly at the warm fingermarks the President's hand had left on the shining head of the silver figure.

'I see you two have already made acquaintance,' he said, grinning broadly.

'I don't know what you mean,' replied the President, avoiding Badezimmer's eye.

'Helga will be in soon to start straightening you out,' countered Badezimmer, grinning broader than ever. Still grinning he turned and left, locking the door behind him.

The President stared after him. Then he looked at his watch. It was two-thirty, a bit late for lunch. Five hours since he was kidnapped from the Western side of the Wall. He looked at the tray: caviare and toast, a frosted bottle of vodka, some strong-smelling goulash and, a concession to his life-style, a chilled glass of orange juice.

He had no hunger, but he swallowed the orange juice at a gulp and sat back trying to imagine how the crisis was being handled in his absence. He imagined the Special Actions Group of the National Security Council would be meeting by now, the hot line to Moscow would be chattering, the Western world would be on full alert.

The silence around him made him uneasy. Day and night for six years he had been surrounded. The little black bag had never been more than a few paces away, the red telephone had been close and his entourage had shadowed him constantly. He kept expecting the door to open and admit one of his staff with an option paper. Then he realised that for the first time in years he had no options. He looked around unconsciously for his customary yellow note-pad to jot down his thoughts on the situation. It added to his sense of disorientation that it wasn't to hand. And no defibrillator!

Suddenly, for the first time in his entire life, he was fearfully conscious of the presence of a heart in his chest. It seemed to swell within him like an inflated balloon. God, what would happen if it chose now to do something silly? He felt unaccustomedly mortal, frail and defenceless. Unconsciously he began to curve his back over his clenched hands in a defensive, foetal position.

He remained sitting hunched in this way, unaware of the passage of time, his mind blank. He was conscious only of the sharp shrieking sounds that greeted every slightest move that he made on the shiny black PVC surface of the sofa.

At the end of eternity the door opened quietly. He looked up and the nerve deep inside him thrummed abruptly for the second time that day.

The girl-woman with the pale and powerful face stood motionless in the doorway. As he watched she closed the door behind her and locked it before moving across the cellar towards him.

Chapter Nine

'*Dobro pojalovat*, Mr President.'

She stopped on the opposite side of the low table and offered her hand. The President got to his feet and touched the cool fingers gingerly as if he expected to receive an electric charge from them.

'Excuse me, ma'am, I don't understand Russian.' He stepped back, clasping his hands behind his back like an erring schoolboy awaiting punishment.

'It means "Welcome". Please sit.'

Two of the bulbs sunk in the ceiling brightened abruptly sending white columns of strong light shafting down into the dimness of the cellar – one onto the President's sofa and the other onto the middle of the three shiny U-shaped chairs facing him.

The shiny PVC screamed shrilly as they sat down into their respective spotlights.

'We shall make love soon, but first we must talk.'

She spoke the words with a gentle throatiness, arching her right eyebrow fractionally to emphasise the word 'talk'.

Speechless with fright the President gulped and stared at the wondrous apparition of womanhood seated before him in a golden pillar of light.

'Are you frightened?' asked Marlene Dietrich, Lauren Bacall, June Allyson and Lisbeth Scott in a Russian-accented undertone voice.

'Frightened, me?' The President blurted his lie unconvincingly. 'Why, no, not at all.'

'I know you have not been successfully alone with a woman for at least ten years.'

God, was it that long? thought the President. A red blush spread upwards over his face and into the widening tributaries of baldness reaching back into his thinning brown hair. He didn't dare ask how she knew. He decided to try to steer the talk away from this area of personal embarrassment.

'Look, would you be kind enough to explain why I'm being held here and what your purpose is. The world is hovering on the brink of a terrible abyss.' He wished at that minute that his speech-writer had been allowed along on the kidnapping.

The PVC of her chair screeched a protest as she shifted her hips slightly, lifted her right thigh and eased her right knee up on top of the left one. The black leather matador pants she wore were an additional skin from the waist to the calf before they flared. She held her arms folded, her head quite still, as she regarded him with midnight-dark eyes emptied of all expression. Her black shirt was open at the throat contrasting sharply with the alabaster white of her skin. But it was buttoned well above the high-water-mark swell of her breasts.

'I have had you brought to me here in the interests of peace and freedom for the whole world.' She looked intently into his eyes for a long moment then raised her face to the light. A deep breath flared her nostrils and her eyelids closed as though she were moved by a deep passion.

'My name is Helga Mikunov,' she said softly, still holding her eyes closed. 'I am a Russian woman. I am aged thirty-two years and I have recently dedicated my life and body to bringing peace to the world through physical love.'

Her eyes did not open. Silence broke out in the cellar, and the only sound they heard was each other's sibilant breathing.

'I am an American man, aged fifty-nine, President of the United States,' stuttered the President foolishly not knowing what else to say.

She opened her eyes again and looked at him for a long moment without speaking.

'I see the lined, anxious face of an ageing, insecure man,' she said with great gentleness. 'I see tired eyes around which the creases of years of political suspicion converge like the spokes of a cartwheel. I see a mouth bunched into an aggressive pout by a blind lust for that political power behind which a man can conceal his fading potency.' She paused and closed her eyes again. 'Caesar, Hannibal, Mussolini, Hitler, Stalin all spread death and destruction around them because they did not love enough and were not loved in the right way.' The rounded weight of her breasts resting on her folded forearms rose suddenly as she breathed deeply again and her voice became more urgent. 'But now the world cannot afford the folly of such men. It can be destroyed totally by them.'

The President at last found a small, protesting voice: 'The world is locked in a struggle between two diametrically opposed social systems. One, mine, stands for individual freedom, private enterprise and human dignity. The other, yours, for oppression.' His voice had come out pitched higher than he intended but he sat back on the PVC with a loud squeak, quite pleased with his succinct, unaided statement.

'Social systems,' she sighed. Heavy, voluptuous lids drooped lazily over her eyes and she moved her head in an almost imperceptible nod of resignation. 'If only everyone could be taught individual integrity, social systems would become irrelevant—'

'Our ideologies are totally irreconcilable,' began the President earnestly leaning forward and gesturing characteristically with his right hand as he did in television addresses to the nation at Serious Moments. The sofa squealed again under his shifting weight.

'No opposites are irreconcilable,' she interrupted quietly.

Her eyes became wide and bright. 'If they were, man and woman would never come together.'

Her right eyebrow arched in dramatic emphasis on the word 'together' and the President was struck afresh by the calm power which the broad, high cheekbones and the firm line of her wide full mouth gave to the beauty of her face. Looking at her his mouth became dry and he swallowed involuntarily.

'But they do come together in the exquisitely beautiful pain of reconciliation which is both mutual and exclusive to each,' said Helga Mikunov. 'All opposing ideologies are equally reconcilable if the desire to be reconciled can be aroused.'

She stopped speaking and stood up. She pushed the long dark hair back from her face and paused, her hands at her neck, her head thrown back, looking steadily down at him over those superb cheekbones.

The sofa made noises like the screech of a fast car skidding at high speed as the President squirmed across the plastic and twisted to look up at her. 'I represent a system,' he said, retreating desperately once more into the arid non-sexual field of politics, 'whose deepest principles and beliefs are violated to the utmost by this removal of my freedom. I demand that I be released. Kidnapping me is a moral admission of the inferiority of your system. If you value peace and freedom as you claim, release me.'

With the words out he removed his abstracted gaze from knee level and his eyes travelled up the undulating contours of the challenging female body silhouetted against the pool of light two feet from his nose.

'Can't you see?' she said quickly, exasperation deepening the throatiness of her voice. 'The systems don't matter. Man in his stupidity has always divided the world against himself, always created causes, and banded himself into tribes, nations, races, regiments or parties to pursue them.'

She paused for breath, her eyes flashing, her breasts heaving. She slapped her hands against the front of her thighs and stood, feet astride, looking fiercely down on him.

'But man has not realised or will not admit that the human race has created a combination of forces that could guarantee its destruction. He has not realised that these causes, nations and parties are led by men who ascend to absolute power at a period of their lives when their physical powers are waning. Now for the first time in history weapons of mass destruction are at their disposal in the years when their vital, stabilising potency ebbs from them. They are left bewildered, unbalanced – and dangerous. And because of their stupid pride a worldwide conspiracy of men conceals this truth—'

'But how can you be sure this applies to all—?' the President interrupted nervously.

'I am sure,' said Helga Mikunov with absolute conviction. 'And to compensate for their lost virility, in their arrogance, they may destroy the world! Now only woman can save mankind!'

'How can they do that?' asked the President, doubtfully.

She looked challengingly into his eyes. 'By making you aware of the danger – and arousing you to ... acts of *reconciliation*. I will show you.'

She turned quickly, walked to a wall in the shadows and reached out to press her hand against it.

Chapter Ten

A multi-stage Inter-Continental Ballistic Missile stood poised erect on its launch pad, smooth, sleek and long, with what looked like one of America's total of 5700 nuclear warheads loaded on its rounded nose. An explosion at its base sent it straining slowly upward on a ballooning cloud of smoke. Soon it was pushing rapidly and unstoppably into the dome of the heavens.

A long, fat, barrel-like Poseidon submarine thrust its snub nose through the surface of the ocean, trembled, then in a sudden spasm launched skywards what looked like a stubby lipstick container with a pointed end. The Multiple Independently Targetable Re-entry Vehicle quickly penetrated the borders of space where its potent nose charged with ten 50-kiloton warheads exploded, sending the cluster of minnow-like missiles darting away on a frenzied swim back to a destructive fusion with earth.

Long, thin, tubular Anti-Ballistic-Missile missiles rose through traps in the ground to proud firing angles and were launched with shivering recoils; slender nosed B-1 strategic bombers pushed inexorably through the upper atmosphere to their targets while tactical fighters jerked clear of the ground and hurled themselves aggressively upward.

The President glanced guiltily sideways. The silvery light from the screen reflected on Helga Mikunov's pale broad face as she sat absorbed in the film shots of test firings of the full range of the United States missile weaponry.

'Approximately 1054 ICBMs, 200 ABMs, 656 submarine-launched missiles,' she said, listing Soviet Intelligence estimates of US might without turning her head. 'Do you begin to believe me?' She turned to him, eyebrows raised interrogatively.

The President avoided her glance. While watching the film he had suddenly been struck by a thought of even greater desolation. Having a finger on the button of such enormously destructive phallic weaponry was not sublimation worthy of the name since so far in his years of power he had never pressed that button either.

Helga Mikunov rose and walked to the panel of switches on the wall that she had operated earlier to remove one black, corrugated screen. 'In case you need convincing further,' she said and pressed another switch.

The screen flickered and another film began. An SS9, one of the great bulbous-nosed rockets that were trundled through Red Square on May Days, stood fatly erect with its giant warhead clamped at its end. As they watched, it thrust menacingly upwards belching flame – as 1599 others could do in a war situation, according to a subtitle. IRBMs and ABMs rose on the screen in concert with the Communist version of submarine-launched missiles – 580 of these – and strategic and tactical aircraft.

The President sank squeakily into his PVC support and put a hand over his eyes until the film finished. 'I've seen enough pornography,' he said hoarsely.

The overhead lights came on again and Helga Mikunov rose and walked to the table. She poured a strong shot of vodka from the frosted bottle and took it to him. He received it without looking up and she returned to the table to pour vodka for herself in the other glass. She came back to where he sat, carrying the drink in her left hand.

In her right hand she carried the silver statuette with the bald head.

When he looked up he saw she was holding it at eye

level in front of him. He started, blushed then sank into a sea of confusion.

'How do you know about that?' he asked, his voice shaking. He gulped down some vodka, making himself cough.

Her face suddenly changed. An expression he had not seen on it before took over.

She smiled.

'Don't tell me you didn't know that Mr Conroy has the CIA bug your bedroom. Even your dreams are monitored. They're too important not to be.' The wide sensual mouth became wider in smiling. Her eyes were bright with compassion and tenderness. 'And all intelligence information is buyable at a price.'

'Oh, my God,' said the President, putting his glass down and his face back into his hands.

She smiled at him for a moment longer. Then she reached out her hand and gently stroked his thinning hair, speaking one word very quietly as she did so.

'Reconciliation.'

He sat bolt upright. The PVC shrilled. He stared up at her wild-eyed. She stood as if frozen, her hand half withdrawn.

'You're taunting me, trying to humiliate me and my country and the whole Free World,' he shouted.

'All men share your fears, not just those in your so-called Free World.' She spoke fiercely, hands on hips. 'I believe your problems are at least partly imaginary. I believe in the future of the human race. I believe with the aid of my body I can help ensure that it survives—'

'Then set me free!' he shouted, running a hand through his hair. 'Before it's too late. Before those movies on your wall become reality.' He gestured towards the screen.

'Peace and freedom are not won without taking risks,' she breathed, her breasts rising and falling quickly. 'Or without sacrifices.'

'You're out to humiliate me. You're probably filming me too, to humble me in the eyes of history—'

'The insufferable arrogance of men like you,' she exploded. Then she stopped. After a moment she went on in a quieter voice. 'If you go from here as you are now, the world will be in even greater danger. I need time in which to inspire in you a gentler spirit of reconciliation.'

'I don't believe you!' yelled the President, a desperate edge to his voice. 'This is a trick, a plot. This is a subtle, despicable Commie plot.'

Helga Mikunov flushed with anger. 'I want to give love to you, to help you,' she said forcing the words out through clenched teeth. 'To save you from yourself, to save humanity from you and men like you.'

'I just don't believe it,' screamed the President, hysterically.

Her hands flew to her face. She clawed at her hair on either side of her head. Suddenly the long black wig of luxuriant hair came free. She flung it from her into the shadows and stood motionless before him in the bright shaft of light from above.

The smooth, rounded contours of her naked head shone voluptuously under the bright illumination.

The President stared at her, unbelievingly.

'For you,' she breathed.

'What?' he croaked.

'I have done it for you. I want you and I know you want me. We must. For the future of the world.'

'I don't believe it,' whispered the President.

Instead of replying Helga Mikunov tore at the mother-of-pearl buttons on her black shirt and pulled it undone. She wore nothing underneath. She shrugged quickly out of it, allowed the garment to drop to the floor then turned and stood jutting gloriously towards the President of the United States, entirely naked to the waist.

'For peace, freedom and all mankind,' she said huskily.

The lights swam in the President's eyes. The Rockies heaved and surged in the grip of a convulsive earthquake. The Sierra Nevada rose and fell, its peaks juddering and its foothills dancing to the shock waves. New jagged mountain ranges were thrown up in the bright glare and the very earth itself seemed to tremble beneath his feet.

White-faced and shaking, the President rose from his squeaking seat and reached for the outstretched hand of Helga Mikunov. He stared transfixed at the shimmering eyes set in the broad pale face, then at the blooming glory of her naked breasts.

Their hands met, their fingers tightened. She led him to the wall in the shadows and reached out to press another switch. The black PVC corrugated screen on the other wall slid back soundlessly. The President screamed.

From behind the plate-glass wall, bald-headed female plaster dummies gazed blue-eyed and long-lashed into the room. Petrified in mid-stride wearing expensive furs, they were swinging in a wide circle round a big divan bed draped in white.

'No, no,' whimpered the President, trying to detach his hand.

'You must,' whispered Helga Mikunov fiercely. 'For the future of the world. The dream must be broken. You can do it.'

She turned to face him, still holding his hand. Her long legs made her an inch taller. She smiled into his eyes, reached up with a free hand to smooth the hair at his temple, and leaned towards him. 'For peace – but also for me,' she murmured. 'Only *you* can do this for me.'

They ran fast towards the wall, hand in hand.

The Cellophane paper, stretched from ceiling to floor to look like plate-glass, burst inward with a loud *crack* under the simultaneous impact of their two bodies.

The President swept the nearest plaster model aside with his free arm and it smashed to the floor just before their knees struck the side of the divan.

The hairline crack that had just opened up in the ten-year-old dam around the President's libido widened. The mighty pent-up body of water behind the dam shivered faintly.

They sank down.

The light of triumph shone in the eyes of Helga Mikunov as she looked up at the President. His were the amazed and delighted eyes of a small boy rediscovering a much-loved toy long since given up for lost.

'For the future of mankind,' he gasped as she pulled his trembling body tenderly down upon her own.

Chapter Eleven

Later, in the cellar by the Müggelsee, the dome-headed female dummies stood guard in a silent, unseeing ring around the bed in which the President and Helga Mikunov slept peacefully. They lay apart at rest. The President stirred occasionally, smiling a smile of seraphic serenity in his sleep. She lay flat on her back, her voluptuous eyelids closed and still.

The single white sheet that covered them fell into contours like the foothills of the Alps beneath her chin. The snow-covered slopes heaved into rhythmic little avalanches in time with her unruffled breathing.

The President opened his eyes. They widened in panic at the first sight of the plaster figures round the bed. Then he relaxed and grinned delightedly to himself as the memory flooded back. He turned to look down at Helga and felt an immediate tumult in the reservoir of his libido. The finest fuzz of pale hair shone on the naked roundness of her head and this imparted a wild and disturbing sensuality to her broad face, even in sleep.

He reached an impulsive hand towards her. Her eyes flickered open and she smiled sleepily when she saw his expression. Withdrawing a hand from under the sheet she took hold of his outstretched fingers.

'Don't try again yet, my warrior. Make haste slowly. Conserve your new-found strength.'

'You're right, Miss Mikunov,' said the President formally, relaxing back onto his pillow.

'Please call me Helga, Mister President.'

'All right . . . Helga,' he said shyly.

'What shall I call you, Mister President?' she asked, softly. 'I'd like to use a very private name that nobody else uses. Did you have a nickname as a small boy?'

The President crinkled his brow. 'I guess I must've done.'

She waited expectantly, a mischievous smile turning the corners of her mouth. 'What was it, tell me.'

'Guess it sounds kinda silly,' said the President at last, 'but in school the boys used to call me "Squeaky".'

'Squeaky?' echoed Helga.

'Yeah, sounds ridiculous now doesn't it?'

'But why "Squeaky"?'

The President hesitated, looking embarrassed. 'My voice was kinda high-pitched. And on my first day at school, my new shoes squeaked too . . . The other kids never stopped laughing at me for a week. And after that *everybody* called me Squeaky.'

She closed her eyes and bit her lip. 'Poor Squeaky.' She propped herself on one elbow and looked down at him, letting the sheet slip from her naked breasts. 'Is that why you became determined to be President – because everybody called you Squeaky and laughed at you?'

'I don't know,' said the President averting his eyes. 'I've never told anybody that before.'

'Perhaps you should have done, Squeaky,' she said huskily. 'It might have helped.'

He smiled at her, his whole face lighting up. 'Helga,' he said suddenly, then stopped in embarrassment.

'Yes?'

He blushed. 'These last few hours have made me see things kinda different. It's been the first time for over ten . . . I didn't think I'd ever . . . I'd given up—'

She leaned over him and dammed the uncertain flood of words with a finger on his mouth. 'Good, you've made me very happy.' She pulled the sheet up round her again.

'I've almost forgotten I'm a hostage. For the first time in years I feel I've broken out of an invisible cage. I feel a new freedom, a new clarity...' His voice rose and his eyes gleamed brightly.

'You are a new man,' breathed Helga Mikunov soothingly. She was becoming faintly alarmed by his fervour, wondering at the force she'd apparently unleashed.

'I can't tell you how different I feel. I see everything, everything, differently because of you.'

'You've seen that the world was caught fast in the grip of rogue-male politics?' she asked, her voice and face becoming serious.

He started at the new steeliness in her voice. 'Yes — I hadn't thought it through in quite those terms. But I guess that's something like how I feel.'

He looked into her eyes noticing for the first time her remote, almost glazed expression. He fancied that her eyes had changed colour from a deep, dark blue to an unfathomable sea-green, taking on a quality that seemed faintly hypnotic. But even as he looked at her, her face softened again and her eyes seemed to revert to a paler, friendlier blue.

'Do you really understand the spirit of reconciliation I talked of?' she asked softly.

'Yes, yes,' said the President, eagerly eyeing the heavy swell of the trembling Alpine foothills. 'But tell me about you, Helga. You are a most remarkable woman. Your face alone...' he hesitated, searching clumsily for the ultimate compliment in his threadbare repertoire, '... it's a face that could launch a thousand ICBMs,' he ended with a rush.

She looked sharply at him. 'Never say that again,' she commanded. 'That is precisely what we are trying to avoid.'

He grinned sheepishly.

'I *am* a remarkable woman,' she went on slowly without a trace of self-consciousness. 'Physiologically and intellectually I received, all in one body, a concentration of talents that are normally spread thinly among hundreds of thousands of people.'

The President searched the clear skin of her face and shoulders but could find no flaw, not the tiniest mole or blemish.

'By the age of four I was a child prodigy in my village in the Urals. I had mastered chess and the balalaika. By the age of nine I had learned all that could be taught me there of mathematics and science, and had read every book in the district library. I could run, climb and fight better than any of the boys in the village, so I was sent to Moscow. At the age of twelve I entered Moscow University—'

'And you were more beautiful than everybody else too,' said the President in an awed voice.

Helga Mikunov flung back the sheet, sprang out of bed and stood up. The sight of her long-legged, flawlessly naked body dazzled and overpowered him. He turned his face away, his eyes squeezed tight closed.

'More beautiful, perhaps,' she said, standing with her hands on her hips, her feet astride. 'But, more important, at Moscow University I studied first history and psychology and then, because of my good fortune in being able to absorb my studies so effortlessly, I went on simultaneously to study political science, medicine, drama and the ballet. By eighteen I was doing advanced research in all these subjects.'

The President turned back, opened one eye gingerly, decided to risk it, and opened the other. He tried to concentrate his attention decently halfway between the fair shadow at the apex of her loins and the pale, temple-throbbing outcrops of her bosom.

'My unique combination of academic disciplines and the gift of rare sexual attractiveness qualified me uniquely both to diagnose the political ills of mankind – and to apply the antidote.'

Her voice had become husky again and the President shifted uncomfortably beneath the sheet. 'I don't quite understand . . .'

'Think of a sailor charting his position on a map, taking fixes, and drawing lines of calculation. His vessel is invariably found where the lines converge.' She paused, picked up her black shirt and shrugged into it. 'I was able to take a fix from positions of advanced research in four widely separated disciplines – history, male psychology, medicine and political science.'

She slowly buttoned in the jutting female outcrops. The President continued to watch her, faintly saddened by this concealment.

'For me the lines converged to a point where perhaps nobody had seen them converge before. I noticed that the tumultuous whirlpools of history swung and eddied around men who, at certain times in their lives, behaved consistently like wounded rogue elephants, scattering their herds and despoiling their forests in paroxysms of outraged impotence . . .'

She reached out and removed an ankle-length bathrobe of pink silk from one of the bald-domed plaster model girls. Watching the President carefully through narrowed eyes, she wrapped it slowly around herself.

His gaze fastened briefly on the plaster limbs of the dummy, but swung back quickly to the reliefs of her live warm body. Seeing this, she let out an imperceptible sigh of satisfaction.

The President, not realising he had passed a test, asked, 'Me? A wounded rogue elephant?'

She smiled at him warmly and he basked openly for a moment in the healing ultra-violet light of the smile. 'Not any more, my fine warrior,' she said softly. 'But before you came here, because the pressure on modern political leaders has increased to a degree unprecedented in history, your own personal potency as a man had vanished. And because of the enormous forces of destruction at your fingertips the possibility of your going on the rampage like a wild rogue elephant increased day by day.' She smoothed the pink silk over her breasts and down the swell of her flanks. 'Now I think your virile instincts for augmenting the herd have been revived and restored. The jungle's a safer place for us all.'

The President remained silent for a moment as if something still puzzled him. 'But who are your helpers – Badezimmer, Kafferty? How did you organise the kidnapping? You must have an army behind you.'

Helga showered smile-warmth on him again and when she spoke it was as though she was explaining something patiently to a child. 'Power, my sweet Squeaky, means only one thing to a man – massive numbers of followers, violence, explosive force, large organisations, the threat of pain and death. But to a woman, power is a much more subtle concept.' As if to illustrate her point she tightened the belt of the pink silk robe, making herself a narrow-waisted egg-timer shape. 'In Moscow my talents were employed naturally by the Party. Therefore I came to know all the so-called powerful men at its head. But power, my Squeaky, in the hands of a woman can be embodied in the subtlety of a promise, a promise of ecstasy, a promise of joy. Man can't find joy alone. So the promise of helping to discover that joy – or deny him it – becomes power.'

The President stared captivated at the egg-timer, his eyes flicking up and down as though watching the invisible grains of time draining silently down into her loins. He became aware suddenly that he had lost all track of time since he plunged through the trapdoor of the viewing stand. And in the same moment he became intensely aware that the sands of time were running faster now through his own life. There was not much time left in the upper cavity, but what there was he felt he wanted to spend with the woman standing before him.

'With only a few helpers,' she said, 'a beautiful and determined woman can exploit large organisations, plug into the lines of their power resources, play rivals off against one another – employ, in fact, the politics of man. But with her sexuality she has a quality ultimately more powerful than nuclear weapons because man has an irresistible, age-old obsession with the soft charms of a woman.'

'But how big is your organisation?' asked the President in an awed voice. 'And are you the head of it?'

'Many other carefully chosen females have been trained by our worldwide organisation in both the East and the West. The work has been done at scientific research establishments ostensibly concerned with other things. You might think of them as modern angels of mercy. I am the co-founder of the movement and its leader in the Communist world. It was born when I met a brilliant Western mind at a seminar in Moscow. He saw the possibility of employing my theory and my talents to the full.' She smiled slowly at the President. 'He is from your own country. We aim to insert our trained "angels" into all levels of government throughout the world as an antidote to this most pressing of dangers—'

'Why,' the President began slowly, looking down at the bedclothes covering his chest, 'did you start with me rather than the leader of your own country? It would have been easier, wouldn't it?'

There was a long silence and Helga Mikunov began pacing back and forth at the foot of the bed, passing slowly between the petrified female dummies. Halting, she swung round the naked one from which she'd taken the robe and leaned over its left shoulder, her own sensually-naked head cheek-to-cheek with the frozen-featured plaster dome. 'I didn't start with you,' she said quietly.

The President looked up sharply. 'What do you mean?'

'I *did* start with the leader of my own country.'

'You didn't go with that bastard ——!' shouted the President, his voice rising almost to a falsetto on the name of the First Secretary of the Communist Party Union of Soviet Socialist Republics. For a moment his fists gathered the sheets into two great bunches. His face worked nervously. Then he leapt out of bed, flinging the bedclothes aside and dashed towards her.

She started back holding the nude dummy at arm's length between her and the naked President of the United States. He grabbed at the dummy and held it tight.

'With – with—' the President spluttered as if on the brink of an epileptic fit. The First Secretary's name clearly would not pass his lips a second time. Gripped by the blind rage of jealousy he began to move round the dummy, still gripping it tightly. But Helga moved crabwise around it too, keeping it between them. They both clung to the dummy, their eyes locked on each other and little high-pitched hiccup noises escaped the President's lips.

'I did it for peace and freedom,' said Helga urgently. 'But it was not the same as with us.'

'Not the same? How was it not the same?' demanded the President.

'I failed.'

'Failed? Impossible! No man could resist you.'

'He did.'

'How? Why?'

'I don't know.'

'You must know.'

'I suppose he is in a more advanced state of...' Words failed her for want of delicacy. '... He's not so much of a man as you are, I suppose,' she said, suddenly inspired. 'He could not...' Her voice tailed away.

The blood rushed back into the Presidential knuckles as his grip on the dummy relaxed. A look of smug satisfaction began to steal across his face.

'Really? You really think he's not such a man as...' His voice was that of a little boy seeking approval for his deeds.

'Yes, I'm sure of it,' she said quickly. 'He set me up in a luxury flat near the Kremlin – but only to make others think he needed a mistress. He visited me, brought me presents but never touched me. It was for peace and freedom but he never once touched me.'

The President's hands fell from the dummy. 'He just couldn't make it with you, huh?' The President laughed an unpleasant little laugh. 'Couldn't make it,' he repeated and laughed again. He walked back to the bed, a swagger creeping into his naked stride. 'I can't say I'm surprised, mind you,' he added, his voice becoming more relaxed and expansive.

The President turned round to face her again, spreading his arms wide, hunching his shoulders and grinning: 'Just shows how that Marxist crap really saps a man's energy, huh?' He laughed again. Then he looked down and became fully aware of his full frontal nakedness. Hastily he flung himself back under the bedclothes.

Helga Mikunov, fully relaxed and in control again, smiled indulgently from behind the dummy's shoulder. 'Why so shy, my Squeaky? Why so shy?'

The President blushed crimson, the flush speading rapidly upward into his scalp through the thinning tributaries in his brown hair.

'Come on, tell me,' she urged soothingly.

The President stared into every corner of the cellar to avoid her eyes. After a long silence, he said, 'For the Most Powerful Man in the World I guess I feel—' he stuttered and began blushing again '. . . feel kind of underprivileged in a certain department, kinda lightweight . . .' His voice tailed away and he pressed an embarrassed fist to the space between his eyebrows.

For a long moment, silence fell in the cellar.

'The First Secretary is smaller.'

Her voice was hardly a whisper and she spoke with her chin still resting on the dummy's shoulder. The words didn't sink into the President's brain for a moment. When they did, his face split from ear to ear in a huge, delighted grin. 'No kidding?'

'No kidding.'

'Hey, how about that,' yelled the President jumping out of bed again.

He danced across to Helga and planted a bold kiss on her cheek. 'You know, Helga, you really understand how to make a guy feel great,' he said. He pulled back and they looked smiling at each other. Suddenly he leaned forward and planted a second kiss – on the cold cheek of the dummy. 'Goodbye, girls, no more will you bother me.'

'Shall you,' said Helga.

'Shall I what?' asked the President.

'No, "shall" you: it should be "shall you" to be grammatically correct.'

'Oh, yeah,' laughed the President and they went back arm in arm to sit on the bed. 'You're even brilliant at English grammar, too.' Then his face became serious. 'But I don't get it. Okay so . . .' the President choked over the name again, 'so . . . the First Secretary couldn't make it with you. How did that lead to me? Does he know that you're doing this? Does he approve? Is he protecting you and your friends?'

'He probably suspects me.'

'Only suspects?'

'When he rejected me I told him I would go to you – or rather, have you brought to me. I told him I found you more attractive anyway.'

'You're playing the two of us off,' said the President, his voice hollow with amazement.

'How could you think such a terrible thing, Squeaky?' she asked, pouting exaggeratedly. 'It's not like that at all.'

'Why hasn't the KGB found this place, then?' the President demanded.

Helga smiled. 'Perhaps we are too clever. Perhaps some of our top men have already succumbed.'

'Succumbed to you personally?' queried the President.

She shook her head. 'No, as I told you, many "angels of mercy" are being trained . . . and many have naked heads like those visions you see when you sleep . . . You're not alone, you see. Many, many other men like you suffer as you have done.'

As the President sat alone on the PVC sofa, reflecting on all the extraordinary things that had happened in those cataclysmic twenty-four hours, he remembered most clearly the expression on Helga's face when she had made that particular announcement. It was a half-smile that combined compassion, tenderness and a hint of triumph. The release of anxiety that came with the full realisation that many other decent men shared his secret agonies had, at that moment, given him a heady, overwhelming sense of new-found freedom.

He had stared at her in amazement, at a loss for

words, and now he found he had difficulty remembering the rest of their conversation in detail. It was at that point that she had revealed that he was soon to receive a visitor, a British journalist. He had agreed to her suggestion that he should tell the journalist he had been taken hostage 'in the name of humanity, peace and freedom' and she had shown him the communiqué that was to be given to the reporter.

Helga had then tenderly brought him fresh clothes, all exactly the right size and fit. Moments later Badezimmer had entered bringing a tray of beluga caviare, buttered toast and a frosted bottle of vodka. She had run a soothing hot bath for him in an adjoining luxury bathroom, then disappeared, leaving him to begin the process of accustoming himself to his new sense of well-being.

She had promised to return later to talk further of 'reconciliation' and, as he sat waiting on the PVC sofa, he realised he was looking forward to the prospect of her return with the same eager sense of anticipation that he had experienced every year as a small boy in the days leading up to Christmas. And yet at the same time he realised that the thought of all those colourful, glittering presents beneath the Christmas tree had never been quite like this!

At that second the door behind him opened. The PVC sofa shrieked shrilly beneath him as he swung round. His eyes widened joyously as Helga moved forward slowly from the shadows and stopped, smiling down warmly at him.

She was a vision of unparalleled beauty. This time she wore only a coat of snowy white mink and her gloriously unadorned head shimmered brilliantly in the overhead light. Quite deliberately she had matched herself to the recurring central image of his dream!

As he looked at her she lifted her arms towards him in a silent gesture of invitation. He rosed unsteadily from the PVC sofa, making it squeak wildly once more, and stumbled towards her. Before he reached her arms, she slipped out of the mink and let it slide slowly to the floor. With it heaped carelessly about her ankles she stood wondrously naked from head to toe, waiting for him.

'Helga,' he gasped as he reached her. 'Helga!'

'Squeaky,' she murmured in response, drawing him tenderly against her. 'My very own dear Squeaky.'

Chapter Twelve

'God only knows, genitalmen, what torture and humiliation the President may be undergoing on behalf of Western Democracy at this moment.'

The Vice-President of the United States of America spoke through lips pursed with his interpretation of tense concern. He paused, his brow crinkling into crazy-paving patterns and brushed at his left shoulder, sending specks of dandruff that gleamed silver in the fluorescent light showering over the front of the immaculate uniform of the long-suffering Chairman of the Joint Chiefs of Staff. 'Therefore, genitalmen, we must redouble our efforts to find a way out of this impasse and lay to rest the spectre of world destruction that hangs over us like the sword of Demosthenes.'

'Goddammit,' said Conroy. 'It was the sword of *Damocles*. But let's stop pussy-footing around this whole thing. I reiterate, nobody should be allowed to hostage the President of the United States with impunity. Let's act. Let's stop talkin' and do somethin'.' He hunched his shoulders twice and gazed pugnaciously round the table.

To save wear and tear on the lungs and blood-vessels of CIA operatives, the anti-bugging device like a silent dog-whistle had been set up on an improvised music stand and attached to a foot-bellows. Beside Conroy an agent stood pumping his leg on the bellows as though reinflating the tyre of some invisible car. Outside the glass dome the four uniformed colonels stood guard with their backs to the deliberations of the Special Actions Group of the National Security Council for the Repatriation of the American President. Already it was known popularly by its initials and newspapers on sale in the streets outside carried banner headlines announcing 'SAGNASCRAP MEETS AGAIN THIS PM'.

'What exactly do you suggest, Conroy?' asked Stanley George.

'I propose we snatch the First Secretary of the Communist Party of the Union of Soviet Socialist Republics and hold him hostage against the safe return of the President,' snapped Conroy.

The five men under the glass dome stared goldfish-mouthed at Conroy. Nobody spoke. The man on the foot-bellows gaped too – and in his astonishment stopped pumping.

'Pump!' yelled Conroy turning an ugly wrathful face on the agent. 'For krissakes keep pumping!' He turned back to the table only when the man had begun jerking his leg on the bellows with a redoubled frenzy.

'Conroy, are you crazy?' asked the Vice-President. 'Kidnap the First Secretary! You want to start World War Three for sure?'

'I sincerely believe that should be the scale of our response. We gotta act fast,' insisted Conroy. 'The report by that screwball journalist Groot shows in my view that the President is already in a state of drugged delirium.'

'Why drugged delirium?' asked George.

'Have you ever heard the President refer to crap like "peace, freedom and humanity" when talking about the Commies?' asked Conroy scornfully. 'We gotta act now before they damage his mind permanently.'

'Have your operatives been able to turn up anything independently on the group that did the kidnapping?' asked the Chairman of the Joint Chiefs of Staff sarcastically. 'Or are we relying exclusively in this crisis on the intelligence provided by a Limey gossip-writer?'

Conroy's face flushed purple and veins bulged at his temples. 'I assigned six of my top Communist-bloc operatives to work Groot over and follow up the trail to its source.' He paused dramatically. 'Those men are now all dead.'

'We read that in the papers,' said Garstenmeyer. '"Dozen Die in Sauna Slaying Mystery". Seems there were six of ours and six of them. Couldn't you at least have disguised our boys to make 'em all look like Russians? Better public relations, I'd have thought!'

Conroy glowered at Garstenmeyer. 'I did – disguised 'em all as KGB men. The KGB men are the ones the newspapers identified as Americans. They disguised their men too.' He breathed quickly and loudly through his nose several times in quick succession like a boxer landing a flurry of blows and the other men recoiled instinctively in their seats. 'D'ya see now that it has to be official Kremlin policy? D'ya see how ruthless these goddamned Commies are? They're using Groot as their stooge.'

'Genitalmen, genitalmen,' said the Vice-President quietly, demonstrating his ability to pour oil on troubled waters in a chairman-like way. 'Before you chew each other's heads off, I think you should hear my report.'

'Sure, sure,' chorused George, the Chairman of the Joint Chiefs of Staff, Garstenmeyer and the emboldened Secretary of State. Conroy looked contemptuous. His expression implied nobody could tell him anything he didn't know already.

'The United States Ambassador to Moscow had an audience with the First Secretary in the Kremlin an hour ago,' said the Vice-President in measured tones. 'His report is significant.' He looked round unblinking for five full seconds. At least two men round the table shuddered at the prospect of his becoming President if the Group failed to achieve Repatriation. 'He reports that the First Secretary behaved in a very agitated fashion and assured him repeatedly that this was not an act of the Soviet Government or the Soviet Communist Party or any of its agencies. Despite great efforts, his intelligence services had been unable to locate the President on Communist territory.'

'Bullshit,' said Conroy quietly.

'He assured our Ambassador that if the President were in Communist territory nobody in the Soviet Union would sleep until he were found and returned safe and well and the culprits were punished.'

'Crap!' said Conroy, a little less quietly.

'What is more, genitalmen, the First Secretary of the Communist Party of the Union of Soviet Socialist Republics has given the following undertaking.' The Vice-President glanced meaningfully at Conroy. 'He assured our Ambassador that a site had been cleared on the north side of Red Square and that at twelve noon precisely tomorrow, Moscow time, he and the Soviet Premier will personally carry out the ceremony of laying the foundation stone for the Moscow Playbaby Club.'

He paused dramatically.

The meeting gasped. Conroy muttered an even greater obscenity but it was obscured by the communal drawing of breath. For a brief moment the CIA agent ceased his foot movement. But he recovered rapidly and continued pumping faster than ever as Conroy began to turn his head towards him.

'The First Secretary said he was doing this to demonstrate the concern and goodwill of his country in the united effort to restore the US President to his homeland.' The Vice-President sat back smirking as if he were personally responsible for this political coup. 'So, Conroy, you will see that your proposal to kidnap the First Secretary is not in step with current developments.'

The others nodded their emphatic agreement. But Conroy made no attempt to hide an expression of non-conviction.

The Defense Secretary ran quickly through the present deployment of the armed forces which hadn't changed much except that the aircraft carriers had now reached stations in the Baltic off Rostock.

'So genitalmen,' said the Vice-President, 'I think our decision here and now is a formality. I propose we await tomorrow's foundation-laying ceremony and hope that it will lead a few minutes later to the return of the President. All those in agreement?'

Hands went up round the table. Only Conroy's hand did not join the others in the air. He continued to sit conspicuously on his palms, staring straight ahead with a concentratedly blank expression on his face.

In Moscow, one window remained lit high up in the walls of the Kremlin long after all others had been extinguished. The silhouette of a bulky man staring out into the night was framed in the square of yellow light. Below in Red Square, bulldozers, earth-movers and mechanical grabs worked by floodlight, clearing the last remnants of the building that had until yesterday stood on the site.

The clank of metal and the roar of engines drifted faintly up to the lighted window. The silhouetted figure stood for a moment as though listening, then shrugged, turned away and walked over to the large desk in the austerely furnished office.

He stood looking for a moment at the silver statuette in the shape of a naked female that was acting as a paper-weight among the pile of Party files, folders, memoranda and option papers.

He crossed suddenly to the door, opened it and looked out. Sitting on a chair in the dingy corridor outside was a Russian four-star general carrying a black attaché case. The general smiled thinly at the First Secretary, raised the case and patted it meaningfully. The First Secretary nodded at him and the man seated on an adjoining chair clutching a portable Soviet defibrillator, then closed the door wearily.

For a second or two he leaned against the closed door, his deeply lined, vodka-ruddied face grey with exhaustion. Then he walked back to the desk and stood irresolutely in front of it. He looked musingly again at the silver statuette, picked it up and ran his thumb absent-mindedly over the smooth, rounded dome of the figure's bald head.

'Helga, Helga,' he muttered distractedly. He replaced the statuette on the desk sighing and shaking his head, then turned and raised his eyes to the portraits hanging above the empty fireplace. 'Vladimir Ilich,' he said softly, looking up at the broad, spade-bearded face of the balding man who had started it all, 'why is there nothing in your writings about this? You left nothing to guide us.' He rubbed his hand agitatedly over his face. 'You were lucky to die so young.'

His gaze moved to the arrogant face with a walrus moustache in the next frame. He nodded wordlessly at the portrait for a full half-minute as if realising too late a great and underlying truth that made everything comprehensible. 'Joseph,' he said quietly. He stopped nodding and instead began shaking his head. 'Man of steel, you may have been. Better had you been flesh and blood.' He laughed shortly, humourlessly. 'Helga might have made you a king.'

He turned from the desk and stopped at a large stone bust on a pedestal, his hand resting on its shoulder. He looked at the lined face, the bushy mane of hair, the flowing beard. He ran his forefinger over the inscription on the plinth. 'Workers of the world unite,' he murmured resignedly.

He stood, his shoulders sagging, gazing vacantly at the bust. 'Defect, yes, but how?' Then, with a surge of resolution, he straightened and walked quickly to his desk and picked up the telephone. He gave instructions for a meeting to be held in his office in half-an-hour's time. The letters KGB were never actually mentioned in the conversation but the cautious nature of the phrases employed told the tape-recorder men on the end of the bugging equipment precisely what sort of meeting it was going to be.

As SAGNASCRAP dispersed from the White House basement on the other side of the world, Conroy hurried away to a private telephone. He spoke into it for a few minutes using cautious guarded phrases and never once mentioning the letters CIA as he convened a meeting of a very select number of people. Then he left the building by a door which avoided the three hundred journalists waiting for news and drove off towards the river.

The gathering came to order half an hour later at the computerised headquarters of the Central Intelligence Agency across the Potomac.

At exactly the same time the bulky silhouetted figure looking down on Red Square from the last lighted window in the walls of the Kremlin was joined by four other shadows who came into his office on wary, furtive feet.

Chapter Thirteen

The private DC9 luxury jet 'Playbaby' winged in over the rural flatlands of western Russia heading for Moscow. Inside its sumptuously furnished fuselage a man with the facial features of the Playbaby empire's founder was holding court. His broad, hunched shoulders, however, looked as though he wore a quarter-back's pads inside his shirt. He also hissed repeatedly through his nose from time to time like a prize-fighter landing a flurry of blows, rather as Gerrard K. Conroy, Director of the Central Intelligence Agency, was wont to do.

Garstenmeyer, head of the American Secret Service, sat beside him on the white, fur-covered sofa. A low table full of exotic drinks stood in front of them. An eight-girl crew of genuine Jet Playbabies with shiny satin baby bonnets and provocatively skimpy romper suits with fishnet tights and stiletto-heeled shoes flitted in and out on a continuous stream of fatuous errands of service; they smiled, bulged, leaned low over the table to reveal their cleavages, juddered, giggled and wiggled away.

In a separate lounge twelve smooth-cheeked, slender, male CIA agents, obviously selected for those very qualities, sat disconsolately in their seats in pebble-dash sports jackets, looking as if something that they knew would be very unpleasant was going to happen to them soon.

Conroy in the guise of the founding father of the

Playbaby chain of clubs got up and spoke briefly with the pilot. Then he turned and went through to the cabin where the twelve agents sat. 'Okay you guys, get changed, quick,' he barked.

They leapt from their seats as one man, undressed and wriggled into tight, gaudy, silk Playbaby costumes that were padded generously at hip, crotch and thorax. They pulled on long blonde and brunette wigs with satin baby bonnets attached, fixed white collars and black bow-ties around their necks and slipped dainty, white, starched cuffs on their bare brown forearms.

'You're a great gang of pansies,' said Conroy approvingly as they primped themselves back into their seats, giggling and flapping their wrists exaggeratedly. When he had completed his inspection, he hurried back to the luxury saloon where the carpet overflowed into his shoes at every step.

'Okay, Garstenmeyer, let's see that mask once more,' he said brusquely.

Garstenmeyer dutifully hauled a rubber-and-plastic mask from his pocket, stretched it in his hands, then held it up in front of his face. With a resounding *thwock* he let it contract quickly around his head. Then he put a fedora over his hair and looked up at Conroy as the spit and image of the First Secretary of the Union of Soviet Socialist Republics.

'Leonid!' shouted Conroy, sticking out his hand towards Garstenmeyer. 'How are yer, guy? Nice to see yer. Welcome to bondage.'

Garstenmeyer grinned and the mask grinned with him. 'Yer like it, huh, Conroy?'

'Sure, it's great. Big improvement on yer own face, fellah!'

Garstenmeyer pulled it off and growled like a dog at the CIA chief. The pilot announced they were beginning their descent into Moscow's Sheremetyevo Airport and Conroy went back to check his men's romper-suit costumes and baby bonnets one last time.

'Any final questions, you fellahs?' he roared. Twelve long-haired heads shook shyly. Slender wrists pulled cute little baby shawls made of fleece around slender shoulders.

The additional shawls had been designed to counteract the Moscow cold – and to conceal the genuinely flat chests of the CIA agents at the point where their own flesh became visible.

The DC9 taxied in to a welcome from a fleet of shiny black Zil VIP limousines. Conroy, Garstenmeyer, the genuinely female Jet Playbabies and the agents in drag crowded to the windows to look out at Moscow's main international airport. The door was opened and steps were wheeled into place. A sensational blonde female Playbaby in a flame-red costume stepped to the door and waved to the frozen-faced group of black-coated Communist leaders below.

Conroy noticed the airfield was ringed with troops, and clusters of MiG-21 fighters were parked round the perimeter. But nobody seemed to notice the black-coated man who raced quickly up a second set of steps that had been wheeled to the rear door of the DC9.

Suddenly somebody who looked very much like the First Secretary of the Communist Party of the Union of Soviet Socialist Republics tapped Conroy on the shoulder as he gazed through the window.

'Excuz me. Could you tell me pleez who is the senior CIA officer on board?'

Conroy turned round, blue in the face with rage. 'Garstenmeyer! For krissakes get that mask off. We're here! Do you want them to rumble us. Get it off, get it off!'

Conroy, almost foaming at the mouth, turned his attention to the welcoming party standing irresolutely outside at the foot of the gangway.

'But, pleez, you don't understand . . .' continued the man who looked like the First Secretary, tapping Conroy's shoulder again.

'Great accent, Garstenmeyer, just great,' said Conroy sarcastically without turning. 'But get that mask the hell off your face quick.'

Conroy ignored the further tapping, so the man who looked like the First Secretary shrugged and hurried back along the plane and out of its rear exit just as Garstenmeyer emerged from a luxury loo smelling of expensive after-shave and scented soap.

'We ready to go, Conroy?' he asked innocently.

'Yeah, wise guy. Glad you decided to take the mask off and not ruin the whole operation.'

Garstenmeyer stared at Conroy uncomprehendingly.

At the bottom of the steps the First Secretary, a little out of breath, waited with outstretched hand to greet the disguised Conroy. As the CIA director descended towards him he congratulated himself silently on the quality of the mask he'd provided for Garstenmeyer. The man who stood at the gangway bottom was a mirror image of the one who'd just tapped him on the shoulder in the plane.

The First Secretary's obviously unenthusiastic bear hug knocked Conroy's wig very slightly awry. Behind him, the twenty giggling Playbabies of both sexes crowded noisily down the gangway, but he quietened them by turning a ferocious scowl over his shoulder.

The Russian leader cleared his throat nervously, then addressed himself to the founder of the Playbaby empire. 'We welcome you in a spirit of concern to save the life of the President of the United States,' he said through thin lips. Then, without waiting for a response, he turned abruptly and led the way to the row of shiny official limousines.

No photographers or pressmen had been allowed on the tarmac to witness the humiliating arrival on Russian territory of the representative plane-load of Western decadence.

The American ambassador to Moscow stepped forward to introduce himself briefly without hiding his distaste for the cultural level of the visitors.

The windows of the streetcar-size Zil limousines were curtained in green so that Conroy and his party sat unseen in the shadowy jade light of the rear seats as the motorcade sped into Moscow behind the First Secretary at ninety miles per hour.

The onion domes and minarets of the Kremlin shimmered in the pale autumn sunshine and the huge crowd of Muscovites filling Red Square stirred with excitement as the motorcade swung into view.

Conroy and his Playbabies drew back the curtains at the car windows to gaze out in awe at the Lenin Tomb and the high fortress walls. The set faces of the crowd stared in at the windows in silent curiosity, ignoring the waving and flirtatious winking of the limousines' gaudily dressed occupants.

Russian soldiers in stiff peaked caps, khaki jackets, royal-blue trousers and black knee-boots stood guard expressionlessly every few yards along the front of the crowd, looking curiously like lion-tamers — except that they held submachine-guns clamped across their chests instead of chairs and whips.

'Jesus,' breathed Conroy in an uncharacteristic moment of doubt. 'What have we got ourselves into? This is kind of scary, ain't it?'

Garstenmeyer let the curtain on his window fall back into place. 'Yeah,' he said wiping his damp brow. 'You're too damned right. You and your crazy ideas. Why don't we get the hell out now, before it's too late?'

'It's already too late,' said Conroy as the cars sighed to a halt and rocked gently on their expensive springing. 'You've got both masks, you sure?' he asked for the hundredth time.

'Yeah I got 'em,' said Garstenmeyer. 'Leonid's in my left pocket,' he said, pulling at his left jacket pocket and uncovering the florid, hooked nose of the First Secretary, 'and I'm in the right.' He pulled at his right pocket to show a bluish pasty-faced piece of mask approximating to two square inches of the jowl beneath his own right ear.

'Great,' said Conroy. 'The plan can't fail. Take it easy.'

He sat back in his seat, the confident pugnacious glint coming back into his eye. 'Nobody hostages the President of the United States with impunity,' he muttered fiercely to himself just before the door was opened to let them out into the sunlight of Red Square.

The First Secretary's stone-laying speech was brief. He

stood on a raised platform, the rails of which were decorated with bunting of the national colours of the United States and the Soviet Union. Beside him the Premier and other leaders from the Party and Government stood impassively in long dark coats and trilbies or fur hats. The expressions on their faces were those of men in a nightmare hoping to wake up soon before they crashed down on whatever in their own particular horror they were falling towards.

'This foundation stone of the Red Square Playbaby Club,' said the First Secretary waving a silver trowel in his left hand and wincing as he spoke, 'will be seen by history as a foundation stone for peace and freedom for the whole world.'

The gaggle of genuine and impostor Playbabies drawn up round the stand postured coquettishly, clapping and tittering. The wind was gusting and rocking the microphone making it difficult for the crowd to hear the First Secretary's words over the loudspeakers. The noise that came from them in fact was a garble sounding very much like a hen-run at feeding time. The Western press roped off in a nearby enclosure were following the speech from typed English translations handed out beforehand. Conroy and his party were reading from similar sheets handed to them as they left the cars.

'In permitting a licentious bourgeois institution, entirely alien to our ideology, to be built and opened here in Red Square,' the First Secretary continued, glancing straight down the cleavage of a 42–23–38 Cleveland Playbaby of the Year standing deliberately below him, and breaking out into an immediate sweat, 'we are demonstrating that our country is capable of making a supreme sacrifice in a time of crisis, in fact at the time of the greatest threat to world peace that has arisen in this nuclear age.'

The First Secretary licked his dry lips and tried hard not to look down again at the ideologically alien bosom beneath him. He glanced up at the half-ton concrete block suspended on chains a few feet in front of his face over a waiting bed of cement.

'I will read the inscription on this foundation stone,' intoned the First Secretary. 'For the introduction of Playbabies to Moscow. To be laid in the name of peace and freedom. Dated this twenty-third day of October—'

Conroy's roving eye suddenly noticed a blonde, Slavonic-looking Playbaby with a blue chin tugging at the hair of one of his fair-skinned agents in drag.

'Psst! KGB!' he whispered fiercely to Garstenmeyer pointing to the blue-chinned Playbaby. 'I think they might be on to us.'

'Hell's teeth,' said Garstenmeyer.

'Get him,' mouthed Conroy.

'How?' pleaded Garstenmeyer frantically.

Conroy's eyes darted around like tongues of flame seeking combustible material.

'The block!' he hissed, inclining his head towards the foundation stone.

Garstenmeyer moved away and whispered hurried instructions into a shell-like ear. The twelve slender, fair-skinned male Playbabies-in-drag exchanged meaningful winks and began moving surreptitiously but purposefully to surround their blue-chinned opponent from the KGB. Simpering and giggling up towards where the First Secretary stood and holding their fleecy little wraps with one hand they engulfed the KGB Playbaby in the middle of their girlish gaggle and edged him in front of the stand.

They giggled even louder as the First Secretary stopped speaking and with his little silver trowel began flicking symbolic amounts of mortar down onto the oozing cement bed beneath the block. As he scooped up the mortar from a ceremonial salver on a lectern beside him, the CIA Playbabies giggled hysterically pretending they were being showered with specks of mortar.

In their midst the KGB man fought with concentrated desperation to free himself. He cut about him with karate chops and jabbed his bony knees repeatedly into various groins. But the padded costumes of the CIA special wardrobe department and the press of bodies absorbed most of the blows harmlessly. His shouted cries were carefully drowned out by the well-drilled shrieks and giggles of the American agents around him.

The anguish in the KGB man's face turned to horror as the First Secretary raised his arm as a signal for the chain around the foundation stone to be released in the control cabin of the crane from which it was suspended.

At that precise moment the crowd of girls appeared to stumble and panic and some of them fell to their knees. Then, as the chains around the block loosened and fell away, they all screamed loud screams of fright.

The great oblong block of Siberian stone zonked down into its gooey bed, shuddered for a moment on the surface, then sank in hard and square.

From the top of the ceremonial stand the leaders of the Communist world, to their horror, could not be sure whether they had seen one or more of the symbols of Western sexual decadence fall under the stone or not. This was due to the speed with which three deceptively slender pairs of arms with muscles like whipcord had supplied the final deft push to the blue-chinned Playbaby before the block compressed him neatly into the cement.

To distract attention, the remaining nine Playbabies-in-drag had flung themselves to the ground shrieking and kicking their legs wildly in the air like demented can-can dancers.

The eyes of the Russian leaders popped out on stalks at this unprecedented Red Square scene.

'Ees anybody hurt?' yelled the First Secretary in a panic. Men rushed from the stand to help the struggling agents to their feet.

'I don't think so,' yelled Conroy. 'Stand still, everybody, let me count ya.'

He made a big charade of counting heads. 'No. All present and correct,' he told the First Secretary. 'Kinda lucky, I guess.'

The Playbabies-in-drag recomposed themselves quickly and with the real American females began mobbing the

First Secretary and cheering his laying of the stone in shrill, excited voices.

The Western press photographers began firing off their flashes to record the unprecedented scene for posterity with the Kremlin's onion domes as a backdrop.

When the giggling and screeching had risen to a high pitch again, Conroy plucked at Garstenmeyer's sleeve. 'Get the hell in there with the masks,' he ordered out of the side of his mouth.

'Okay, wish me luck,' muttered Garstenmeyer and he advanced unnoticed on the apparently all-female swarm seething around the Russian leader. As he went, he pulled a rubberoid mask from the left pocket of his jacket.

Conroy watched tensely from the quiet fringes of the storm. He had lost sight of Garstenmeyer. He began counting. Sometimes he thought he saw the head of the First Secretary bobbing wildly; sometimes a male arm clutched at the air above the boiling ruck of Playbabies as if its owner was drowning in female flesh. Ninety-eight, ninety-nine, one hundred, a hundred and one ... still no sign of Garstenmeyer or the First Secretary. Were the twelve being too enthusiastic? Conroy measured with his eye the distance to the line of shiny black Zil limousines waiting to whisk them back to the airport and the DC9. Their Russian drivers stood by watching the scene open-mouthed.

The crowd of Muscovites, moved by the girlish adulation of their leader – whom they had never thought of before as a sex symbol – began cheering on the Playbabies. In their excitement they strained at the rope barriers behind which they were marshalled, threatening to break free. Conroy saw that at any moment chaos would swamp his carefully laid plan. He began to moan quietly; then suddenly a portly figure reeled from the ruck holding his head in his hands.

But, dammit, who was it? he wondered desperately. Garstenmeyer had been chosen for the job because he was the same overweight, running-to-fat build as the First Secretary. Had Garstenmeyer managed to fix the mask of his own face over the head of the First Secretary so they could spirit him away?

Conroy rushed towards the reeling figure and tore the hands free of the face.

He had done it!

The rubbery features of 'Garstenmeyer' looked twisted and unnatural enough for Conroy to know that it was the First Secretary underneath. He flung his arms round the stunned man. 'Nobody hostages the President of the United States with impunity,' he muttered fiercely and hustled 'Garstenmeyer' over to the nearest limousine, yelling over his shoulder for his twelve men and the Jet Playbabies to follow.

Immediately the ruck began breaking up and rushing for the cars.

Conroy looked back and saw Garstenmeyer, now wearing the mask of the First Secretary — and, thought Conroy, looking very much like him, too — standing dazed and bedraggled on the cobbles of Red Square, looking after them.

Conroy thrust 'Garstenmeyer' into the back of the first Zil and followed him in. He jabbed a hypodermic into the stunned man's forearm and watched with satisfaction as he slumped back against the soft cushioning, immediately semi-conscious. As they swung out of the square he wound down his window and waved. 'So long, Leonid, my thanks,' he yelled to the little group that had now surrounded the bemasked Garstenmeyer by the foundation stone to the Red Square Playbaby Club. 'Hope to see you again soon.'

'Can you move this heap any faster? We're running behind schedule,' said Conroy, sliding open the glass partition between the driver and the back seat.

'I try,' said the Russian, and with a surprising willingness pushed the Zil up to one hundred miles per hour as they sped through the drab outskirts of Moscow.

Conroy closed the partition again and pulled aside the curtains on the back window. Behind them, he saw the six other cars carrying his male and female Playbabies accelerate too. Then he tensed.

Flying along the long curving road half a mile behind was another great black Zil obviously coming in pursuit.

He looked at 'Garstenmeyer', slumped bemused and semi-conscious in the corner of the limousine's back seat. He had not spoken a word since they left Red Square.

'You okay, Leonid?' asked Conroy, gloatingly. He didn't really expect a reply. 'Course y'are baby, you're fine,' said Conroy answering himself and banging the drugged man on the shoulder.

Then he peered out of the window again. The lone Zil was gaining.

'Move this Commie crate faster, comrade driver,' he yelled through the partition. Surprisingly the driver again obliged and pushed the speedometer up to 120 miles per hour.

Conroy began sweating. Nothing more than a few miles of Communist road lay between him and the greatest coup in the history of the CIA – the kidnapping of Russia's leader from the heart of Moscow. And he had almost brought it off single-handed!

He looked out of the window again. Surely nobody could suspect yet. The plan had been perfect. Garstenmeyer had done a great job masking the Soviet First Secretary with the likeness of his own face then putting on a mask that made it seem he was the Communist leader. It should be hours, or even days if he was careful, before they tumbled him. When they finally unmasked Garstenmeyer, Conroy reflected gloatingly, he would probably be in for at least a show trial and a few years of Russian hard labour. The Secret Service chief had sunk into a strange, listless mood since losing the President before the eyes of the world's press and had seemed to welcome the opportunity of taking part in one last act of glorious self-destruction.

But when he checked the rear window again Conroy saw the Zil was still chasing them and he banged on the glass partition again. 'Faster, faster, you comrade bum,' he yelled. Incredibly the Communist driver again obliged, putting his foot flat down to the floor and sending the limousine careering along the narrow road, weaving in and out of carts and bicycles at close on 130 miles per hour.

The pursuing Zil was still about a quarter of a mile behind when the motorcade of six limousines carrying the Americans screamed into Sheremetyevo Airport.

'Straight to the plane, comrade,' ordered Conroy, waving towards where the DC9 stood with its engines roaring.

The line of Zils screeched to a halt beside the aircraft, their doors flew open and the twenty brightly dressed Playbabies tumbled out onto the tarmac and rushed helter-skelter towards the plane's steps like coloured confetti blown on a gusting wind.

'Quick, for krissakes,' yelled Conroy as he ran at their head holding the arm of the stumbling 'Garstenmeyer'. He thrust the still-comatose man up the steps, then paused to look round. The Zil that had chased them from Red Square was hurtling through the gates onto the airfield.

'Faster, you turkeys,' he yelled again over his shoulder. 'Or I'll leave y'all here with these Commie bastards.' He disappeared inside the plane with his charge.

The welter of human confetti blew up the steps in a kaleidoscopic stream and one of the crew leaned out waiting to slam the hatch closed behind the last man or woman as the Zil hurtled across the runways towards them.

'Come onnnnnn!' yelled Conroy from inside with the voice of a man falling into a thousand-foot crevasse.

The last wiggling American – the Cleveland Playbaby of the Year 42–23–38 – juddered up the steps and collapsed breathless inside the plane. The crew man slammed the hatch shut. The DC9 began rolling as the Zil that had chased them left a noisy set of black tyre tracks on the tarmac and halted shuddering under the wing. Its doors immediately flew open and emptied black-coated men onto the runway. From among them, one figure ran forward, frantically waving up at the cockpit to stop the DC9.

'It's Garstenmeyer,' yelled the pilot suddenly. 'He's made it.'

Conroy rushed forward and stared down from the flight deck. Sure enough the unmistakable vodka-ruddied mask of the First Secretary of the Communist Party of the Union of Soviet Socialist Republics was recognisable on the madly waving man below.

'Get the door open, I'll stop,' shouted the pilot.

Conroy looked coldly down again at the figure dancing frantically under the nose of the plane. 'Crap! Leave the bastard!'

'But you can't do that,' yelled the pilot.

'Can't I?' shouted Conroy. 'I'm running this show. Fly!'

Conroy drew a pistol from a shoulder holster under his left arm and stuck it in the pilot's left ear.

'Where to – Cuba?' asked the pilot laconically.

'Shaddup!' screamed Conroy. 'Fly!'

The DC9 was still rolling slowly. The man in the First Secretary's mask just escaped being run down by one of the jet's landing wheels.

'Screw the Secret Service!' shouted Conroy through the perspex of the cockpit and gave the hopping man a V-sign. 'I hope you get twenty goddamned years in Siberia.'

Garstenmeyer seemed to be managing a pleading, beseeching expression inside the plastic–rubber mask covering his face. He dodged under the slowly moving plane, looking up and making dumb mime signs of supplication with his raised hands.

'Screw you, too, Garstenmeyer,' yelled Conroy again and jabbed the muzzle of his gun deeper into the pilot's ear. 'Fly!'

The DC9 accelerated smoothly over the man and the Zil and started out across the taxiing area towards the holding point.

The waving man and his companions jumped back in the car and began to chase the plane.

'Faster, faster,' yelled Conroy, jabbing the pistol deeper still into the pilot's ear and drawing blood.

The Zil shot by and pulled over in front of the DC9.

'Change direction,' shouted Conroy.

The pilot veered to the left and opened the throttle, sending the jet scudding round the limousine and on towards the holding point. The Zil followed, weaving in and out under the wings, twice almost colliding with the undercarriage.

'The bastard is trying to wreck us,' screeched Conroy, beside himself. He looked back briefly at 'Garstenmeyer'. He was slumped in his seat in the luxury salon, still only half-conscious. He, Gerrard K. Conroy, had got the Soviet First Secretary and he would damn well get him home! To hell with the head of the Secret Service in that damned limousine down there.

The DC9 continued to avoid the weaving Zil, turned in the holding area and began to race forward along the north–south runway of Sheremetyevo. As it gathered speed Conroy noticed that unaccountably the Russian troops ringing the airport and the MiG-21 fighter-pilots were taking no action to intervene in the drama being played out before them.

'Great!' yelled Conroy, looking back through a side window of the cockpit at the Zil a hundred yards away. 'We're losing them.'

As the jet gained momentum, Conroy rushed back into the salon. He stopped, breathing heavily and sweating before the slumped figure of 'Garstenmeyer'. He savoured his moment of triumph for a second as the jet rushed forward nearing take-off speed. Then he reached out to tug the mask of Garstenmeyer from the First Secretary's face. His fingers went under the jawline behind the ear lobes, fumbling for the edges of the thin rubberoid disguise.

He stiffened.

He dug his fingers in again behind the rim of the mask and pulled. And pulled. And pulled again without success.

Then at last his fingers got a purchase. He tugged hard and his fingers flew free, brightening wetly with blood. He stared down first at the thin slivers of flesh embedded in his fingernails; then back at the face, which had no mask on it now and never had.

The shock of the facial lacerations revived the Secret Service Chief. 'For hell's sake, Conroy, lay off!' he yelled. 'Are you trying to kill me or something?'

'Garstenmeyer!'

Conroy's anguished cry was that of a man hitting the bottom of a thousand-foot crevasse.

'Garstenmeyer!' The scream rang out a second time in the racing plane. 'You creep! You f—ing dozy goddamned creep!'

Conroy reached forward and felt in Garstenmeyer's right-hand pocket. He cursed when he pulled out the pallid mask of the Secret Service Chief's own likeness. He dived his hand into Garstenmeyer's left-hand pocket and froze. The lining of the empty pocket came inside out.

'If you're you and you haven't got the First Secretary mask, who is that out there in the mask?' shrieked Conroy, staring white-faced at Garstenmeyer. When he received no reply he raced back to the flight deck to jab the barrel of his pistol into the pilot's left ear once again. 'Stop!' he screeched.

'I can't!' shouted the pilot, trying to hold the jet as it thrust forward at well over a hundred miles per hour.

'Stop,' screeched Conroy again. 'We haven't got him. You've gotta stop!'

The pilot jerked forward wrestling the controls with both hands. Then he reared back in his seat and forced his feet down on the brakes. When the jet began to slow, he put it into a dangerous turn at around sixty miles per hour and careered off the runway onto the perimeter track. He slowed the aircraft to a crawl as the shiny black Zil caught up with them and drew it to a halt beside the stationary limousine.

The slowly moving DC9 stove in the Zil's offside and stopped.

The man in the First Secretary's mask jumped from the limousine again and ran over waving. The navigator opened a hatch and flung down an emergency ladder. The man rose puffing and panting through the hatchway as the Zil reversed away.

Conroy rushed forward to pull him in. Hauling him to his feet, the CIA chief grabbed him by the head and tugged at his mask.

Again nothing.

'Who are you, you bum?' yelled Conroy.

He tugged once more. Once more his fingers flew free. Once more they were sticky with blood and clawed flesh.

'I want to defect,' said the real First Secretary of the Communist Party of the Union of Soviet Socialist Republics, wincing in pain.

Conroy stared.

'I want Helga. I want to defect,' he repeated again dully. 'You wouldn't listen before. There's nothing left for me here.'

Conroy suddenly remembered the tap on his shoulder before he disembarked from the DC9. The face before him was the same, more real than any mask. Suddenly, as he looked at the First Secretary, he realised why their 'escape' to the airport had been so simple.

'Yahooooo!' screamed Conroy. 'Let's get the hell off this Commie bastard airport. We've got him!'

The DC9 surged forward again along the perimeter track, turned on to the east–west runway, spurted and lifted off into the darkening skies above a Moscow that would never be quite the same again.

'Nobody hostages the President of the United States with impunity,' breathed Conroy, as he grabbed the wrists of the First Secretary of the Communist Party of the Union of Soviet Socialist Republics and snapped handcuffs on them.

Chapter Fourteen

The members of SAGNASCRAP sat motionless beneath the transparent maximum security dome like a selection of stale cheeses on display under a perspex cover. And like cheeses kept covered too long they were all sweating visibly.

'Whaddaya all starin' at?' demanded Conroy. 'Why are you all getting so hot under the collar? We've got a real bargaining counter now.'

His fellow members continued to stare with undisguised animosity.

'Is this group concerned with repatriating the President or not?' he demanded, pointing to the long name-plate running down the centre of the table. 'It wasn't set up so we could sit around and talk and do nuthin'. Somethin's been done at least — somethin' commensurate with America's prestige and standing as the most powerful nation on earth.'

'Where is he?' asked the Defense Secretary in a flat voice.

'Felixstowe.'

'Felixstowe? Where in hell's Felixstowe?'

'Felixstowe, England. It's a sleepy little seaside resort on the East coast populated entirely by pensioners enjoying concession rates for late-season Old Folks' Weeks. It's perfect cover. Nobody'll ever look there.'

'What kind of security is he being held under?'

'The First Secretary of the Communist Party of the Union of Soviet Socialist Republics is staying...'

Conroy paused and looked round to check that the two men on the foot-bellows, one at either end of the table, were pumping steadily. The second man had been added to ease the strain the meetings were putting on CIA knee-caps. The number of whistles had been increased to six and were attached to six identical music-stands placed close by each Council member's elbow. On seeing Conroy peer round at them, the two agents accelerated sharply under his gaze.

'... Is staying at Seaview boarding house, Number Six, Highcliff Road, Felixstowe, Suffolk, England, with two of my oldest and most reliable operatives. The First Secretary is, as you know, sixty-five years of age. My men are sixty-seven and sixty-three respectively. Muffled in their hats and topcoats they take constitutional walks along the sea-front. As a precaution my operatives keep their small-arms trained on him through the pockets of their coats. They thus merge inconspicuously among the old-age pensioners of England without attracting any attention whatsoever. The First Secretary is in fact proving to be amenable and I, in all modesty, believe this is the greatest natural cover I've ever devised.'

Garstenmeyer sat with his eyes lowered self-consciously leaving Conroy's ego to weather the storm of opprobrium.

'Genitalmen,' said the Vice-President in a voice so tight it threatened to choke him, 'this Group can do nothing but censure the Director of the CIA and the head of the Secret Service for their actions.' He paused for breath. 'This criminal act flies in the face of the democratic principles of the Free World. Perhaps the Group feels the two men concerned should be arrested immediately and relieved of their posts. They have brought shame to the good name of America.'

'Crap!' said Conroy. 'At least, with respect, Mr Vice-President, may I suggest, crap,' added Conroy hurriedly. 'This is a time of crisis when resolute action, courage and quick strong decisions are required. Remember Cuba?'

'This does not compare remotely—' began the Vice-President.

'All right, all right,' said Conroy, 'but all we gotta do is announce that the First Secretary was kidnapped by a dissident group of Americans. Disclaim responsibility, pledge not to sleep until we find him.'

'But that's not true,' exclaimed the Secretary of State who prided himself on his honesty if not his loquacity.

'True?' said Conroy incredulously. 'That's the kind of crap they gave us about the hostaging of the President. Do you believe those lying Commie bastards?'

There was silence for a moment save for the hiss and crump of the pumping bellows and the heavy breathing of the agents operating them.

'Send police to the Playbaby headquarters in San Francisco,' said Conroy confidently, 'and there you will find the movement's founder bound and gagged and locked up in a bedroom with all his many Playbabies. His plane was hijacked by the same dissidents who flew disguised to the Red Square ceremony in his plane and snatched the First Secretary. Let the police take the press with them. Announce it to the world now. Even apologise, if you like!'

Conroy purposely made no mention of the First Secretary's expressed desire to defect.

'Announce it now,' repeated the Defense Secretary with heavy sarcasm. 'And apologise – now that the armies of Russia and its Warsaw Pact allies are rolling in full mobilisation across Eastern Europe to the Iron Curtain frontier with NATO. Announce it and apologise now that the entire Russian navy has been mobilised in the Indian Ocean, the Mediterranean, the Atlantic and the Pacific. Announce it and apologise now that the tanks on the East Berlin border have been reinforced by several hundred more and infantrymen have been moved up in support, now that all of Russia's destructive rocketry is poised and aimed at the heart of our beloved America, primed and ready to be fired.'

The human cheeses under the maximum security display cover began sweating even more profusely at the Defense Secretary's words.

'I think Conroy, along with Garstenmeyer, should be

removed from his post and arrested,' said the Secretary of State, waspishly. 'He is making it impossible for my Department to function in a diplomatic fashion.'

'Democracy and freedom,' shouted Conroy. 'Does that mean you have to rob yourselves of your only resolute leaders at a time when the world is on the brink of destruction?' Droplets of spit flew frustratedly from his lips. 'Oh, for an American dictatorship, a totalitarian dictatorship that would really make America great again.'

'Perhaps, genitalmen,' said the Vice-President hesitantly, 'Conroy is right, what we need at this time is solidarity and concerted action. Perhaps if we can live through this crisis we might see the happenings of the last hours differently.'

'You're goddamned right I'm right,' said Conroy. 'Thank you Mr Vice-President for that shaft of sanity in these doom-laden times.' He paused and drew a sheet of paper from his brief-case. 'I have here a draft of the suggested dissident manifesto setting out the terms for the return of the President. It is concise and succinct.'

He handed it to the Vice-President who glanced at it, then began to read it to the meeting.

'In the absence of firm action by the United States government we have kidnapped the First Secretary of the Soviet Communist Party in the name of peace and freedom. True peace and freedom, which are desired by all decent peoples, is directly threatened by the criminal kidnapping of the President of the United States by Red Commie bastards . . .'

The meeting winced but Conroy was unabashed.

'Thought that touch would make it sound genuine,' he grinned.

The Vice-President continued reading. 'The First Secretary will be freed and returned to his country immediately that the President sets foot safely in the West . . .'

He gasped aloud suddenly and paused before reading the next and last paragraph.

'Here's a fine bit of diplomacy, Secretary of State,' cut in Conroy *sotto voce* by way of a trailer and sat back grinning unpleasantly.

'In compensation of, and recognition for, the goodwill shown in Moscow's Red Square by the Soviet authorities, we also demand that the US Government immediately erect a one-hundred-foot-high monument of solid gold in the shape of a hammer and sickle in the centre of Times Square. This monument shall be guarded with maximum-security measures day and night for ever by the US Marines.' The Vice-President's voice grew faint. 'Signed, The Group for Power through Unfettered Private Enterprise!'

'That gold hammer and sickle trick makes the dissident angle look kinda genuine, doesn't it?' Conroy asked his colleagues rhetorically.

Their chance to express an opinion was sabotaged by one of the uniformed colonels gesticulating outside the sound-proof glass dome. The meeting was halted and the dome raised.

'Sir,' said the major addressing the Vice-President, 'there is a call from a rooming house in Felixstowe, England, sir. The caller insists he is the First Secretary of the Communist Party of the Union of Soviet Socialist Republics and he insists on speaking to you personally, sir.'

The Vice-President signalled for the red telephone to be passed in and the dome lowered again. Conroy, looking worried, motioned the two bellows-pumping agents to move the Vice-President's music-stand up to the phone and point the silent dog-whistle towards the ear- and mouth-pieces.

'Pump harder, damn you,' hissed Conroy to the two men as the Vice-President lifted the receiver to his ear.

The temporary Chief Executive's face expanded in disbelief as he listened to the distant voice. His eyebrows almost disappeared into his hairline. 'Okay we'll consider it and call you back,' he said at last and put the phone down.

'Genitalmen,' he said gravely, gazing round the table, 'that was in fact the First Secretary. He is demanding political asylum in the West! He said he will resist any attempt to repatriate him to Russia! He wants to defect!'

* * *

As the Vice-President replaced the telephone receiver, a closed-circuit television camera in the blast-proof, sound-proof, flash-proof underground bunker half a mile beneath a suburb of Moscow was turning by remote control to focus on a four-star Russian general. With calm deliberation he was swinging the two-foot-thick lead door of the Ultimate Deterrent Chamber closed behind him.

A group of high-ranking officers and civilians bent almost double with anxiety watched on a television monitoring screen in an adjoining chamber as the general replaced his revolver in the holster on his belt and leaned for a moment against the inside of the secured door, wiping the perspiration from his brow.

They watched in horror as he listened to the frantic sounds of hammering on the outside of the door, then walked forward across the chamber, his chest heaving, his breath coming in long shuddering gasps. Their fingers and hands froze into claw-shapes of agony as his eyes roamed over the panel of buttons and switches on the wall before him and came to rest on the large, red star-shaped button set apart on its own.

Through the wonder of closed-circuit television they could read the warnings printed in red Cyrillic script by the button: 'Extreme and Ultimate Danger – For Use Only In The Event Of Armageddon.'

They saw what appeared to be the gleam of unbearable sexual frustration brighten in the four-star general's eye. Then, over the sensitive sound-monitoring system, they heard General Vladimir Korsov muttering to himself in his thick Armenian accent. 'Nobody hostages the First Secretary of the Communist Party of the Union of Soviet Socialist Republics with impunity.'

The group of agonised men bent even further forward uttering little bird-like cries of anguish as they watched General Korsov reach out a hand towards the button shaped like a big red star.

* * *

Meanwhile at that same instant the door of the cellar by the Müggelsee in East Berlin was opening to admit a diffident Gilbert Groot for the second time within twenty-four hours.

The scene before his eyes was almost the same as on his first visit. The President of the United States sat beneath a spotlight in the centre of the darkened cellar, flanked this time by two black-clad, hooded figures.

They motioned him to a black PVC-covered chair opposite the President, which squeaked as he sat down.

'Hello again, Groot,' said the President affably. He seemed very relaxed and self-possessed.

'Hello, Mr President, nice to see you again,' said Groot, wondering what to ask first. He was going to ask what the President had had for breakfast but sensed that the occasion demanded something more searching, more of an interview-in-depth type of question.

'I'm gonna defect, Groot,' said the President, speaking before Britain's most famous gossip-writer could fashion a query.

Groot scribbled furiously. He did not notice that one of the black-clad figures had tensed suddenly as the President spoke and had taken a pace nearer his chair.

'I can quote that, sir, can I?' he asked respectfully.

'Of course,' said the President folding his arms, and sitting back oozing self-satisfaction.

'You know the foundation stone of the Red Square Playbaby Club was laid earlier yesterday, sir, I suppose,' asked Groot tentatively, 'and that presumably means you could go free?'

'I do, Groot. But I've decided to spend the rest of my life in the Communist half of the world for . . .' he looked round at the slender long-legged figure on his right, still anonymous but distinctly female despite the hood, '. . . for private reasons.'

'No, no! You cannot!' The vibrant female voice from under the hood set a nerve jangling deep inside Groot's viscera. 'You will be freed immediately now that the purpose of our mission has been fulfilled.'

'We've been through this all before, Helga,' said the President patiently turning to look round. 'If your organisation believes in peace and freedom for humanity I must be left to choose. If you take me from here I will go to the Soviet Embassy to ask for asylum.'

Groot wrote frantically on his pad.

'What do you think of the kidnapping of the First Secretary from Moscow?' asked Groot.

'It's somehow irrelevant to me,' said the President easily.

'No, no, it is madness, folly, supreme male conceit!' The voice interrupted in an uncontrolled rush from beneath the hood. 'It destroys everything our organisation is working for.' Her voice dropped to a whisper. 'We miscalculated. There was clearly another dangerous man in Washington who required attention and I overlooked him. Somebody should have been sent, Moira perhaps...' Her voice died away and the head in the hood fell forward for a moment in an attitude of despair. 'The President must go home...'

Groot stiffened, wondering if he'd heard correctly. Before he could make up his mind the door of the cellar burst open and Badezimmer rushed in without a hood to whisper frantically in the ear of Helga Mikunov.

'It's Moscow. Korsov's locked himself in the Ultimate Deterrent Chamber alone!' In his agitation Badezimmer's frantic whisper carried clearly to Groot and the President. It never occurred to them that it was strange he would whisper in English so that they understood.

'He has locked everybody out but they are watching by closed circuit television and ringing the red telephone trying to speak with him. He is not answering and they want you to try to stop him! They think you're the only person in the world who can do it!'

Helga Mikunov thrust Badezimmer from her and rushed to the telephone extension on the wall of the cellar. She picked it up and listened.

'He hasn't answered yet?' she asked tensely. 'Keep ringing, it's the only chance.'

Groot, the President, Badezimmer and Kafferty stood and sat motionless, held fast in the fist of suspense that gripped the silent cellar.

Seconds ticked by with agonising slowness. Helga Mikunov slowly raised herself taut on the tips of her toes, her back arched, voluptuous eyes closed in what appeared to be a supreme effort to will the man a thousand miles away in Moscow to answer the telephone instead of pressing a button. Her nostrils flared wide as she breathed deeply and her lips formed an almost silent word that to her small male audience in the cellar seemed like 'Vladimir'.

In the bunker below Moscow, the stubby fingers of General Vladimir Korsov still hovered shakily over the large red star button in the centre of the panel. The watchers in the adjoining chamber could see and hear through their closed-circuit communications line that the red telephone beneath the switch panel was jangling. The General's concentration was faltering; deep breaths shivered through his nose and throat and a noise like a puppy whimpering reached the ears of the trembling men clustered round the closed-circuit television screen. For a long time the telephone continued to jangle, Korsov continued to falter and the watching men continued to tremble like aspen leaves in a strong breeze.

Helga Mikunov turned a face distorted with anguish to the men in the East Berlin cellar. 'Badezimmer, take Groot to the checkpoint and the President to the Embassy,' she said urgently, then returned her whole attention to the silent telephone.

As they were ushered reluctantly to the door, Groot and the President heard Helga Mikunov gasp and open her mouth as though to speak into the receiver. Badezimmer hustled them out and the door closed behind them before they could hear what she said.

For a moment she simply breathed excitedly into the telephone. Then she spoke. 'Valodi,' she said, her voice so husky that it was barely audible. 'It's Helga. We met at that party in the Kremlin, do you remember? I have never forgotten you...'

Outside, Badezimmer pushed Groot and the President ahead of him towards the car. Once he was seated in the back seat, Groot began to rough out his news dispatch on a pad resting on his knee. 'The President of the United States,' he wrote, 'told me today in an exclusive interview he was defecting from the West to live under Communism. Behind him as he spoke the startlingly beautiful woman for whom he was making the sacrifice was on the phone to Moscow trying to sweet-talk a Russian general out of pressing a nuclear button that would destroy the world.'

He stopped and read over what he'd written. Not a bad story, he thought. He began to feel he was getting the hang of this foreign correspondent business although he wasn't sure he didn't prefer interviewing those film-stars in negligées over breakfast in the Dorchester after all.

Beginning a new paragraph, he continued: 'In a cellar somewhere in Communist territory the President, wearing a white shirt and blue trousers and surrounded by Communists sporting sinister black hoods—'

'Time for the masks to go on,' said Badezimmer and curtailed Groot's writing by snapping a mask on his face. He did the same to the President. 'No talking,' ordered Badezimmer. When Kafferty had climbed in to join them, he drove out along the rutted lane through the trees.

The stubby forefinger on the right hand of sixty-one-year-old Vladimir Korsov stiffened before the concave crimson button. The telephone behind him was still ringing but he ignored it. Two sharp cries split the silence of the bunker and the stiffened forefinger jabbed forward hard. Once, twice, three times the finger prodded and three times the red button yielded.

Forty miles away one of forty giant SS9 missiles standing straight against the fading sky, armed with a massive nuclear warhead, shuddered and rose on a cloud of smoke and flame. It was precisely the same weapon the President had watched on film earlier. But this time it was real. It thrust slowly upwards into the darkened sky, and gathered speed heading out to the West trailing a hellfire wake of burned gases.

Exactly forty minutes later it passed forty miles high over East Berlin while below the unknowing President of the United States was knocking on the door of the shuttered Russian Embassy to ask if he could defect, please. A cleaner holding a mop and bucket opened the door to him, invited him in and closed the door again.

In the cellar by the Müggelsee, a few minutes before, Helga Mikunov had still been talking into the telephone. 'You've what, Valodi? You've already fired one ICBM?' She paused, lowered her voice to a new note of huskiness. 'Well listen, Valodi, I want you and only you. Just don't press it any more. You'll spoil it for us both. Don't hang up, keep talking to me and don't press the button again. I am going to go on talking to you and I'm coming to you by supersonic jet and I'm going to talk to you all the way. Have you got that? I want you. Do you understand? I desire you, I want you and I want you to want me. So don't press it again, will you?'

'Aw, all right, so I'll admit it,' said Conroy, with ill grace. 'Sure I knew the First Secretary wanted to defect. But I didn't think it was priority relevance right now. It's all to do with some dizzy dame named Helga or something. I couldn't make much of it; he gibbered on about her a lot, I guess. Said she would have to come to the West now and wherever she was he wanted to be too.'

The inside of the dome was misting heavily and SAGNASCRAP looked weary and irresolute.

'I propose,' persisted Conroy, 'that the go-ahead be given for the gold hammer and sickle monument in Times Square anyway. We can deal with this crazy request for asylum later, try to make him change his mind.'

The uniformed colonels outside the sound-proof dome went into their dumb mime of wild gesticulation again and SAGNASCRAP and the bellows men all breathed a sigh of relief and waited for the comparatively fresh air to flood in from outside as the Vice-President called another halt and signalled the dome to be raised.

'Breathing you guys' breath is a great sacrifice to make for security,' muttered the Chairman of the Joint Chiefs of Staff.

Ignoring the sour remark the Vice-President signalled for the dome to be lowered again and looked down at the sealed note he had just been handed. When he opened it his face blanched to exactly the same colour as the crisp white triangle of handkerchief protruding from his top pocket.

'Groot's seen him again! He reports that the President is defecting to the East,' he croaked.

SAGNASCRAP sat paralysed by the news.

'Groot says it's got something to do with a Russian dame named *Helga*.'

The members of SAGNASCRAP sat as if they had been turned to stone. 'An eternal triangle of apocalyptic proportions,' breathed the Secretary of State.

'Groot also says that some nutty Russian general has gone berserk in Moscow and has got his finger on the damned button,' added the Vice-President hollowly.

A sudden deafening clatter on the outside of the glass dome was made by the four colonels all banging on it at once. When it was raised they all rushed forward, the first one holding out a sheet of teleprinter paper from which the customary seal was missing. Forgetting to lower the dome, forgetting to expel the colonels, forgetting all security measures completely, the Vice-President took one look at it and blurted out its contents.

'The first Russian ICBM,' he croaked, 'is on its way towards Washington!'

Chapter Fifteen

In Times Square, rush-hour crowds of New Yorkers stopped in their tracks under the garish neon lights and gazed up at the hundred-foot-high gold statue of a hammer and sickle being winched upright on quivering cables. Scattered and half-hearted cheers broke out as smartly turned-out contingents of US Marines marched forward to mount an honour guard at the four corners of the monument.

'Instituted in the spirit of Cultural and Sexual Reciprocity in return for the unique American erection in Red Square, Moscow,' read an inscribed plaque at the base.

'A reminder to us all that tools are all-important in this life, buddy,' a yellow-cab driver who had read Groot's report of the President's recent doings told his fare as he drove him by.

At the same moment on the sea front at Felixstowe, England, a burly, florid-faced man wearing a pearl-grey Homburg hat and a dark overcoat pulled a tattered photograph from his inside breast-pocket.

'Me shooting duck at Dneprodzerzhinsk where I was born,' said the First Secretary, pointing proudly to the picture of himself sitting in a boat grasping the business end of a double-barrelled shot-gun with both hands.

'Great, Leonid,' said the ageing CIA operative with the lined face and sunken cheeks on his left. 'Great weapon – if you could use it.' He nudged the pistol in his right coat pocket into the First Secretary's left kidney. 'Let's keep walking, huh, Leonid.'

The defector coloured slightly but said nothing.

The ageing CIA operative with the rheumy eyes and a toothless grin on his right fell into step and the trio moved with brisk senility along the promenade. The two men on the outside, who also wore Homburgs and dark coats, cast suspicious glances at the stick-wielding visitors enjoying the late-season economy of the Old Folks' Weeks. Those in wheelchairs received particularly close scrutiny.

'Can't be too careful with your KGB babies,' said the CIA operative on the right, grinning a totally toothless grin. 'They're bright boys some of them. Good at disguises.'

The First Secretary was hardly listening. He brought his distracted gaze back from the horizon. 'When can I see her? Where is she now? Where is Helga?'

'Don't keep asking the same question over and over, Leonid, willya?' snapped the toothless agent.

At that very same instant in West Berlin the long-suffering Dutch businessman was banging on the wall of his hotel room again trying to attract the attention of the man who once more seemed to be over-revving his Porsche.

'Moira,' asked Groot slyly between noisy bursts of acceleration, 'do you know anybody named Helga?'

'Yes, yes,' gasped Moira. 'But, for hell's sake, not now! If the world is going to end in three minutes let's not waste time.'

She returned to her gasping and threshing with renewed enthusiasm and the Dutchman began banging loudly on the wall again but neither of them heard him.

In the bowels of the White House, SAGNASCRAP had moved to the Emergency Operations Room and the original six members were now the centre of a crowded cellar containing the full National Security Council. Maps were spread on tables, coloured lights flashed on and off behind glass maps on the walls, telephones bleeped and grey-faced men and women drank coffee from paper cups. Despite the air-conditioning, cigarette smoke, stale breath and the smell of sweat engulfed the gathering, overlaid with the more elusive odour of fear. Men and women no longer looked at one another but all eyes turned repeatedly to the large red blob moving very slowly westwards across the biggest glass map of the world.

An air force general thrust a long roll of teleprinter copy into the hands of the Vice-President. 'From the hot line, sir,' he panted and retreated a respectful distance. The crowd pressed around closer. Conroy tried to read it over the Vice-President's shoulder.

'Inter-Continental Ballistic Missile SS9 launched without authority Soviet Government,' the Vice-President read hoarsely. 'Not, repeat not, part of Soviet Union's Assured Destruction Capability nor of Invulnerable Second Strike Capacity. Urge you not, repeat not, to respond. Dissident element at large in firing centre. We are attempting to eliminate him. Hopeful of early success. Meanwhile invite you to destroy SS9 which flying altitude 40 miles 29 degrees west 10 degrees north over English Channel. Good luck with destruction.'

It was signed in the name of the Russian Prime Minister.

The Vice-President looked up gravely, raising his eyebrows at those clustered around him in a mute question. They nodded back gravely.

The big red blob was now moving out into the Atlantic.

He beckoned the Chairman of the Joint Chiefs of Staff and seven other officers of exalted rank around him. They went into a rugger-scrum huddle, heads bent, whispering. Several seconds passed while the rest of the Emergency Operations Room looked on. Different officers in the huddle were seen holding up different numbers of fingers. Eventually they all straightened up.

'Genitalmen – fire ten Anti-Ballistic Missile missiles!'

The Vice-President's voice rang clearly and incisively through the fetid air.

Bells rang. Buzzers buzzed. The coloured lights flashed

faster behind the glass maps on the walls. People scurried like lemmings.

In the middle of it all the Second Most Powerful Man in the World leading the Most Powerful Country into battle stood uncomfortably in his grey lightweight civilian clothes with his hands in his pockets looking at his highly buffed custom-made shoes and doing nothing.

Twenty seconds passed.

'Ten Anti-Ballistic Missile missiles launched, sir!'

The announcement came from the Chairman of the Joint Chiefs of Staff who stood warily three feet back from the Vice-President to avoid further besmirching of his freshly valeted uniform.

'Good,' said the Vice-President because he could not think of anything more appropriate. He looked down and nudged a squashed cigarette end along the carpet with the toe of his shiny shoe. It had lipstick on the tip. Now who would be careless enough to squash cigarettes out on the floor of the Emergency Operations Room at a time like this when there were perfectly good ashtrays provided, he wondered, as ten of the most powerful weapons ever launched in the history of the world soared out through the night searching for the nuclear juggernaut that was their prey.

The Vice-President looked round at his closest colleagues. None met his eye. All were nudging something or other around on the carpet with the toes of their highly polished shoes.

The history books would never get this detail, thought the Vice-President. Too mundane. Then he realised that the chances were pretty strong that there would never be any more history books in which to record tonight's events, let alone the human interest detail.

An air force general thrusting a telephone into his hand forced him to abandon the lipstick-stained cigarette end before he had pushed it completely into the shadow of the operations table.

'Moscow personally by word of mouth on the phone,

sir,' said the officer reverently. 'They wish to establish voice contact to replace the teleprinter hot line.'

The Vice-President took the red telephone, held it to his ear and listened. He set his face into the steely, no-nonsense uncompromising mask he felt everybody in the Emergency Operations Room expected of him. Who knew, somebody there might survive to describe to some newspaper somewhere how he handled the greatest crisis the world had ever known.

The Russian Prime Minister announced himself. 'Ve vish to 'elp as moch as possible et thees time of great trial,' he said speaking in English as a sign of courtesy and goodwill. 'Ve urge yew to be calm and eggcept ower deepest apologees for zees zituashun. I hev some practical meazures to suggest to breeng thees matter to suckcessful conklusion,' he added. 'Pleez be kind enuff to employ interpreyter.'

'We will listen, Mr Premier,' said Vice-President uncompromisingly. He signalled for a Russian language expert.

A thin, white-faced air force officer, of moderate rank, hurried forward wearing on his lapel a security clearance badge marked 'Maximum Security: Translation'. He listened into the phone, his face working in agitation at the momentousness of his task.

'The Russian Premier says telephone contact has been established with the General in the—' the officer's face twisted in anguish as a nervous stutter strangled him. He fought it and, after a silence decorated with amazing facial contortions, the last three words of the sentence rushed out of his shivering mouth, '—button-firing bunker.'

He listened again. His eyes widened.

'He says that the General is at present engaged in conversation with a woman named Helga Mikunov, who, it is believed, was responsible for the—' The words dried up again and his face muscles went into more silent overtime. The Emergency Operations Room waited in an overwrought brittle stillness. '—the kidnapping of our President,' he gushed. 'Her name was found scrawled all over the walls of the General's room after he went berserk, sir.'

The officer listened again.

'Haven't we a better translator?' hissed the Vice-President to the Chairman of the Joint Chiefs of Staff, spraying his medal ribbons once more with irritated spit.

'Plenty, sir,' hissed the newly appalled General jumping back to a distance of ten feet and whispering at the top of his voice, 'but none here now with Top-Level Emergency-Operations-Room clearance.'

The interpreting officer was speaking again. '... amnesty for her for the time being because they believe this woman is the only person who can prevent total holo—total holo—holo—' The pause grew longer.

'Caust!' shouted Conroy and the Vice-President impatiently in concert.

'Yes, yes—caust—holocaust,' stuttered the air force man, 'since she is known to possess unbelievable powers of sex—' The cellar held its breath.

In straining to break the constricting dam of his stutter the last two words, when they came, burst out in a deafening high-pitched shout. '—SEXUAL ATTRACTION!'

The cellarful of sweating bodies shifted uneasily.

'She is at present being flown in a supersonic transport from East Berlin to—' Again the well of articulation ran dry, again the entire Emergency Operations Room waited. '—Moscow and is actually in voice contact from the plane with the deranged General in the Ultimate Deterrent Chamber. She will continue to talk to the General and is expected to arrive in Moscow one hour from now.'

The officer held his hand over the mouthpiece and looked up at the Vice-President. 'The Premier is offering a direct link to here, sir, so that we may listen to the ccc—ccc—' Impatient fingers drummed noisily all over the silent cellar. '—ccconversation, if you would like, sir.'

'Yes,' snapped the Vice-President.

'*Da*,' said the officer to Moscow.

'Don't listen to these crummy Commies,' interrupted Conroy viciously. 'They're just trying to intimidate us so we return their damned First Secretary.' He paused, breathing loudly. 'Fire one of our own ICBMs to show 'em we're not intimidated.'

'Conroy, shut up,' said the Vice-President quietly, winning himself more respect from the rest of the room than he had done during the entire crisis so far.

Conroy glowered silently, his ego momentarily squashed out of shape.

'By the way, sir,' said the air force officer, covering the phone again, 'the Premier said the President is—' The group of men round the room stood staring at the vibrating jaw of the stuttering man. '—at present in the Russian Embassy in East Berlin where he is being accorded—' They waited again. '—VIP treatment.'

'Great,' said Conroy with deep and bitter sarcasm. 'Let's get ourselves plugged into the obscene phone-call.'

He hurried away to arrange for the conversation to be relayed over the Emergency Operations Room public address system. The Vice-President meanwhile went into a whispered huddle with the Secretaries of Defense and State.

'A new development, sir,' shouted the linguist officer on the phone. The Vice-President turned back.

'The SS9 has—' The officer's lower jaw went into an apparently unstoppable flapping motion.

After twenty seconds the Defense Secretary stepped forward and held it closed with his hand. When he stepped back the jaw was clamped closed. After ten eternal seconds the muscles thawed and the officer continued in a low voice. '—has changed course and gone into orbit around the earth. The woman Helga Mikunov has persuaded General Korsov to put it into orbit until she gets there.'

'Is that right?' screamed the Vice-President to the General by the glass plotting map on which the red blob moved. Everybody rushed to crowd round the glass map.

Ten yellow lights were moving steadily out eastwards across the Atlantic. But the large red blob moving westwards had disappeared.

'Seems right, sir.'

'Deactivate and ditch the ABMs!' yelled the Vice-President.

Out in the moonless darkness of the Atlantic night ten long, thin, phallus-shaped missiles headed abruptly downward and pierced the calm surface of the sea in a series of sibilant splashes. Silently they jammed themselves nozzle-first in the soft mud of the sea-bed 400 fathoms deep and stood stiffly upright, their tail-fins spread like a glade of petrified metallic trees. Fishes swam incuriously among them, never suspecting the recovering operation would occupy a fleet of ships and seven thousand men and eat up the better part of a hundred million dollars over the next four years, while enraging the anti-pollution lobbies in all the countries of the world.

On the glass map in the White House Emergency Operations Room the ten lights began going out one by one halfway between Europe and America. As the last one extinguished itself there was a smattering of applause. But it died away quickly when the plotter re-located the red orbiting blip of the SS9. At first it was a firefly speck. Then it was tuned in large until it looked as if the planet Mars had come into close orbit around the earth.

The entire assembly watched mutely as the large red disc swung lazily over the United States at a safe distance out in space and on into the Pacific.

'Launch some more ABMs, for krissakes,' said Conroy staring round aggressively.

'We'll wait,' said the Vice-President quietly. 'It won't help to have that SS9 detonated, even out there in orbit. It looks like they're getting things under control in Moscow.'

Silence followed this exchange. It was broken at last by the crackle of the public address speakers on the walls. The stuttering air force officer holding the red telephone to his ear nodded eagerly to indicate that the link with the Mikunov–Korsov conversation had been successfully made.

'Valodi, *niet*. *Niet*, Valodi . . .'

The husky female voice came clearly into the cellar,

electrifying the male members of the National Security Council without exception. They listened rapt as Helga continued to cajole and persuade in alluring tones.

Then silence fell and Valodi seemed to be considering his answer from the Moscow bunker. The silence stretched and stretched until it became almost unbearable.

'Valodi . . . Valodi?'

The voice of Helga Mikunov spoke again, the throaty flow of words uttered in tantalising supplication. The female officers and secretaries stuck their hands on their hips and glowered darkly at the loudspeakers on the whitewashed walls. They looked round contemptuously at the transfixed members of the National Security Council, with whom they'd tried unsuccessfully to have affairs.

'What's she say?' snapped the Vice-President, closing his mouth at last and turning to the air force officer.

He blushed. When he tried to reply his lower jaw began quivering again and not a word came out.

The Defense Secretary stepped forward, held the jaw closed for a few seconds then retreated.

'She said, "Think only of the time you stared at my— b-b-b— at my — b-b-b—breasts— at that Kremlin cocktail party. Don't bring it in from— o-o—orbit. I am coming to be with you."'

'Helga!'

The strangled croak from the loudspeaker was obviously the stricken Valodi replying. 'Helga . . . *da . . . da* . . .' His strained voice rambled for a minute or more with the hint of a sob breaking through every second word.

'What is it? What is it?' said the Vice-President, tugging the sleeve of the air force man.

'He is promising to do nothing until Helga is with him in the bunker. He says he thinks only of— h-h-h—her,' stuttered the officer.

'Of her what?' demanded Conroy, his lips glistening wetly.

'Just of h-h-h—her,' stuttered the officer.

The throaty voice of Helga husked out again starting on a long, low, caressing monologue. The cadence of her voice rose and fell in the hypnotic rhythm of warm, rolling surf plying passionately over the hot sands of a palm-fringed beach.

'What's that, what's that?' The Vice-President's eyes had taken on a bright gleam.

The officer blushed and stuttered again for a full minute before replying. 'She is— telling him that at that last Kremlin cocktail party she noticed that whenever he looked at her his left knee began to tremble making the finely creased, very masculine leg of his uniform pants flutter. She says she found it very exciting and she asks him if he was aware his knee was— t-t-t— t-t-t—trembling.'

'Turn that crap off,' yelled the Vice-President, colouring to the shade of beetroot and breathing heavily. 'They're trying to take revenge on us for that Playbaby Club in Red Square.'

The loudspeakers clicked and went silent.

'You listen to it on the telephone,' said the Vice-President to the interpreter. 'Tell me if they say anything important. I don't think listening to that's healthy for us. It's goddamned subversive.' He turned away, pulled out his handkerchief and mopped his brow.

All over the room the middle-aged officers and politicians also pulled out their handkerchiefs and dabbed at their sweating faces. The air force interpreter continued listening goggle-eyed into the telephone, blushing and trying unsuccessfully to control his shuddering jaw.

'I guess what we all need is some air,' said the Vice-President. He glanced towards the glass map. The red blob was swinging slowly and harmlessly through its orbit over India. 'Let's take a two-minute break outside,' he said, heading for the door.

He led the rush of uniformed and civilian men waving handkerchiefs through a door towards the washrooms – and the stairs that would lead up to a breath of fresh air on the south portico of the White House.

Chapter Sixteen

The Prime Minister of the Union of Soviet Socialist Republics ushered Helga Mikunov along the brightly lit, underground corridor. His eyes flickered shiftily to the smooth rumpling movement of her hips beneath the tight leather pants as she walked before him along the passageway. The red telephone receiver was cupped to her ear under a tumble of long black hair and from time to time he heard her murmur the name 'Valodi' among an unending stream of endearments and intimacies. The Premier carried the telephone receiver, and a third man paid out the cable carefully behind him.

The eyes of green-uniformed armed guards stationed in narrow niches along the passageway flicked through their maximum arc of vision as she passed by them. Without moving they breathed deeply on the delicate wake of musky perfume that she trailed behind her. Every fifty paces they were stopped by black-uniformed security men who checked the dayglo badges pinned to their chests bearing photographs and 'Kremlin Topmost' security clearances in red lettering.

Twenty feet short of a blood-red door at the end of the passage they were stopped by three more black-uniformed security men. 'I'm coming, Valodi, I'm coming to you, my love,' whispered Helga breathily in the face of the startled security men. 'I'm twenty feet from you. Don't do anything until I'm with you.' They stared suspiciously at the telephone receiver half hidden by her hair.

The senior of the black-uniformed men exchanged inaudible words with the Premier, checked and rechecked their badges, then pressed a little red rubber stamp onto them before standing aside.

'I'm going to stop speaking for a moment, Valodi,' Helga Mikunov breathed into the receiver. 'I'm outside. Please open the door. Don't destroy the world now. There's no trick. I'm coming in alone.' She stopped speaking and sighed long and deeply into the mouthpiece. Then she turned crisply and handed it to the senior security man to hold.

The Premier held out his free hand. 'Good luck, Comrade Mikunov,' he said gravely. 'In the name of peace and freedom.'

She touched his fingers briefly, took a deep breath which made her breasts rise dramatically, then began walking slowly towards the door. Suddenly she stopped and returned to face the Premier. Without a word she reached up and swept the long black wig from her head and in a single movement draped it over the Premier's face.

She looked at him steadily for a moment, her naked head reflecting the light, her dark eyes magnificently expressionless and even a little glazed. Then she turned and walked towards the door again. The man who had been paying out the cable of Helga Mikunov's red telephone handed the Premier a green instrument.

'Hello. Emergency Operations Room, Washington.' The Premier paused for the acknowledgement then added in a tight voice, 'She's going in now.'

As he spoke the red door swung open and Helga Mikunov slipped inside. Immediately the door closed behind her.

The Premier held the green phone to one ear and the red phone to his other ear so that he was simultaneously in contact with Washington and the inside of the Ultimate Deterrent Chamber.

In the Emergency Operations Room in Washington forty people stood motionless.

'She's going in now.' The voice of the Russian Premier came clearly over the loudspeakers in English. Then silence.

The red blob on the glass wall map representing the nuclear juggernaut out in space was swinging over the Atlantic again heading for the east coast of the United States for the fourth time.

For an achingly long minute the Emergency Operations Room strained its forty pairs of ears listening for the sign of release from the Russian Prime Minister. But they heard nothing because he was standing without breathing in the whitewashed passage outside the Ultimate Deterrent Chamber. He held a telephone receiver to each ear but he too heard nothing.

The Emergency Operations Room also found itself holding its breath – a jumbled, anxiety-ridden tableau of modern American figures.

The sound of her voice, when it came, electrified all who heard it in both Washington and Moscow.

'This is Helga Mikunov speaking.'

The loudspeakers in the Emergency Operations Room crackled briefly in the pause that followed. 'I speak to you with my finger one centimetre away from the Armageddon button which, if I pressed it, could set in train a series of actions that would lead to the destruction of the world. Thirty-nine more SS9 KBMs can be launched from here within seconds.'

The men in the Emergency Operations Room turned to each other, their faces crumpling with expressions of dismay. The sexual saviour of the world had to their horror become an avenging angel.

'My kind helper, General Vladimir Korsov has played his role magnificently. Now I can and *will* press the nuclear button unless certain conditions are met.'

'Oh no,' moaned the Vice-President, covering his face with his right hand. 'When will it end?'

The agitated voice of the Russian Premier cut in, 'I assure you the Soviet Government had no prior knowledge of thees.'

'Nuke them now, before it's too late,' shouted Conroy. 'Nuke the bastards!'

135

Helga Mikunov's calm throaty voice was heard again. 'We have carried out this desperate plan to demonstrate to the world the enormous danger it faces from ageing male politicians and military leaders who seek violent solutions to international problems in sublimation of their own vanished virility. Ladies and gentlemen of the world, I submit that our entire existence, because of the horror of modern weapons, is threatened by these sexually unstable ageing males.'

Expressions of outrage, incredulous disbelief and embarrassment chased each other across the faces of all the mature men in the Emergency Operations Room.

'Vladimir Korsov could have been a tragic example – but in fact he found reconciliation with me several months ago and agreed to act the part of his former self to help us.'

The Vice-President and many others again started paying great attention to chasing cigarette ends around on the carpet with the toes of their shoes as Helga Mikunov paused to take a seductively drawn breath.

'I have dedicated myself to correcting the imbalance in the minds and bodies of the world's most important men,' she went on. 'I believe the problem is largely psychological and correctable. That is why the President of the United States was kidnapped and brought to me. That is why indirectly the First Secretary of our Communist Party has allowed himself to be abducted to the West.'

The red blob on the glass wall map crossed the coast of the United States exactly on the meridian of Washington.

'To ensure peace and freedom I now demand certain solemn assurances from both the Vice-President of the United States and the Premier of the Soviet Union. As a safeguard against the dangers I've outlined, they must make certain compulsory arrangements at all major political meetings held henceforth anywhere in the world. The male participants at these meetings must invariably be separated around the negotiating tables by females, selected and trained by me. Their presence will constantly remind male politicians of the need for a spirit of gentleness and reconciliation. I have highly trained units of such girls waiting ready in Britain, France and other main international centres.'

Gasps from forty throats ran round the Emergency Operations Room like the staggered firing of rifle salvoes at a state funeral.

'I have one further demand,' the voice of Helga Mikunov continued confidently. 'In order to try to tempt the President of the United States to return home – his defection is against my will and my purpose – the Vice-President should instruct all females in the United States of America to shave their heads at once. This will create the necessary sexual ambience to attract him home. This must be effected by means of a nationwide television broadcast.'

The Vice-President let a little moan escape his lips.

'I shall wait thirty seconds for the appropriate assurances from both the Vice-President and the Soviet Premier.'

The Vice-President shot an agonised glance at the wall map. Out in space the red blob was approaching a point almost directly over Washington.

He gesticulated wildly towards his speech-writer across the room to prepare a television address to the nation, then snatched the red phone from the translation officer.

'Hello, Mr Prime Minister. Are you agreed to the demands?'

The frantic Russian's 'yes' came back immediately.

'Okay, Miss Mikunov,' said the Vice-President, 'we give you the solemn assurances you ask for. In return we demand equally solemn assurances that you will vacate the Ultimate Deterrent Chamber forthwith.'

'Please make the television broadcast immediately. You are in no position to bargain.' Her voice had become crisp, uncompromising.

The Vice-President dropped the telephone receiver and dashed out to the emergency television studio set up in the White House basement for addresses to the nation. As he seated himself, his speech-writer thrust two hastily typewritten sheets into his hands.

Sweating, with collar awry and hair dishevelled, the Vice-President moved into view on sixty million television screens from coast to coast to make his historic appeal. Gazing directly and honestly into the eyes of sixty million families, he read the address of his speech-writer unseen.

'Ladies and genitalmen, bald is beautiful – that is my message to America's female population tonight.' Sixty million set owners tried unsuccessfully to adjust the sound to correct what they thought was garble. When they failed they settled back again.

'Ladies of America, for your country and your President, I want you to go to the bathroom—' his voice choked with emotion at the enormity of such a request in a democratic society '—go to the bathroom and with your husband's razor, shave off all your cranial hair. This will help repatriate our President and save the world.' He paused before attempting the speech-writer's closing exhortation. 'Remember, you gotta shave if you wanna save...'

Within seconds, all across the great American nation, female cranial hair began to tumble from patriotic heads in razored chunks. As the Vice-President hurried back to the Emergency Operations Room, telephones began ringing in the White House and television studio switchboards were jammed with calls from women and girls confirming that they had already done their patriotic duty.

The Vice-President snatched up the Moscow telephone. 'The broadcast has been made and thousands of loyal American women are phoning in guaranteeing they've already shaved their heads,' he reported.

'Good,' replied Helga Mikunov laconically. 'Now I can announce to you that General Korsov deactivated the warhead before launching. But as it must be brought down somewhere he is already in the process of doing that. He's aiming at the marshes of the Potomac – but there will be a surprise for you.'

Alarm sprang to the faces of the watchers again.

The red blob on the glass map was now directly

above Washington. And it had stopped moving! It began to grow rapidly larger indicating it was descending fast in a straight-down trajectory from space.

'It's a filthy Commie plot,' yelled Conroy. 'Nuke 'em now before we're put out of action completely.'

The basement Emergency Operations Room suddenly shuddered. The ground trembled as if shaken by an earthquake. But as soon as the shock passed all was still again.

Every eye in the room flew anxiously to the wall map. The red blob had gone out!

'Kee-rist,' said Conroy, 'it's down.'

'But not detonated,' breathed the Vice-President quietly.

Major Franklin Grubner leading the amphibious patrol across the squelching marshes of the Potomac under a moonless sky halted the column of vehicles and ordered them to switch on their mounted searchlights in the direction of the black mound.

White beams stabbed through the darkness and illuminated the enormous long hulk of the SS9 steaming and crackling four hundred yards away as its hot metal contracted in the cool dampness of the swamp.

The Major lifted his walkie-talkie to his mouth.

'Contact!' he yelled. 'Sizeable cylindrical object located half buried in mud of Potomac swamps, three miles east of estuary. No fire. No other noticeable activity.'

He listened to a voice from the White House for a moment.

'Roger. Will proceed forward to inspect.'

As the column of vehicles drew nearer Major Grubner lifted his walkie-talkie again. 'Warhead appears to be split in two. Payload substance oozing out. Approaching to identify.'

The Major rode over the squelchy ground in a jeep with his Sergeant. He jumped down twenty yards from the SS9 which towered above them as large as a house against faint and distant stars.

He walked over and shone his flashlight on the broken

warhead that was the size of a church steeple. The split in it was wide enough to drive a bus through, and the glistening black payload was still spilling slowly out into a growing heap on the surface of the swamp.

Major Grubner ran his Geiger counter over the nearest point of the payload material and got no reaction whatsoever. He bent and scooped some up with his trench shovel and studied it at close quarters with his flashlight.

'Sergeant,' said Major Grubner at last. 'Do you know what I think this is?'

'No sir,' said the sergeant dutifully.

'Take some on your finger and identify it.'

'If that's not an order I'd rather not, sir,' said the sergeant backing away a step.

'Okay, sergeant,' he said, 'but you're missing a treat you could have told your grandchildren about.'

The sergeant gulped. 'I'm happy to take your word for it sir.'

'This, I believe,' he said, scooping up a fingerful of the oozing black payload and holding it first to his nose then to his lips then placing it on the tip of his tongue, 'is the freshest consignment of Russian caviare ever to have reached the United States.'

He gobbled down a small handful and nodded. 'Yes, sir, and real beluga too.'

He turned to the still dubious-looking sergeant. 'Detail a couple of men to go back to the jeep immediately for three frosted bottles of vodka and lots of hot buttered toast. We'll set up camp here to guard this.'

Major Grubner picked up another fistful of the glistening black globules and crushed it into his mouth before taking up his walkie-talkie to report to the White House.

Chapter Seventeen

'Hell's teeth, Undrupuv!' said Gerrard K. Conroy clamping his hands over his eyes as a striptease dancer with a double-jointed pelvis bumped and ground freakishly towards the climax of a bizarre act ten feet from their table. 'Why did you drag me to this place?'

'Relax,' said Yuri Undrupuv. The Director General of the KGB's eyes, shining with perverted brightness, were riveted on the strangely gyrating figure. 'The best bit is just coming.'

Conroy opened a crack in the visor that his closed fingers made across his eyes. Through the V-shaped frame he saw the dancer fling away a light cape of chiffon and reach up behind her back to the fastening of her brassière. Her large crude features and heavily rouged mouth sagged with simulated ardour as the strident music from a small brass combo clawed frantically hand over hand towards a crescendo. Long frizzy blonde hair swung around the dancer's face but didn't conceal the sweat springing through the thickly applied make-up.

'Goddamn!' muttered Conroy, closing the visor again as the dancer began to swing her hips and cross one knee gracelessly in front of the other while pretending to struggle tantalisingly with her bra hook.

Because his hands covered his eyes Conroy actually missed the poleaxing climax. But Undrupuv didn't. His fleshy lips sagged apart wetly as the dancer finally snatched away the inflated bra and pushed a hairy male chest towards the audience. The long, frizzy blonde wig came off at the same moment to reveal an old-fashioned short-back-and-sides haircut.

Undrupuv applauded the semi-naked man immoderately. His jowls quaked and a small amount of saliva dribbled down his chin. Conroy uncovered his eyes to see the man grinning grotesquely and posturing left and right holding the wig and bra. The CIA chief grimaced and shuddered, as if he'd swallowed a quart of vinegar, and turned his back to the stage.

'Good, eh, Conroy?' said Undrupuv beaming broadly at his opposite number. 'I thought you might like it. On your card in our file against "Sex" it says: "Unmarried. Nothing known. Tendencies: presumed unnatural."' The Russian grinned broadly. 'Me too. Have I brought you to the right place?'

Conroy swallowed noticeably. 'Let's discuss what we came here to discuss, namely how to get my President and your First Secretary back on the right sides of the Iron Curtain.' Conroy's voice rasped like a draw file on a jagged edge of sheet tin.

Undrupuv raised his bushy Georgian eyebrows. 'Iron Curtain. What quaint old-fashioned terminology – but I thought they had both defected.'

'Right,' said Conroy. 'We know all that crap. But neither you nor I, nor the patriotic services we represent can afford to allow the image of our countries and our ways of life to be tarnished and besmirched in the eyes of the world by the whims of a couple of odd-ball politicians, right?'

'Maybe,' said Undrupuv quietly. He glanced uneasily round at the other shadowy patrons in *Chez Nus*, West Berlin's best-known transvestite club. 'But keep your voice down, for Marx's sake! Every single customer here is probably a secret agent of some sort.'

'The dancing turns too?' asked Conroy.

'Correct,' said Undrupuv. 'That's why I suggested here.

Everybody expects everybody else to be an agent and on their guard so they can all relax. Nobody expects to hear anything here. It's a kind of rest room for spies where they come for their quiet hours. But it won't help to shout our conversation. There might be the odd one who isn't already drunk.'

A tall, willowy dancer with long blonde hair and a real-looking bosom of generous weight came on in a sequinned costume and began immediately to take off bits of it in an unskilled fashion. His face was surprisingly, serenely female and he won rapt attention from the audience by the little breathy gasps he emitted as he spun and turned and dropped frilly things.

Conroy and Undrupuv swung round to look and to their amazement Moira winked lasciviously at them before turning away and wiggling her shapely bottom in their direction.

'Hey, that guy's really some woman,' said Conroy loudly.

'Yeah, really some swell guy,' said Undrupuv in his best, but still not very good, imitation of an American accent. He laughed uproariously at his wit, jerking shoulders, jowls and saliva around spasmodically.

Conroy scowled and turned back to continue the discussion.

Moira was a late addition to the bill and she'd had to bribe the stage manager heavily to get on at all. Half an hour earlier, wearing much less than she was now, she had been relaxing beside her assignment in his hotel room. Then the phone rang. When she'd replaced the receiver she stood up suddenly beside the bed. 'Grooty,' she began dramatically, 'I'm going to shock you.'

'Impossible, luv,' said Groot lazily through a euphoric post-coital haze. Then he shot up into a sitting position as Moira calmly removed the long blonde wig of hair he'd always imagined was her own. The naked dome of her head blazed an ineradicable image into his mind.

'Wha—what goes on?' he asked in a shocked voice.

'I'm one of Helga's girls, Grooty,' she said. 'I was

assigned to stay close to you on their behalf. Now I must leave on another mission.'

'What do you mean?' asked Groot dimly.

'She's been recruiting for two years. I signed up to help save the world.'

'Then you're not working for British Intelligence after all?' said Groot slowly.

'Yes, them too. I've infiltrated the organisation and I've got to carry out their orders to protect my cover.' She grimaced comically and replaced the wig. 'You didn't suspect I was a girl with a mission to bring peace to the world with my body, did you?'

Groot laughed uncertainly. 'Nah, it hadn't struck me. You only really seemed interested in . . . in one thing really.'

Moira smiled affectionately. 'The training in the Organisation has been hard. I haven't ever worked with anybody as virile as you. To learn how to save the world we had to . . . well, you know what Helga said.' She started to pick up articles of clothing scattered round the room.

Groot knew a stab of regret as he watched the two snowy white spinnakers of her bra fill and billow out taut. Perhaps this was the last time he would see those great sails run out.

When she was fully dressed she came over to the bed. 'It's been a great assignment,' she said, placing a finger to her own lips then pressing it against his naked right nipple in a tender farewell. 'But a high-ranking American in need of reconciliation programming has just arrived. I must dash. Perhaps we'll meet again. I hope so.'

Twenty-nine minutes later she was on stage at the *Chez Nus* ogling Conroy and Undrupuv.

'Where is the President now?' asked Conroy brusquely, unaware of Moira's ogling.

Undrupuv smiled. 'You want to try to snatch him.' He raised his hands, palms upward above the table. 'Should I, the chief of the KGB tell you, the head of the CIA, such a thing?'

'Yes.'

'Okay. He is still in our embassy not five miles from here – behind the Berlin Wall.' Undrupuv laughed uproariously. He stopped suddenly when he noticed the entire audience was looking at him and not Moira, who by now was suggestively detaching her chiffon tail.

'Where is the First Secretary?' he asked in a practically inaudible whisper.

'In England.'

'Come on, that is not good enough. I have told you exactly where your man is. You only tell me the country.' Undrupuv grinned inanely.

'Save it, Undrupuv,' said Conroy. 'It would be easier for you to find the First Secretary in a day in England than it would be for us to get the President out of your East Berlin Embassy in a hundred years. You Commies all live in natural prisons. Our world is the *Free* World remember.'

Undrupuv's neck went red. He opened his mouth to say something but Conroy cut in again.

'More important. Where is this dame Helga now?'

'She is under house arrest in the Kremlin with General Korsov.'

'Guarded?'

'Guarded, yes.' Undrupuv smiled a smile that was nearer a leer. 'By seven eunuchs. Such a woman would wind any real man round her finger. So I found the answer in our Special Operatives Section.'

'Shouldn't be hard to find guys like that anywhere in your outfit,' said Conroy. 'You've got almost the entire service to choose from. None of 'em's got any balls.'

Undrupuv's neck went red again and some veins in his temple bulged.

'Ours is a dedicated, idealistic service and a unit of such men is deemed necessary to resist the blandishments of certain sections of your own thoroughly degenerate organisation!'

'What's gonna happen to Helga?'

'At present she is being allowed to deploy her small army of beautiful, naked-headed girls at all major political meetings, in accordance with those solemn assurances given by the temporary leaders of our two countries. But otherwise she will remain closely confined.'

Moira waggled her shoulders pointedly at them from the stage. Conroy, noticing the movement out of the corner of his eye, turned uneasily to stare at the rippling tumult occurring within the sequinned brassière.

'He must have had a transplant from Raquel Welch,' yelled a voice from the shadows. Loud guffaws rolled towards Moira who ignored them with a calm confidence which her audience assumed was born of years of female impersonating.

The United Nations Special Committee on the Question of Defining Aggression, which had been striving unsuccessfully for a semantic formula acceptable to all nations for over twenty years, sat down to its ninety-eighth meeting at UN Headquarters by the East River in New York at the moment that Moira lost her chiffon tail.

The Committee president opened the meeting by welcoming thirty-five new members who had doubled the size of the committee. He cleared his throat nervously and expressed the hope that the presence of thirty-five curvaceous, naked-headed girls in scoop-necked sweaters and matador pants would add a new dimension to the Committee's deliberations and lead to an early and successful outcome.

The Communist delegate from Bulgaria attracted thirty-five adoring glances when he won the race to be the first to his feet. 'The proposed draft definition of aggression submitted three years ago by the six Western powers is abstract and artificial in character,' he said.

From the side of his eye he noticed that all the girls had suddenly leaned forward to rest their arms on the table thus revealing the warm shadowy canyons that separated their rounded bosoms.

'... the Western draft enlarges the concept of aggression beyond the provisions of Article Two, paragraph four of the United Nations Charter,' he added, his eyes darting round the table from one semi-revealed bosom to another like a nectar-starved bee at midsummer, '... and I submit that the definition should be restricted within the meaning of Article Fifty-One of the Charter but covering economic and political pressure and subversion of the kind constantly applied by the ruthless imperialist and capitalist powers on a worldwide basis—'

The Bulgarian sat down abruptly before he had finished, half falling towards the naked-headed female on his left, who seemed to have her arm in a stranglehold round his left thigh.

The United States delegate, a tall distinguished man with iron-grey hair, jumped up. 'I submit,' he said, 'that the draft definition proposed by the Soviet Union and her allies ignores the fact that the Security Council is the organ with primary responsibility for preserving world peace—'

Before he could go any further a commotion around the Algerian and Canadian delegates and their female companions distracted the attention of the meeting. The gavel of the Committee president echoed through the chamber and when silence was achieved he invited the Algerian delegate to explain the commotion. After a moment's hesitation, the Algerian stood up, looking abashed.

'Mr Chairman, I apologise but some misunderstanding arose with the new lady delegate on my right. She wishes it to be said that she does not believe that the Security Council is the most important organ for maintaining world peace ... She says in her opinion the most important organ—'

The president, scenting something unpalatable, suddenly banged his gavel and hurriedly invited the American delegate to continue.

'In the twenty unsuccessful years of debate on this issue Mr Chairman,' said the United States delegate, 'the intransigence of the Communist delegates and the inept insistence of the non-aligned nations on establishing multi-faceted criteria for defining aggressive intent has—'

His proposal, which seemed destined to go on for at

least an hour, was interrupted by the shaven-headed girl on his left tugging at the cloth of his trouser leg and fluttering her false eyelashes up at him. 'Sir, you've got lovely thighs,' she murmured.

This whispered compliment carried clearly across the room that had been built with acoustic considerations in mind and the American delegate, blushing furiously, excused himself and sat down to 'consult'. The softly rounded dome of his companion's head moved close to his neatly cropped iron-grey hair. She whispered again in his ear while apparently running her hand gently back and forth along his thigh under the table.

The president looked round aghast as he realised that the large chamber, normally the scene of cold, embittered charge and counter-charge, was seething below table-level with surreptitious caresses and counter-caresses. The attention of all delegates without exception had wandered far from the problem of defining aggression. And suddenly the president himself felt a hand on his left knee.

'I call the United Kingdom delegate to the floor,' he shouted desperately.

'My government believes,' said the angular Englishman, rising and tucking his chin self-consciously into his chest, 'that aggression should be a term applicable without prejudice to a finding of threat to the peace, or a breach of that peace...' He paused and without taking his eyes from his notes slapped at the bare female arm creeping round his waist. '... to the use of force in international relations, overt or covert, direct or indirect by a state against the territorial integrity—'

The attention of the Committee president who was himself squirming in his seat under the assault of unseen hands was caught by the beautiful, bald-headed companion of the United States delegate. She gazed directly into his eyes and stood up to reveal herself as a living Venus de Milo with arms.

'Mr Chairman,' she said interrupting the United Kingdom

delegate, in a cool, confident voice, 'I propose that "aggression" should be simply defined as follows: "Any act of mental or physical violence which impedes the natural union of attracted males and females in an environment of peace anywhere in the world".'

The overhead lights flashed on her naked head as she sat down. Thirty-five male delegates stared at her mesmerised. Then the Bulgarian delegate jumped up, holding the hand of the bare-headed girl next to him in full view.

'I second that, Mr Chairman,' he said breathing hard. 'And anyone who opposes this resolution is himself guilty of aggression.'

The president asked for a vote and when seventy hands showed unanimously he declared that aggression had been finally defined.

Cheering immediately broke out and the delegates leapt from their seats to embrace in turn all the new female members. Then the meeting broke up in a disorderly rush for the door, each delegate clutching the hand of his own dome-headed girl.

Similar scenes were occurring simultaneously at meetings of the European Economic Commission in Brussels. British, French and German delegates who had argued furiously for many years about farm support policies, sovereignty and monetary union dashed madly from their conference chambers in full agreement and with their clothing disarranged. They clutched the hands of various naked-headed girls to them and disappeared swiftly in the direction of the lifts to their hotel rooms.

'Look,' said Conroy leaning across the table in the *Chez Nus* and jabbing his finger into Undrupuv's chest, 'hear what that guy said about Raquel Welch? Well, that's what I propose we do to get the two hostages back where they belong.'

'Transplant women's breasts onto them?' asked Undrupuv, his voice rising querulously.

'No, transplant their brains, you schmuck,' said Conroy

viciously. 'If the First Secretary wants to stay in the West and the President wants to stay in the East what must we do? Simple. A brain transplant – change their minds for them.'

'Change their minds for them? Yes, I like the idea.' Undrupuv burst into quietly insane laughter that sent a chill down Moira's beautifully curved spine as she fumbled onstage with the fastening of her sequinned brassière.

'That's what the world struggle is all about today, eh, Yuri,' said Conroy. 'A battle for men's minds – which in this case we both win. Is it a deal?' He stuck out his hand towards the Russian.

The smile on Undrupuv's face froze solid for several seconds as he stared at Conroy's hand; then it abruptly disappeared altogether. 'Tell me, Conroy, why does the mind of the First Secretary need to be changed if, as you claim, the First Secretary was kidnapped against his will by the brilliance of your organisation?'

'Ah, well, I was coming to that,' said Conroy, his expression a delicate fusion of craftiness and shiftiness. 'You see, after he got to the West and saw how good it was compared with your own dreary life-style, he asked for asylum.'

'Crap, Conroy,' said Undrupuv quietly, 'if I may be permitted to borrow from your colourful vocabulary. The First Secretary felt humiliated because he thought Helga Mikunov would have to move to the West. He had decided to defect two days before you came to Red Square in disguise – a disguise which, needless to say, we penetrated as soon as you landed.'

'Impossible,' said Conroy.

'The First Secretary unfortunately persuaded a number of high-ranking agents in my service to help him defect,' said Undrupuv ignoring Conroy's suggestion. 'Your bungling almost ruined his very carefully laid plans. How would you feel if we told the world that he had to chase the CIA plane all over Sheremetyevo airport to try and get aboard. And was constantly refused entry?'

Conroy's face turned magenta in the dimness and he felt the chill of a deathly humiliation at the prospect of the disclosure.

'Nobody would believe KGB crap like that. It would be obvious it was empty propaganda. And anyway, the First Secretary's mind is made up – now he definitely wants to stay in the West.'

'Okay,' said Undrupuv. 'Maybe you are right. We both have an equal interest in putting something new into their heads...'

The world's two leading spymasters were so intent on their whispered conversation that they failed to notice the hush that had fallen on the rest of the audience as Moira finally freed the fastenings of her sequinned brassière. She turned her back on the audience, slipped out of it and let it fall to the floor. Then with her back still turned, she did something totally unprecedented in the history of the *Chez Nus* transvestite club – she slipped out of her G-string and stood completely naked facing the back curtains.

The audience stared goggle-eyed from the darkness, waiting for their man to turn round. Below the stage the pasty-faced musicians blew screeching high notes through their brass instruments. Then with slow deliberation Moira reached up a hand to her wig.

'Helsinki,' said Conroy to Undrupuv, completely oblivious to the climax that was being reached behind him.

'Why Helsinki?' asked Undrupuv.

'It's neutral,' replied Conroy. 'Helsinki with Rory Rymerson, the top American brain specialist, as our man and a Russian surgeon of your own choice. I have a totally secure operating theatre prepared...'

At that second the saxophones wailed and Moira turned. She snatched at her blonde wig, flung it aside and stood dramatically naked-headed in the spotlight, raised her arms triumphantly aloft. Her glorious, unmistakably female breasts trembled perceptibly from her out-of-breathness and her lips were parted seductively in a manner no transvestite could have matched.

The confirmation of her sex provided by her naked loins plunged the audience into a palpable state of shock. This lasted for some ten seconds; then tables and chairs were overturned in a noisy, panic-stricken scramble for the exits. Within seconds the club was empty save for Conroy, Undrupuv and Moira who remained motionless and entirely naked in the spotlight on the stage, listening to their conversation.

'Okay, Helsinki it is, then,' said Undrupuv still looking straight into Conroy's eyes and wondering whether it was foolish to trust him. 'How do we go about getting them there for the transplant?'

'I suggest . . .' began Conroy, then realised the place had gone quiet. Without taking his eyes from Undrupuv's he lowered his voice to a whisper, inaudible even to Moira. The conversation continued as a murmur of unintelligible sound.

After two minutes Moira tired of standing with her arms upraised attracting no attention whatsoever. She stepped down from the stage and walked naked to where the two men sat staring fiercely at each other and talking in whispers.

Without speaking she sat down at the table and pressed the length of her bare calf against Conroy's trouser-clad leg. But still the two men continued their rapt discussion. When Conroy eventually turned to find a real naked-headed woman sitting at his elbow he screamed and tried to move away.

'Get this guy off me!' he yelled hysterically. Moira pushed harder against his leg and leaned over to try to spear her moist tongue into his ear. Conroy screamed again and the table fell over as he jumped up.

'It's a woman!' shrieked Undrupuv.

In shared panic they ran stumbling and gasping towards the door, leaving Moira in sole possession of the eerily silent, smoky basement. When they had gone she shrugged and walked back to the stage. Picking up a wrap-over robe from behind a curtain, she slipped into it, went to a telephone by the bar and dialled the hotel.

'Gilbert? It's Moira,' she said when a male voice replied. 'Book two seats to Helsinki on the first available flight.'

'You had a change of mind, luv?' asked Groot.

'No, but I think the President is going to have one,' she replied and hung up.

The door of a second floor bedroom in the Seaview boarding house in Felixstowe, England, burst open at 3.30 a.m. and six men in long black raincoats and trilby hats fell in babbling in Russian. They grabbed the First Secretary of the Soviet Communist Party and, ignoring his protests that he wished only to see Helga, rushed him downstairs.

'Why you CIA men go to such trouble to dress up like this I don't understand,' said the First Secretary as he was hustled into a car drawn up at the kerb in Highcliff Road.

His captors ignored the remark and one of the men lifted a large hypodermic syringe into view. Pulling back the First Secretary's sleeve he injected him wordlessly and moments later the First Secretary's eyes fell closed . . .

The President of the United States wakened at the same time in his room in the Soviet Embassy in East Berlin to find six clean-limbed, crew-cut, open-faced young men standing round his bed. One of them also held a syringe.

In the gloom the President could see they wore pebble-dash sports jackets and knitted ties with white, button-down-collar shirts. They chewed gum and invited him to accompany them in chummy Texan accents.

Without a word he got out of bed, dressed and went with them. The President of the United States knew better than to argue with KGB agents.

Chapter Eighteen

The President of the United States and the First Secretary of the Communist Party of the Union of Soviet Socialist Republics lay side by side on twin operating tables but the sheets covering them were not regulation white. At Conroy's insistence the President's already unconscious figure was draped with the red, white and blue of the star-spangled banner while the form of the First Secretary reclined similarly anaesthetised under a blood-red flag with a large yellow hammer and sickle emblazoned on its top left corner.

'Are we about ready to go?' rasped Conroy.

The Director of the Central Intelligence Agency stood in a predatory, on-guard position at the head of the President's table, his bulky quarter-back shoulders bulging under a gown of white sterilised cotton. Beside him stood the American brain surgeon, Rory Rymerson. He too was dressed all in white, save for a small replica of the United States flag sewn on the front of his medical skull-cap. He also wore red, white and blue striped rubber gloves.

'Guess I'm ready,' said Rymerson.

He was a powerfully built man with a barrel chest and a leathery face the colour of strong, dark tea. He glanced in the direction of his chief nurse. Moira, unrecognisable in mask cap and gown, closed her left eye an eighth of an inch in a sly wink of response, indicating she was ready for Rymerson at any time.

Groot noticed this and felt a slight pang of jealousy. He knew Moira was dedicated to her mission. But did she have to go to work immediately on every man she met over forty-five?

'Your team ready, Undrupuv?' asked Conroy out of the side of his mouth.

Undrupuv, who had assumed a similar on-guard position ten feet away at the head of the table on which the unconscious First Secretary was lying, turned to the Russian surgeon, Alexei Drugonov, who was distinguished by the small red flag with its hammer and sickle emblem on the front of his head cover, and blood red gloves. 'Ready, Comrade Drugonov?'

'*Da.*'

As he spoke Drugonov turned to his chief Russian nurse and raised an eyebrow at her for confirmation. The nurse's broad, dramatic cheekbones filled out the gauze mask like no other face in the operating theatre. Her dark, strangely hypnotic eyes narrowed slightly with the tiny nod of affirmation she gave in Drugonov's direction and Groot, who was watching her carefully, wondered again at the irresistible conqueror of seven KGB eunuchs who had managed to free herself and get back into the middle of the action so quickly.

'Helga will find a way,' Moira had told him on the plane to Helsinki and her power to undermine and penetrate any organisation of males was amply illustrated by the fact that, unknown to the chiefs of the two largest security services in the world, Britain's most famous gossip-writer was now standing anonymously among the team of twelve secret American observers. They were ranged in a semi-circle opposite a similar number of secret Russian observers under the glaring lights of a maximum security Helsinki operating theatre.

Like the other twenty-four observers, only Groot's eyes were visible between the gauze mask and white skull-cap.

A sterilised white gown reached down to the floor and his rubber-gloved hands hung clear of his sides, giving him, like the others, the appearance of an immobilised penguin.

'Okay,' said Conroy, still speaking out of the corner of his mouth in Undrupuv's direction, 'if we're both ready, begin brain transplant!'

The American and Russian surgeons advanced simultaneously on the skulls of their respective leaders holding little drills in their right hands. They were followed closely by their national teams.

Groot noticed a sudden rumpling movement as the hands of half a dozen of his fellow American observers disappeared under their white gowns. The gowns suddenly distended and stretched tight as though six small tents had been erected pointing into the centre of the theatre.

Groot looked quickly across at their opposite numbers and saw that six Russian observers had similar ominous bulges under their gowns. All twelve gowns poked out towards the inert figures of the President and the First Secretary and the teams about to operate on them.

A series of clicking sounds indicated that the safety catches of twelve shrouded machineguns had been removed.

Conroy and Undrupuv exchanged hostile but understanding glances and nodded for the operation to proceed.

Small white bald patches had been shaved on the heads of both patients, slightly forward and to the right of the centre of their heads.

'What are you gonna do, for krissakes?' asked Conroy in a squeamish voice as Rymerson made quick incisions to lay open the scalp, clamped the edges of the incision, inserted the drill inside the perimeter of the bald patch and began boring a small hole in the Presidential cranium.

'Make a series of holes four centimetres apart in a horseshoe shape in the President's skull,' said Rymerson laconically, his voice muffled by his mask.

A buzz like a dentist's drill from the next table indicated that Drugonov was boring holes in the First Secretary's head too. Conroy's face began to turn a pale shade of green as he watched the drill complete the horseshoe ring of holes. He moved a pace back as the surgeon took a tiny wire saw from Moira and inserted it in the first hole. Then he began sawing gently, joining the holes together. Moira and her fellow nurses stepped forward regularly to swab the operation area and pat away sweat before it could appear on the surgeon's brow.

'What next?' croaked Conroy.

'Next I shall insert a scalpel under the bone flap and break it open but the base of the horseshoe will remain attached to the covering muscle which will act as a hinge.' Rymerson's voice had a flat, sadistic tone and his eyes darted sideways as he spoke. He noted Conroy's pallor with satisfaction. 'So you see we shall have a little trapdoor in his skull through which to work.'

Conroy's scalp tingled in sympathy and he broke out into a cold sweat. He sneaked a look sideways at Undrupuv who was watching his own man. Conroy drew considerable comfort from the slit of definitely greenish skin visible around the Russian's eyes.

Rymerson motioned one of his nurses forward to plug the edges of the cut bone with wax to prevent bleeding.

Groot, standing twelve feet away, felt his mouth go as dry as the desert in June. He was glad he could not see more.

Rymerson darted a glance at the CIA chief to check the greenness of Conroy's face. 'Now,' he said, taking a pair of scissors from Moira, 'I am going to cut through this soft covering inside the skull – the dura mater – and expose the brain itself which has the consistency of soft cheese.'

He cut busily with the scissors and Conroy watched aghast as a section of the moist greyish-white brain of the Most Powerful Man in the World came into view.

He shuddered. Could that muddy-looking cream cheese really choose among all those complex issues outlined in those complex option papers and decide the fate of America and all mankind? Did his own actions, thoughts, ambitions, perversions, stem from similar mouldy cheese inside his own head?

Because he crumpled limply, Conroy hit the floor without much sound.

Two of the masked and gowned CIA men who weren't busy pointing sub-machineguns across the operating theatre moved forward, dragged Conroy clear of the table and began trying to revive him. As they did so Undrupuv straightened up from peering into the hole in the First Secretary's head, swayed and sagged noiselessly to the floor in a similar faint.

Two KGB men stepped forward, hauled him aside and began working on him.

Rymerson smiled smugly over his mask at Moira and carried on working through the hole in the President's skull. Two minutes later he stopped, looked up and beckoned to one of the CIA gunmen. He pointed to the President's head. 'Guard that hole,' he told the man and walked over to Drugonov to consult.

As he approached, Drugonov summoned up a KGB gunman to stand guard at the opening into the First Secretary's brain.

The muzzle of the KGB machinegun held under the white smock was trained steadily between Rymerson's eyes as he bent and peered into the Russian cavity with Drugonov.

'Your hole's a little jagged round the edges,' said Rymerson lightly. Drugonov glowered at the American. 'Otherwise not bad. You seem to have hit the correct area of the thalamus and hypothalamus all right. Like to come and look at mine?'

Still scowling, his professional pride wounded, the Russian surgeon followed Rymerson back to the President, cautioning the KGB man with his eyes to continue guarding his aperture.

Conroy and Undrupuv, restored to shaky consciousness by their cohorts with glasses of sterilised water, tried to slip back unnoticed to the heads of their tables.

'Where have we got to?' asked Conroy, muzzily.

'We are just inspecting each other's digging,' said

Rymerson, 'prior to removing approximately sixty grammes of the thalamus and hypothalamus from each head and exchanging them.'

'Sixty grammes? Two ounces? Is that all?' asked Conroy. 'You're not gonna transplant the whole brain, huh?'

'Not unless you want a Russian-speaking Communist President of the United States and a capitalist First Secretary of the Soviet Communist Party preaching the American Way of Life.'

'Cut the wisecracks, Rymerson,' snarled Conroy, 'what's this thalamus and hypothalamus stuff?'

'Little is known for sure about the functions of various parts of the brain,' said Rymerson breathing an exasperated sigh as if his patience was being tried severely by a small tiresome child, 'but my own experiments have made me – although I hesitate to say it myself – the foremost authority in the world—'

'Yeah, yeah, Rymerson, we know,' said Conroy nastily. 'Never mind the propaganda, just give me the facts.'

The surgeon bit back sharp words. 'The thalamus and the hypothalamus beneath it, my theories suggest, help control the emotions and the affections and I believe the tendency to wilfulness. They also, by the way, play a vital role in relaying viscera nerve messages of taste and smell and have a direct if still mysterious connection with the stomach.'

'Yeah, yeah,' said Conroy rudely, 'so after all the mumbo-jumbo what does it mean?'

'It means,' said Rymerson quietly, 'that by carefully calculating which segment of the thalamus and hypothalamus to remove we can exactly exchange the desires of the President to remain in Communist territory for the desire of the First Secretary to remain in the West. After the operation they will both simply want to go home.'

'We hope,' said Undrupuv quickly. 'Hadn't you better get on with it before they both catch a cold in the head through those holes?'

The two surgeons returned to their tables, dismissed the armed guards to their places and took up from their assistants identical instruments that looked very similar to ice-cream scoops. As one man they leaned forward and poked them in through the holes in the heads of the two world leaders.

There was a pause as each surgeon once more left his own manhole – again conscientiously calling forward a guard with a gun – to go and check that the other's instrument was identically zeroed in on the correct area. When they were satisfied, each returned to his own ice-cream scoop and stood listening as though for a prearranged order.

Conroy and Undrupuv looked sideways at each other, and checked their watches.

'Thirty seconds from now,' said Conroy.

'Check,' said Undrupuv.

The seconds ticked silently by. Nobody moved. The twelve guards held their concealed machineguns steady on the surgeons and their assistants.

Groot stood watching anonymously from behind his mask and cap, his Adam's apple moving up and down rapidly with the tension. He was more glad than ever that he was not near enough to observe the operation in minute detail.

Conroy and Undrupuv stood behind and to one side of their surgeons and counted down.

'Five, four, three, two . . . one!'

'Incise for transplant!'

They called the order loudly in unison in English.

The two surgeons, again acting as one man, dug in their ice-cream scoops, waggled them around for a moment then withdrew them. Carefully they transferred the cerebral nuggets to forceps and held them up to the light, revealing what looked like two wetly gleaming segments of discoloured Camembert.

Still looking at their watches, Conroy and Undrupuv opened their mouths for a second order.

'Surgeons turn towards each other and walk forward to exchange brain segments,' they called in one voice.

As the surgeons obeyed, one CIA man and one KGB

agent detached themselves from their respective semicircles and stepped forward producing clipboards bearing sheets of paper headed 'Utmost Top Secret.'

Conroy and Undrupuv moved to stand beside their surgeons. The two Russians and the two Americans eyed each other suspiciously. The surgeons stood holding the discoloured Camembert slices in forceps raised in their right hands.

'Sign here, please, sir,' said the CIA agent holding the clipboard and a pen towards Undrupuv. 'Just under where it says, "Received, one brain segment of the President of the United States in return for identical segment of brain of First Secretary of Soviet Communist Party".'

'Not until I hev got my hands on it!' said Undrupuv firmly. 'I'm not a fool, you know.'

'Lay your filthy Commie hands on it and you'll contaminate it and kill your man within a few days,' said Rymerson aggressively.

'It was a figure of speech meaning "in our possession",' shouted Undrupuv angrily. 'We don't sign until you sign.'

The KGB agent thrust his clipboard bearing a similar cyclostyled receipt towards Conroy.

'Crap to the signing! For God's sake, exchange the brain lumps before they go cold and rot,' yelled Conroy.

'Hey, where is your porous membrane?' demanded Rymerson suddenly of the Russian surgeon, glaring at him.

'Porous membrane? What porous membrane?' asked Drugonov.

'The porous membrane, you dumb Commie,' shouted Rymerson, 'to isolate the brain segments and allow access to nutrition, but at the same time to prevent entry of foreign cells that could cause the transplant to be rejected.'

'We don't need the porous membrane,' screamed Drugonov. 'We have treated both men with maximum immunosuppressive agents, including whole body irradiation.'

'You fool,' breathed Rymerson. The hand in which he

held the forceps and brain segment shook in his rage. 'The degree of immunosuppression necessary to prevent rejection is related inversely to the degree of donor-recipient compatibility.'

'I know, I know,' shouted Drugonov. 'But the ABO red blood cell tests and the leucocyte blood cell tests have shown an unusually high degree of compatibility. These two men have reached their mighty positions precisely because they are physiologically very similar!'

'But don't you see, you Red Commie dunderhead? The degree of compatibility is not great enough to remove all risk of rejection—'

'Don't call me a Red Commie dunderhead,' said Drugonov, raising his forceps and the discoloured slice of Camembert as if to strike Rymerson.

'Complete compatibility occurs only when donor and recipient are identical twins, you Commie airhead,' shrieked Rymerson, 'so we must have the porous membrane to be sure—'

Drugonov lost his temper completely and lunged at Rymerson with his segment.

A nervous CIA man opened fire from under the skirts of his sterile smock and a burst of nine bullets whistled within two inches of the brain segment of the First Secretary in Drugonov's wildly waving hand.

The bullets smashed a cluster of overhead lights in the corner, sending down a shower of glass fragments.

'Stop this, for krissakes! Cease fire!' screamed Conroy lunging in between the struggling surgeons.

Undrupuv moved in suddenly to protect his man followed by most of his observers. Seeing this the Americans moved in too. Only Groot and one other member of the American team, a surprisingly rotund figure, whale-like beneath his mask cap and gown, remained standing by the wall. They watched wide-eyed as the struggling group seethed around the unconscious leaders on the operating tables, the two pairs of forceps containing their vital morsels jerking visibly above the mêlée.

On the fringes of the throng Helga made a quick sign to Moira. In a single movement they slipped out of their sterile robes and whisked the covers from their dramatically shaven heads. They wore nothing underneath them.

Wearing only masks around their mouths for aseptic reasons they moved in from opposite directions pressing their naked bodies into the crush of struggling men. Slowly and gently they pushed towards the two quarrelling surgeons calling one word softly as they went: 'Reconciliation, gentlemen! Reconciliation!'

Chapter Nineteen.

'Schlupp . . . schlupp!'

In the hushed stillness of the Helsinki operating theatre the two squelching sounds, following closely on one another, carried softly to the pricked, journalistic ears of Gilbert Groot. His spine tingled eerily from top to bottom at the thought that he was secretly observing a moment of enormous magnitude in the history of mankind.

He watched without breathing. The little Camembert-like plug of capitalistic brain extracted from the President of the United States was thrust soggily into the head of the First Secretary of the Communist Party of the Union of Soviet Socialist Republics at almost the same moment that the plug of identical size from the First Secretary's brain was similarly pressed home into the hole in the President's head.

Ball-point pens raced smoothly across two clipboards as Conroy for the CIA and Undrupuv for the KGB signed for the exchange of material.

'The President's been waiting to give Leonid a piece of his mind for some time. Now he's really gone and done it,' whispered one irreverent, begowned CIA agent to his fellow standing beside him.

Groot heard the whispered remark and looked sideways along the row of white-masked American profiles. The man to whom it had been addressed wasn't amused. He stared stolidly straight ahead of him as the grin on the face of the other agent faded and was finally shaken away completely with a resigned shrug.

Groot turned back to the operation – then did a quick double-take. There was something about the eyes of the man who was not amused that rang an alarm bell somewhere in the servants' quarters of Groot's mind. They not only stared straight ahead but they possessed the same glazed, hypnotic quality that he had noticed in the eyes of Helga Mikunov. Groot realised that it was the same man who had stood apart with him when the fighting broke out in the operating theatre. He looked along the line again and saw that the man's gown swelled outward over an enormously fat belly. Undressed he would look like a fat white whale, Groot thought suddenly. Then he wondered why the man had not struck him as odd before among the fit, hard-boiled agents.

He was sure the man was aware that he was staring at him and was consciously avoiding his glance. Through a half-closed eye Groot imagined the man naked with a towel wrapped entirely round his head. Could it be the man who had twice rained sweat on him in the Berlin sauna bath? And if it was, what was he doing here?

Groot turned his attention reluctantly back to the operation. Although he continued to glance along the line of faces from time to time, the fat man studiously avoided turning in his direction.

The two surgeons were busying themselves sewing up the inner incisions in preparation for closing the bone flaps with wire sutures. They were helped by their teams headed by Helga and Moira, now respectably gowned and masked again after their successful naked intervention in the East–West battle around the operating tables.

Rymerson smiled a smile of smug satisfaction as he tucked in the edges of the porous membrane – a section of skin from a pig's pancreas – that the Russian had finally agreed they should use to isolate both transplants from the danger of rejection.

Ten minutes later Rymerson deftly sewed up the edges

of the incision in the scalp. 'There, gentlemen of the security services, you see the world's first human brain transplant completed,' he said triumphantly. He paused, his expression saddening. 'Unfortunately this outstanding achievement must remain a secret from the world—'

'Cut the medical bullshit, Rymerson,' cut in Conroy rudely. 'How long before it all takes?'

'The stitches can be taken out in around three days, if all is well.' Rymerson paused again, crinkling his brow in thought. 'Tell them when they regain consciousness they each had a little fall that required a few stitches. They'll have headaches when they wake up, but they won't know they've been operated on.'

'What about the bald patches?' asked Undrupuv.

'Stick little hairpieces over them. Pander to their vanity and tell them it's been put there for the sake of television appearances and must not be touched or removed for one month. By then the hair will have grown again. That should do it.'

Conroy glanced over to Drugonov and saw that he had finished his needlework too. Like Rymerson he was standing back admiring the neatness of his own stitching. The Russian still showed, by the sulky lines pulling down the corners of his mouth, that he had not forgotten having to bow to the judgement of Rymerson about using the porous membrane from the pig's pancreas. But he brightened visibly when Helga Mikunov flashed him an electric, eyes-only smile of approval over her mask.

'Okay, Undrupuv, he's all yours now, take him away,' said Conroy nodding towards the unconscious First Secretary, 'before we decide to put some really nasty capitalist ideas into his head.'

Undrupuv glowered, said nothing and turned on his heel.

Led by the two intelligence chiefs, the flag-bedecked forms of the President and the First Secretary were wheeled from the theatre. The President's trolley, as was appropriate, turned right, followed by the American team, and the First Secretary's went, with the Russian team, to the left.

The distance between the two men and the little alien scraps of brain they had imparted to each other widened rapidly.

The operating theatre, scene of history in the making, stood empty and silent with a little pile of broken glass in one corner and nine bullets embedded deep in its otherwise germ-free walls.

Groot tried to push through the crowd of men in front of him in the corridor. The fat, whale-like man had been on the end of the line nearest the door and had been among the first out. For a moment Groot had lost sight of him in the crush.

The journalist pushed his way past three men and caught sight of his quarry, who was waddling fast about twenty yards ahead in the long corridor.

'Hey watch it, buddy,' said one American agent as Groot shoved him roughly aside in his anxiety not to lose sight of the fat man. 'Say, who are you anyway?'

Groot felt panic at the thought of being unmasked rising in his throat. He slowed his pace and spoke out of the corner of his mouth. 'Ah ain't feelin' too darned good right now,' he said in his best Southern drawl. 'They never told me Ah hadda watch the brains being squeezed outta folks' heads when Ah joined this outfit.'

The man he'd pushed laughed good-naturedly. 'Okay, buddy, maybe you'd better run then.'

'Guess Ah will,' said Groot and immediately broke into a gallop as he saw the fat man turn into a side corridor.

Groot turned the same corner five seconds later. He advanced ten paces then stopped. The corridor was empty and numbered green doors led off it endlessly on either side.

He opened the first door and gazed round at shelves piled high with jars of obscene-looking biological specimens pickled in preservative. He closed it hurriedly and opened the next door, setting a dozen teaching skeletons rattling and clinking in agitation. The next door led to a back stairway to other floors. A further search without attracting undue attention to himself was out of the question. Groot walked slowly back to the main corridor.

It was empty. There was no sign anywhere of the fast-moving fat man with the glazed eyes.

Chapter Twenty

The Dutch businessman who had flown to Helsinki from West Berlin two days before could not believe his ears. Not only was his sales drive to infiltrate the Finnish market with Dutch deep-freeze equipment not going well but that damned engine-revving noise in the next room sounded exactly like the racket that had disturbed him in Berlin, where he hadn't sold much equipment either. It seemed as if it was haunting him. He must be tired, getting old and jaded. He rubbed his eyes. It was clearly a hallucination. Ignore it, he told himself, and it would go away.

Two minutes later as the revving of the Porsche rose to a crescendo he lost control completely and banged his head hard and repeatedly against the intervening wall. Release finally came when he sank down into the deep silence of unconsciousness.

He never knew it but four seconds later the noise stopped abruptly. It was followed by a prolonged sigh.

Moira, too, had found release.

She sank back limply against Groot. He gently stroked the golden nylon fleece of her wig which he insisted she wear on her shining head when in his presence.

'I don't go for you without hair, Moira, somehow,' he said.

'I'm glad,' said Moira dreamily. 'I don't really care how you go for me – as long as you do!'

A long, warm, tactile silence followed in which no words were spoken.

'Want a ciggie, luv?' asked Groot at last when he thought she was strong enough to sit up and take nourishment. He offered her one of his cigarettes and they lit up.

'Now,' said Groot seriously, 'I think you'd better answer one or two questions.'

'Must I?' she asked, moving languorously to a new, fluidly relaxed position.

Groot covered her to the chin with a sheet to help himself to concentrate.

'Yeah. Like, who is the fat man I saw you with last night in the operating theatre?'

'Fat man?'

'Yeah, fat man. Don't be coy.'

'I didn't see any fat man.'

'No, perhaps you were too busy ogling the brain surgeon. But to me he looked suspiciously like the fat porpoise who gave me the original tip-off in that sauna bath.'

'Don't be jealous, Gilbert. Ogling's just my life's work now, my mission.' She pressed herself back against the pillows and closed her eyes. 'But this isn't work, this is leisure, pleasure. Do something else nice to me. Now,' she said softly.

'Look, Moira, I've got to know this – and a lot more.'

'I think I've told you too much already, Grooty,' she said sucking in a deep lungful of smoke. 'I've been indiscreet because you do such beautiful things to me. You know, if women ever take over the world you could lead the fight back. You're irresistible.'

'Where do you fit into all this?' asked Groot, ignoring her blandishments.

'I can't tell you. It's a state secret,' she said, smiling with her eyes still closed.

Groot stubbed out his cigarette half smoked. A calculating expression flitted across his face. He lifted the sheet and slid underneath it next to her.

'Mmmmmmmmmm,' said Moira.

'If you want me to know nothing, why did you tip me off about coming here to Helsinki?' Groot stopped what he was doing, took her cigarette away, put it out then resumed.

'Mmmmmmmmmm,' said Moira.

'Why did you tip me off?' persisted Groot gently.

'Mmmmmmmmmm, because I wanted to see you again. I didn't dream they were going to transplant . . . I thought it would help you to get another good story . . . I like you, Grooty, you know that . . . ooohh, don't stop—'

Groot suddenly became still.

'Go on! Go on!' urged Moira frantically.

'All right,' said Groot slowly. 'But what part exactly are you playing?'

'I can't tell you. Stop talking and just . . .'

Groot stopped again and reached for his cigarettes on the bedside table.

'No, no,' gasped Moira. 'Don't smoke now! Go on with what you were doing. I'll tell you.'

'Are you really working for British Intelligence?' he asked, putting down the cigarettes and lighter.

'Yes, I already told you, didn't I? . . . Go on! Go on!'

'But you have also infiltrated Helga's group?'

'Yes, yes, I have . . . Please, Grooty.'

'Is she the leader, the brains behind it, or is the fat man in charge?'

'Mmmmmmmmmm . . .' Moira breathed. 'That's really nice, but I can't tell you everything.'

Groot stopped.

Moira's voice was frantic again. 'I don't honestly know, Gil. Maybe the fat man is behind it. I take instructions from Helga but London doesn't think Helga could be working entirely alone. We think there could be somebody else but we don't know who he is . . . Please go on now, Grooty, go on!'

'Have you reported back about the transplant yet?'

'No, not yet. It hasn't been possible. There are no secure communications here . . .' Groot bent back to his task, at the same time nuzzling Moira's left ear.

'Ooohh,' gasped Moira, her eyes still closed.

'Do you realise, Moira, we could both be killed – by either side – because we know about the transplant?'

'I don't care! I don't care about anything right now!' said Moira desperately. 'Just don't stop what you're doing . . .'

Groot's eyes narrowed calculatingly. 'Moira,' he said, accelerating her passion gently, 'what put you on to me?'

'Ooohh, Grooty, stop talking.'

Groot relaxed and pulled away from her.

'No, Grooty, no!' she groaned. 'Don't, please. You're torturing me! I'll tell you! . . . The Organisation, Helga's people, they assigned me to stay close to you. It wasn't London, that was a lie . . . Now, Grooty, please, go on.'

'How did you get yourself taken on by the Organisation, by Helga's people?'

'Damn these questions,' moaned Moira threshing around wildly in frustration. 'They recruited suitable women in several countries. They've all been hypnotised during their training. Now, Grooty, please, please . . .'

'Hypnotised!' Groot froze. 'So that's it.'

'Grooty!' shrieked Moira pleadingly. 'For Heaven's sake, do it!'

'Why aren't you hypnotised then, Moira?'

'Because I'm trained . . . to resist such things,' she gasped.

'Then why haven't you been trained to resist this?'

'I have. I have! But it's hell on earth to always resist. Even a highly trained and sublimated naked angel has to fall sometime . . . Go on!'

'What about Conroy then?'

'Grooty, stop talking . . . please.'

'What about Conroy?' said Groot again, easing off threateningly.

'The Organisation tells me they're very worried about him,' snapped Moira. 'They say he's a particularly dangerous rogue male. They sent me to work on him at the Berlin night club. But I didn't get anywhere. Now please, Grooty . . .'

'One more question. How do you intend to find out who is the Big Brains behind it all?'

'I'm working on it with some success,' gasped Moira writhing frantically. 'Helga told me they were pleased with my work on you and at the transplant operation. I've been invited to meet the head of the entire Organisation at a sauna bath here in Helsinki tomorrow morning, to be briefed for a new important assignment ... But, Grooty, please stop talking now – and hurry ...'

'I want to know what happens.'

'All right, all right, I promise I'll tell you ... Now, Grooty, it's agony, pleeease! Do it, do it, do it!'

Groot relented.

The room echoed with deafening pit noises from Le Mans.

Next door at that moment the Dutch businessman regained consciousness and heard the roar coming through at him. Without a further thought he crashed his head against the wall once more and fell back into another long black silent tunnel.

Two hours later Groot left his hotel and took a taxi to one of the main Helsinki banks with a spool of recorded tape in his pocket. He went in and asked to see the manager. Fifteen minutes later he re-emerged, crunched across the frozen snow of the pavement and took the taxi that was still waiting for him to a large private hospital five miles outside the city.

As he motored up the hospital drive he pretended not to notice the thirty or forty men skulking behind the wide trunks of the pines, conspicuous against the white snow in their long black coats and black trilbies. He could spot CIA men anywhere now.

Inside the main door similarly dressed men maintained for some minutes that nobody by the name of Conroy was known to be in the building. But when enough time had passed for the message to go up that Gilbert Groot, the British journalist, wished to see him, there was a sudden change of heart and he was shown up to a makeshift office in one of the hospital's private wards.

'So you're the world-renowned Mr Groot,' remarked

Conroy sarcastically from behind a temporary desk made out of an operating table. 'Front man and fellow traveller for the Organisation. What brings you to Helsinki?'

'I came for a theatre visit,' said Groot.

'See a good show, didya?'

'I'm not sure. It was a very complicated plot. Medical thriller, interchangeable roles, that sort of thing.'

Conroy's eyes narrowed. 'Did you have a good seat?'

'No, I stood. I was one of the chorus.'

'Pity,' said Conroy slowly, 'that means that you won't leave this building alive.'

'Really?' said Groot gulping, although this was precisely what he had expected.

'Yeah,' said Conroy drawing an automatic pistol from inside his jacket. 'We're just starting to clean up the security shambles that went with that operation. These bald-headed dames from the Organisation are making life difficult.'

The foresight of the pistol had become entangled in the soft lining of Conroy's outsize brown pebble-dash jacket. He struggled to free it as Groot stood in front of the operating table watching him expressionlessly.

After thirty seconds of struggle Conroy had to tear the lining to get the gun out. He swung it to point at Groot with at least two feet of torn crimson lining hanging out of the front of his jacket like the lolling tongue of a bloodhound.

'So you were one of the interlopers, were you, Groot? We found two of my men deeply anaesthetised in an empty room four hours after the operation. And later Rymerson's chief nurse was found drugged in her hotel room. Who were your two friends?'

'That's what I came to ask you,' said Groot, doing his best to toss his words out casually like film heroes he'd seen in his youth at the Bethnal Green Odeon. 'Thought you might know who the fat man was – because I think he was a fellah I met in the Heerstrasse mixed sauna in Berlin.'

Conroy looked hard at Groot. 'You mean he might be one of those connected with the President's kidnapping?'

Groot nodded.

'Would you believe that?' Conroy asked himself quietly and followed up with a half a minute of quietly obscene cursing.

'Helga Mikunov was the chief nurse for the other team,' said Groot. 'Didn't you know that either?'

Conroy's renewed muffled cursing was as good as an affirmative answer. 'Okay, Groot,' said the CIA chief, staring balefully at him, 'whose coat-tails did you come in on? You must be working for the Organisation. Therefore I gotta kill ya.'

'I don't work for it,' said Groot, 'but I've got a girlfriend in it. She has infiltrated it for British Intelligence.'

'Has she? Well, she can kiss you goodbye.'

'Why haven't you infiltrated the Organisation with some of your male Playbabies?' asked Groot innocently.

Conroy's eyes went a deeper shade of bloodshot. He gripped the butt of the pistol so tightly that his hand shook and he had to hold it steady on Groot with both hands.

'It's no good asking the British who kidnapped your President,' said Groot hurriedly trying to mollify Conroy. 'They don't really know yet. But they're working on it . . .'

'If you hadn't come and given yourself up, Groot, you might have lived to tell this story,' said Conroy quietly at the end of a long silence.

'I didn't come to give myself up,' said Groot equally quietly. 'I've come to escort the President home.'

Conroy blinked.

'I've recorded an account of everything I know on tape and deposited it in a local bank. If anything happens to me the bank has instructions to make the contents of the tape known to the world through my literary agent. Interesting story of the transvestite CIA chief who transplanted the President's brain. Enough to discredit the CIA for all time.'

'Nobody will believe it,' said Conroyy.

'Right,' said Groot, 'at first. But people are always saying the President needs his head examining — if that's done it will be proved.'

'Whaddaya want, Groot?' asked Conroy, his gun hand shaking even more violently with frustration. 'Whaddaya asking for?'

'Not much. Just permission to take the President back to freedom in my own way.'

'Why?'

'I'm in this for the money. The story I'll be able to tell when this is over will be worth more if I can escort the President on his triumphant return. It will look better for you too. It won't appear then that you snatched him or tampered with his head.'

'How do I know you won't squeal when you get home?'

'You don't,' said Groot. 'All you know is that if you do me any harm here, the truth will come out straight away. Do it my way and I'll give you my word, for what it's worth, that I won't reveal the truth, while you or the President are in office.'

For a while Conroy's face twisted as if his naked body was being dragged over broken glass. Then his expression changed abruptly and a broad familiar smile churned up his heavy features. Seeing it, Groot was immediately uneasy.

'Tell me exactly what you have in mind, Gil, buddy,' said Conroy laying the pistol on the desk and folding his arms.

Groot pulled up a chair and leaned forward to explain what he wanted.

When the door closed behind him five minutes later, Conroy picked up the phone and called his chief assistant.

'Prepare a contingency plan,' he said, 'to murder every bank manager in Helsinki and burn and ransack the entire contents of their vaults. After that, get Groot!'

In Washington the space in the White House maximum security glass dome had become even more restricted. Five naked-headed girls were snuggled with obvious delight between the men of SAGNASCRAP cramped together around the table.

'. . . the worst part of this crisis has finally passed, genitalmen,' the Vice-President was saying, 'but as yet we are still in no position even to guess what the final outcome will be.' He wondered briefly whether he felt a hand on his knee or whether he was imagining it.

'What's the latest from Moscow?' asked the Defense Secretary trying to ignore the bare-headed girl on his left side who was nudging her generous bosom against his left bicep.

'A strange silence about the whereabouts of the President,' said the Vice-President. He was certain now that fingers were toying with the sharp crease in his trousers along the centre of his right thigh.

'Where's Conroy?' asked the Chairman of the Joint Chiefs of Staff.

'There's a curious silence from his department,' the Vice-President began, trying to brush away the marauding hand without any of the other members noticing.

With a surge of relief he saw one of the colonels waving from outside the dome and holding up a message. The other members of the Group saw him at the same time and jumped up eagerly to retreat from the preying hands of the girls. The Vice-President took the paper and read it quickly.

'It's from Conroy. But it doesn't say where he is exactly.' As he read ahead the Vice-President's face, which had remained set in optimistic lines throughout even the darkest moments of the President's ordeal, suddenly caved in. But almost immediately he managed to spread a delighted grin across it. 'Genitalmen! The President of the United States will reappear safely in the West within the next two hours, Conroy says. He recommends that we tune into all the normal news media to discover where and when. Conroy adds, "I can't say more now. He is safe and well."'

SAGNASCRAP became immediately joyous. As one man it grabbed its five new female members and waltzed them deliriously round the interior of the dome. The glass rapidly steamed up completely and this made it impossible for those outside to see what was happening inside under maximum security.

Chapter Twenty-One

Three thousand flag-waving, hysterically happy young music lovers swayed, chanted and clapped the massed orchestra and its conductor on the platform of the Albert Hall in London. Waves of sentimental emotion rolled and billowed above the heads of the crowd as they called over and over again for the stirring national hymn capable of moving all England to tears.

The Last Night of the Proms was reaching its traditional climax in a heaving conflux of nostalgia, national pride, emotional love of music and well-bred hooliganism. When the clamour of the promenading crowd and the more sedate seated audience reached a deafening roar the conductor acquiesced. He accepted the inevitable – the time had come. The opening bars of Elgar's 'Pomp and Circumstance March Number One' were inaudible beneath the din of the crowd but as the musicians sawed, beat and blasted their way towards the strident, soul-stirring opening of the song, the crowd quietened.

The strings flurried, then the whole orchestra deepened its voice to boom out the opening chords with the power of a million confident earth-removers tearing at the foundations of Everest.

'Land of Hope and Glory,' the crowd sang, flinging a solid roar of sound straining against the roof and walls . . .

> 'Mother of the Free . . .
> How shall we extol thee . . .
> Who are born of thee . . .

Banners and flags waved, mascots were hoisted aloft and three thousand people swayed in the grip of the mystical force of music that seemed to bind their hoarse voices harmoniously and blend their individual spirits into a magnificent unity.

> 'God who made thee mighty . . .
> Make thee mightier yet . .

Suddenly the orchestra stopped playing. The audience careered on like a juggernaut out of control for several seconds. Then the sublime moment disintegrated into a shambles of bewilderment and consternation. The united swaying body became three thousand disturbed individual souls again. Never before had the Last Night audience been cut off in the full flood of this legendary hymn of freedom.

They quietened with curiosity as they saw two additional male figures in evening-dress making their way towards the conductor's rostrum. Complete silence had fallen by the time the conductor turned with a grave face and held up a hand for absolute quiet.

The crowd sensed instinctively that a message of epic proportions was being brought. They prepared themselves at least for the announcement of the death of the highest in the land.

'Ladies and gentlemen.' The words of the conductor dropped leaden into the void. 'It has fallen to me to make an historic announcement to you.'

Six thousand eyes in the audience were riveted on the stand. Some thought the figure of one of the men standing silently to one side in evening-dress looked vaguely familiar. Pin-drop silence reigned in every corner of the vast rotunda of the Albert Hall.

'Tonight,' said the conductor, 'here in this hall, it is our enormous privilege and pleasure to welcome back to freedom the champion and defender of liberty, the leader of the Western world, who has just a few short hours ago emerged from the clutches of Communist tyranny ... Ladies and gentlemen, I give you none other than ... the newly freed President of the United States of America!'

The conductor flung his arm wide towards the President. The great audience was caught fast in a stunned and astonished silence.

'And the man we have to thank for restoring the President to freedom in the Western world, for restoring him to freedom, more precisely, here in this very hall tonight ... none other than that great British journalist, the man who has made it all possible ... Gilbert Groot!'

Groot and the President bowed their heads slightly to the audience in the continuing stunned silence.

Then from high up in the back of the hall a ripple of applause and cheering began. It rolled down from the balconies, echoed back from the promenaders and grew slowly to a mighty roar of welcome and approval. The sound washed back and forth across the hall, mounting gradually to a responsible and representative crescendo of pleasure on behalf of the Free World.

Tears gathered in the eyes of Gilbert Groot and the President as they stood side by side staring straight ahead, their wing collars and white ties quivering under the impact of their emotionally agitated Adam's apples.

Suddenly beneath the sustained roar of the crowd excited strains of music were faintly heard. The orchestra were seen sawing at their instruments animatedly as though spontaneously set in motion by a common nerve running deep within the throng.

The ovation began to subside and the drive of the music from a hundred instruments gained dominance. Suddenly the entire body of the hall exploded joyously once more into the national hymn, which had been interrupted by the arrival of the President.

'LAND ... OF ... HO–OPE ... AND ... GLO–RY
MO–THER ... OF ... THE ... FREE ...'

The tidal waves of inspired vocal praise crashed against the stout iron girders of the roof, threatening to tear it free and send it into orbit.

Tears coursed openly and unashamedly down the faces of the President and Groot and everybody else in the Albert Hall.

'GOD ... WHO ... MADE ... THEE ... MIGHTY ...
MAKE ... THEE ... MIGHTIER ... YET'

Chapter Twenty-Two

The television camera zoomed slowly in for yet another enormous close-up with the relentlessness of an ear-nose-and-throat specialist searching for something malignant. Screens across Britain filled with a square grid of Gilbert Groot's facial flesh on a scale of one inch to the millimetre, bordered by his singed eyebrows to the north and his lower lip in the south. The producer was putting into practice the belief long and widely held in television studios that the nation had both the right and the desire to inspect every last skin blemish of people in the news — especially if they were having to pay a thousand pounds to the money-grasping celebrity to interview him anyway.

'The President and I,' Groot was saying, 'are just good friends. We were close for a time but not any more.'

'I see,' said the interviewer, glancing down desperately at the clipboard of questions he held in his lap off-camera. Then he asked, 'Tell me, Mr Groot, from where did you accompany the President to London?'

'I'm afraid I can't reveal that.'

'Why?'

'A journalist must respect and protect his sources,' said Groot grandly.

'How did you come to be involved in the repatriation of the President? The last the world knew he was in the Russian Embassy in East Berlin and wished to defect.'

'My *sources*,' Groot lingered lovingly on the word, 'tipped me off.'

'What, in your privileged opinion, Mr Groot,' asked the interviewer trying a hopeful touch of sycophancy, 'was responsible for the President's reversal of his earlier decision to defect? What made him change his mind?'

'I think probably his mind was changed for him,' replied Groot. 'I can't put it any clearer than that.'

'By whom?'

'It may become obvious later.'

'I can't press you on this point?'

'No.'

'But clearly he suddenly had the brains to see it was in his best interests to return home in exchange for the First Secretary.'

'Yes, I think that's very well put,' said Groot.

In Moscow a performance of Swan Lake was drawing to a rapturous close in the Bolshoi Theatre. As the audience applauded and cheered and the lithe slender dancers took curtain call after curtain call a group of dark-coated figures hurried through the cold night towards the stage door.

The young, beautiful Undrupuva accepted her third bouquet at the footlights, her smile of delight widening as she began to realise such a reception would go a long way towards establishing her as a prima ballerina.

But suddenly the audience stopped clapping and cheering and a deathly hush fell over the theatre.

Undrupuva looked anxiously out into the sea of white, silent faces but found no clue to the frightening phenomenon. Then she noticed they were staring past her to the back of the stage.

She turned and saw a figure clad in a long black coat and black trilby standing alone at the top of the finale staircase. Her hand flew to her face with a little gasp of horror as she realised it was her father. The hushed fearful expressions of the audience were explained.

He had always disapproved of her career in the ballet.

He opposed such degrading exposure of female limbs. But surely he would not now come publicly to rebuke her and ruin her career?

She watched in terror as Undrupuv descended the staircase in silence and walked to the front of the stage. To her amazement he ignored her entirely. In the pin-drop silence he bent and whispered to the conductor of the orchestra and a microphone was handed up.

'Ladies and gentlemen of Russia,' said Undrupuv, clearing his throat. 'I have come here to the Bolshoi Theatre to make an important announcement.'

The audience shrank in their seats. After the new liberalisation begun a few days ago with the laying of the foundations of a Playbaby Club in Red Square, was a new rigid, cultural volte-face to be announced? Was the Bolshoi to be closed? Was a return to the long dark night of Stalinism about to begin?

'It gives me enormous pleasure to announce that the First Secretary of the Communist Party of the Union of Soviet Socialist Republics who was recently plucked from our midst by imperialist dark forces is tonight returned amongst us.'

Undrupuv turned with right arm outstretched.

As he did so the tall, portly figure of the First Secretary neatly dressed in his long dark coat and pearl-grey flat-topped Homburg appeared dramatically at the top of the staircase.

The dumbfounded audience sat and stared in silence. Then the First Secretary began slowly to descend. The audience would not have been surprised if he had swung out on wires above their heads. As he came down the stairs the First Secretary deliberately removed his gloves. Tucking them under his left arm, he suddenly smote the silence by applauding his audience in the best Communist tradition.

His clapping broke the lock-jaw tension in the auditorium. As one man, the audience burst into a frenzied welcoming ovation. Gradually the deep rumble of two thousand feet being drummed fast upon the floors of the theatre added a deep bass dimension of sound to the hoarse cheering and the palm-reddening applause. The cast of dancers began to join in, clapping wildly. Some, in their excitement, began to jump into little entrechats of childlike delight.

In a room in the Kremlin a meal was being prepared at the express instructions of the First Secretary – a thick Texan Steak, blueberry pie, washed down with Coca-Cola. He'd also expressed a request to listen to records of Elvis Presley's old hits afterwards.

The First Secretary and the KGB Chief stood side by side, wet-cheeked but smiling, engulfed by the deafening ovation.

After ten minutes with the wave of sound showing no sign of abating, the orchestra began to play spontaneously as though bidden by the invisible soul of Russia. The haunting strains of Tchaikovsky's 'Dance of the Swans' somehow stilled the tumult, piercing the very marrow of everyone present. With equal spontaneity the dancers began to move ecstatically around the First Secretary and Undrupuv, leaping and flinging their arms wide in welcome and praise.

The tinkling stream of the music's tender passages flooded and swelled towards their torrential climax and the entire company whirled like a tornado around the stationary black-clad figures.

The audience writhed, stamped and clapped, pushing themselves close to exhaustion, as they had been indoctrinated to do over a lifetime, to welcome back the champion of World Socialism.

'How did the President behave on the journey? What was his reaction to freedom?' The interviewer in London was keeping at his task of interviewing Groot unflaggingly.

'He ate a lot of caviare, drank some vodka and asked for balalaika music to be played on the aircraft's musak system,' said Groot.

'Really? So it would seem his recent experience has influenced his cultural and gastronomic tastes in an unusual way.'

'Yes, I would say so.'

'How interesting, Mr Groot,' said the interviewer, wondering whether they were getting a £1,000-worth of interview out of him. 'Now tell me, the President disappeared again immediately after your joint appearance at the Last Night of the Proms in the Albert Hall tonight. Why was this?'

'He was continuing his journey to Washington accompanied by various security personnel and the American ambassador to London.'

'Why did he come to London rather than go direct to Washington?'

'Knowing what a warm welcome he would receive, I managed to persuade his entourage to let him make his first appearance in the West, here.'

'Really, then your influence with the President must still be enormous.'

'Not really . . . As I said, we're just good friends.'

In another room along the corridor, Groot's literary agent sat poring over a pile of contracts while men queued outside the door, making offers in tens of thousands of pounds for the right to interview Groot on television and write his story themselves under his name in their newspapers. Representatives of the United States TV networks and American newspaper chains took their turn in the international queue.

'Coming to the Organisation, which has been responsible for the world crisis of the past few days,' the interviewer continued earnestly, 'what, Mr Groot, is your impression of the people behind it? Do you think they have ensured a real and lasting peace? . . . What is the devastating Helga Mikunov really like? . . . Is this incredible Russian woman the brains behind the new-style international guerrilla organisation or is there somebody higher? . . . Tell me, Mr Groot, we've all seen pictures of the entire female population of the United States with their heads shaved and pictures, too, of what are popularly called "Helga's Naked Angels" sitting in at high-level political meetings. How do you account for the hypnotic effect of these hairless girls on mature politicians? ... Let me put it this way, Mr Groot, there seems to be many unanswered questions in the historically unprecedented series of events of the past few days. How do you explain these events and your own remarkable part in them? ...'

Groot stumbled wearily from the studio at the end of the interview-in-depth feeling he had thoroughly earned his thousand pounds. He looked in for a quick word with his agent who was shuffling the enormous sheaf of contracts into a neat pile now that the queue had disappeared. Groot promised to contact him in the morning, then made for the front door, the street, and some fresh air.

As he passed through the large reception foyer Groot heard the voice of the late-night news announcer coming from a monitor screen.

'... mysterious but apparently unrelated series of bizarre events has been reported from the Finnish capital of Helsinki ...'

Groot stood rooted to the spot.

'... the managers of Helsinki's five major banks have disappeared and are presumed kidnapped. The vaults and the entire bank premises of all five have been burned and ransacked. The Finnish police admit they are mystified since no money was found to be missing.'

Groot stared at the calm face of the newsreader in disbelief.

'Also two of the world's leading brain surgeons, one American, the other Russian, have been discovered wandering in a forest outside the Finnish capital suffering from total amnesia. Police say they found signs that seemed to indicate the two men had been living together for some time in a remote log cabin twenty miles from Helsinki.'

Groot rubbed a hand over his face to make sure he was awake and not dreaming. As he watched, the newsreader turned aside to accept something off-camera.

'News has just come in,' the newsreader said, looking up from the extra sheet of paper he'd been given, 'of yet another strange happening in Finland tonight. This time a fifty-nine-year-old American man wearing garish women's clothing was arrested after a police chase along the pavements of Helsinki's main street. When arrested the man protested that he was the head of the American Central Intelligence Agency and that he had been chasing a blonde British air hostess he suspected of being connected with the now widely famed Organisation. A spokesman for SAGNASCRAP in Washington said, however, that the case had been investigated and the man had been dismissed as a crank. The United States Government would be making no objection to the continued detention of the man, the spokesman said.'

The newsreader looked up raising one well-bred eyebrow in a silent comment. 'Lastly, Helsinki police were called to a local sauna bath tonight on a complaint that a naked-headed girl resembling the description given by the American was being abducted by a fat man. But detectives found nothing except a blonde wig in the sauna bath. And that, ladies and gentlemen, is the end of tonight's late news . . .'

'What can have happened to Moira?' Groot said half aloud as he continued to stand transfixed in the middle of the foyer. Then he looked round, realising that all the people in the reception area were staring at him. With an effort, he gathered himself and pushed through the glass doors into the cool night air of London.

Then he stopped.

On the far side of the street the unmistakable pebble-dash jackets of six crew-cut men caught his eye. He looked to his right. Fifty yards away on his side of the street six men in long dark overcoats and trilbies were walking towards him. He turned to duck back into the television studios, but before he reached the door a screaming gaggle of girls waving autograph books surrounded him.

Screeching loudly, they tugged and pulled at his hair and clothes as if he were a pop idol.

'Gilbert, Gil—bert, Gil, Gil . . .' they shouted and chanted. 'Give us yer autograph!'

Groot took a book and began to sign, looking nervously across the street at the men in pebble-dash jackets who had stopped bewilderedly in mid-stride. Along the pavement the astonished men in black coats had stopped too, waiting for the female whirlwind around Groot to subside.

Groot signed furiously as the crowd jostled against him. At first he didn't realise he was being manoeuvred round the corner of the building. He signed a few more books, playing for time against the rival mobs of CIA and KGB men.

Then suddenly he realised the crowd of girls was pushing him against a large black car parked at the kerb in the side street. He tried to shove them away but they pressed closer and screamed louder. Press photographers appeared and started taking pictures of this phenomenal new object of teenage adulation.

Groot saw that one of the girls had opened the door of the limousine and he felt himself being pushed helplessly towards it. He clutched at the nearest girl to try to prevent them forching him inside. But in the crush he managed only to catch at her long tresses. The wig came away in his hand and Groot's singed eyebrows shot up in alarm.

The girl's head in reality was naked of all hair.

Her accomplices took advantage of Groot's surprise, threw themselves against him in a concerted rush and knocked him bodily through the open door into the vehicle's back seat. The photographers were still taking flash pictures as it shot away with seven of the girls clambering round him on the seat.

When the limousine was clear of the centre of London and speeding towards the motorway-scarred countryside, the girls, one by one, removed their wigs to reveal shining naked heads.

Groot stared at them round-eyed. And they stared back at him with that glazed hypnotic look that he had noticed before in the eyes of Helga Mikunov and the fat man in the Helsinki operating theatre.

Then one of them took a hypodermic from her handbag and reached towards him . . .

The headlines in the next morning's tabloids were three inches high and printed in thick heavy type. They said simply, 'GROOT GONE!'

Chapter Twenty-Three

Groot didn't become completely unconscious as a result of the injection. Instead he slipped into a soporific daze in which he was fully aware of what was going on about him, but at the same time he was gripped by a total, uncaring lethargy which left his limbs, neck and head feeling numbly leaden.

So he didn't move when the seven naked heads shimmering faintly in the darkness began to arrange themselves closely around him, pressing in from either side on the back seat of the limousine as it sighed along a motorway.

Some of the girls huddled around his knees on the floor and one spread-eagled herself across his lap, snuggling into a relaxed position against his chest. Only his head was left free of this blanket of warm female bodies.

But they did not speak a word or move a single muscle. They simply remained inert against him. He could feel the heat of their bodies through thin clothing. But they retained their uncannily still postures without exception. And he could not get any brain-message to his muscles to move himself.

Groot suddenly felt like an egg beneath the hot, cloying feathers of a broody hen. It was as if his soft-bodied captors were trying with their warmth to hatch him, to draw out from inside the shell that was Gilbert Groot, some newer, fresher, younger being that was at present only a deeply buried yolk.

But his sluggish brain could not drag itself any further towards a conclusion of understanding. He rode as though lifeless on the soft back-seat of the limousine, giving himself up to the invasion of the drug and the cocoon of hatching-box warmth all around him. He didn't notice when they began running through narrower leafed-over lanes in the green heart of pre-motorway England.

Neither did he notice the large white signboard with blue lettering on it announcing The Uncommon Cold Research Station as the limousine swung in through gates in a high wire fence. He didn't notice because at that moment he was seized by a paroxysm of multiple sneezes which racked his body and sent the seven girls tumbling from him in all directions. The car pulled up in an underground garage.

Because he was still sneezing violently he didn't notice them exchanging smiles of triumph as they picked themselves up and readjusted their rumpled clothing. He continued sneezing for the next three minutes as he was hauled from the car and bundled into the building.

'Welcome, Mr Groot.'

The resonant American voice reached the journalist through the misty aftermath of the cataclysmic sneezing bout. The last time he had heard the voice it had been through the steam and raining sweat of the Heerstrasse sauna bath.

'Dr Livingstone, I presume,' said Groot, snuffling loudly.

'No, Froggerty.'

As his streaming eyes cleared, Groot dimly recognised that he had been led into a large, book-lined study. The naked-headed girls withdrew and through Groot's haze, the round, hairless head and sagging jowls of Dr Dagmar Froggerty materialised. Perched on the white-coated shoulders of a Humpty-Dumpty body, the head looked as if it had become severely misshapen during its great fall into the chair behind a leather-topped antique desk.

'I hope you've enjoyed your ride here in my personal

incubator,' said the Humpty-Dumpty head. 'A unique device, I think you'll agree.'

'Judique,' agreed Groot, sitting down in a leather wing-chair by the fire and opening his mouth to sneeze again.

'In certain circumstances that incubator could be very pleasurable — but, of course, not with the sensation-depressant additive you had in your injection. In case you're wondering what I've incubated in you on your way here, I should tell you it is a particularly virulent, fast-acting strain of the uncommon cold virus . . .'

'Bastard,' said Groot, exploding the sneeze.

'. . . that, I suspect, might prove fatal in unfavourable circumstances.'

'Bastard!' said Groot sneezing once more.

'And to help my theory, as an experiment, I shall see to it that you are immersed in just exactly the required kind of unfavourable environment about half an hour from now.' He looked at his watch. 'This establishment, Groot, is where the Uncommon Cold War has been waged. Several lives have been anonymously sacrificed in its top-secret cause and yours will make a dishonourable addition to that roll. Whisky?'

Groot's head cleared, not enough for him to speak but enough for him to stare into the moist oyster-shaped eyes of the fat man. The dark centres were tiny black specks in a mottled sea of white.

'You'd better have the whisky because within the hour you are certain to catch your death of cold.'

On the word 'cold', the dark specks of Froggerty's pupils widened hypnotically to eclipse their surrounding oyster whites. Without taking his eyes from Groot's face, he picked up a small brass bell from the desk-top and rang it. The door behind Groot opened quickly, then closed. Groot buried his face in his handkerchief as another sneeze racked him. When he looked up again, Helga Mikunov stood by the desk. She wore the stark, all-black pants and shirt outfit she'd worn the first time in the Berlin cellar.

'Get Mr Groot a Chivas Regal, Helga,' said Froggerty. 'He seems to have developed a nasty chill. I'll have one too.'

Helga obeyed wordlessly. She moved with the eerie grace of a sleepwalker towards a mahogany sideboard on which decanters stood. Froggerty's eyes, the pupils dilating as large as saucers, never left her.

Groot stopped snuffling and sneezing. He stared hard at the fat man, comprehension dawning dimly through the fog of the sensation-depressant. He saw that Froggerty's lips shone wetly as his gaze followed Helga's extraordinarily long legs across the room.

As she placed the whisky in his hand Groot looked for a second into her dark eyes – and fancied he saw a newly enigmatic flicker of expression there.

'Mr Groot,' said Froggerty, sipping his whisky, 'my apologies but you've got to die now because you are a threat to world peace as I plan it. A threat to my anonymous efforts to save mankind. You know too much about me. Public exposure by you would irreparably damage our cause – and I sense in you a growing antagonism.'

Groot's brow crinkled in puzzlement. 'You don't add up, Froggerty. I don't get you.' He glanced at Helga but she was staring absently into the fire as though she was not listening. 'You trick me into publicising your organisation's work, purely for money. That's all I've done so far. There must be something you're very frightened of. If you are genuinely interested in securing peace, why not come out into the open now and take the credit?'

'Prepare another shot of sensation-depressant. It appears to be wearing off,' said Froggerty quietly over his shoulder.

'You just don't make sense, Froggerty,' said Groot in a louder voice. 'You must be scared.'

Froggerty's oyster eyes narrowed. 'We have good reason to suppose that Moira Smith, who we previously thought to be a reliable operative for us, is in fact an agent of British Intelligence. The security services of this world, Groot, are in themselves uncontrollable wild beasts threatening peace with their every plot. You and Moira Smith have spent much time together . . .' he paused, breathing noisily and his eyes filled with an expression of malicious envy. '. . . in various activities which suggest that you, too, are working against us . . .'

'What have you done with Moira?' asked Groot sharply.

'She has been removed for a new intensive course of hypnosis. She will remember nothing of her life before. She will be a perfect asset then.'

Groot stared hard at the fat scientist. 'I think I'm beginning to see . . . I don't think you're working for world peace at all. Bringing me here proves it. You're no different from the other "rogue males" . . .'

Helga turned round slowly from the drawer in which she was seeking a fresh hypodermic. She stared hard at both of them; then the jowl-creases in Froggerty's face trembled. 'Shut up, Groot.'

'Yeah, that's right. You'd be about fifty-nine or sixty. You're probably twice as dangerous as any of the world leaders your organisation aims to save.'

He heard Helga Mikunov suck in her breath sharply.

'I see it all now,' continued Groot, rising from his chair and staring down into the fat man's face. 'You pushed the world to the brink of destruction to try to concentrate absolute power in your own hands – with your hypnotised floozies sitting in at every major political meeting in the world—'

'Shut up!' snapped Froggerty, pounding the desk with a fat fist. His face and jowls had turned puce.

'. . . you're trying to short-circuit all the democratic processes, and the undemocratic ones as well, come to that.'

'You're wrong, you're wrong!' rasped Froggerty, glancing guiltily at Helga.

'You're doing precisely what you claim, when done by the leaders of the major powers, is a threat to world peace,' said Groot vehemently.

'It's not true,' said Froggerty looking wildly towards Helga for support. But she stared back speechlessly at the scientist.

'You're a *no-sex maniac* of the very worst kind,' said Groot in a low voice. 'An enemy of the world.'

Froggerty stared furiously at Groot, fighting to regain his self-control. When he'd mastered his breathing, he turned to Helga. 'Hear... this... well,' he said slowly, his chest heaving. 'Go to the laboratory and get an *augmented* sensation-depressant. I think Groot is becoming delirious.'

Helga glided obediently from the room, followed every inch of the way by Froggerty's dilated eyes. When the door closed behind her Froggerty turned back to glower at Groot once more.

'You are right, Groot,' he said in a trembling voice, 'but you don't know the whole story. Before you die I will tell you.'

Groot sneezed violently twice, but managed to hold back the third with an enormous effort.

'I worked for three years as the psychiatric adviser to the President of the United States,' said Froggerty. 'I enjoyed many intimate confidences and shared the symptoms of the President's fears. I tried to help him but he scorned me and my methods. He refused to admit the truth about his problem...'

Before Froggerty himself noticed, Groot saw that his fat white hands were beginning to tremble on the desk top. Then Froggerty noticed too. As he looked down at them they began to shake violently and with a muffled cry Froggerty tore open the drawer of his desk. He lifted out a large plate of fresh cream cheese and, ignoring Groot, began scooping it greedily into his mouth. He gulped and swallowed obscenely for several minutes concentrating his whole attention on the task. When at last he turned back to Groot, his hands had stopped shaking.

'Yes, Groot,' he said, in little more than a whisper, 'the President of the United States made the mistake of underestimating my scientific mind. When I analysed his problem and told him of my conclusion — that his personal inadequacy could be a threat to world peace — he flew into a rage and fired me on the spot. He fired me although I was the only man in America who could help him. Not only that,' his eyes flared again and his obese shoulders shook with subdued rage, 'he turned the tables afterwards, attributing his own inadequacies to me in despicable lies and rumours that he spread around Washington.'

Froggerty paused to brush a globule of cream cheese from the corner of his mouth with the back of a fat hand.

'What do you mean, lies?' asked Groot. 'They're probably all true. I should think you stuff yourself with food because it's the only appetite you've got left now . . .'

Froggerty clenched his fat, doughy fists in anger. His fleshy lips drew back from his uneven teeth and black venom seemed to fill his eye-sockets. 'I hated him! Do you hear? I still hate him.' The words came out as if they had been stretched on a rack of torture. 'But I hate you even more, Groot! You disgusting sexual athlete.' Froggerty leaned across the desk towards Groot and spat a flurry of words at him through a fine spray of saliva. 'When the President fired me a year ago I took a trip to Moscow. There I met the incredible Helga Mikunov. Since then I have patiently built up my organisation – to show him who is the Most Powerful Man in the World! Now I'm on the brink of achieving total power! Your death will be contemptibly insignificant . . .'

'Great,' said Groot, 'but it won't change anything. You'll still be totally impotent—'

'Shut up!'

Froggerty rose suddenly from behind his desk as the door opened and Helga Mikunov came in carrying a box of syringes. She stopped and stared from one man to the other, her imperceptibly glazed eyes passing expressionlessly over their faces. In the electric silence Groot's hand snapped forward as he sneezed again – three explosive, window-rattling sneezes that shook his frame to its marrow foundations.

'Helga,' said Froggerty, staring intently into her eyes. 'Hear . . . this . . . well.' He paused and Helga Mikunov seemed to rivet her gaze on the fat man's face. When he spoke again his voice had a hollow, echoing quality. 'Hear . . . this . . . well. Take Groot to Number Three

Refrigeration Incubator. I have set the lock for two hours. Place him inside.'

Helga turned and her eyes fell on Groot. She moved slowly towards him on those long, lazily rhythmical legs. Taking a pair of gleaming aluminium handcuffs from the desk, she snapped them onto his unprotesting wrists and led him away.

Chapter Twenty-Four

The President sat irresolutely behind his Oval Office desk in the White House, gingerly touching the top of his head with the fingers of his right hand.

The large, colour television set facing his desk was carrying newsfilm pictures of his triumphant return home the previous night among hundreds of thousands of naked-headed American women of all ages at Kennedy Airport.

He got up suddenly, crossed to the television set and turned it off. He stood indecisively, gazing round the historic room, furnished with antique American chairs and sofas. His glance fell for a moment on the splash of colour that the stars and stripes of the United States flag provided against the wall behind the desk.

'Damn it,' he said softly and crossed swiftly back to sit down at his desk.

As an afterthought he got up again and went to lock the door leading out of the office. Then he returned to his desk and opened up a large drawer. Inside was an executive mini-refrigerator. He opened it and drew out a frosted bottle of vodka, a small-stemmed glass and a glistening plate of beluga caviare. From a Thermos compartment in the same drawer he extracted a plate of hot golden toast.

He glanced round quickly to see that nobody was peering in the window, then heaped the black sturgeon's eggs in large mounds onto successive toast slices and crammed them into his mouth. He washed it down rapidly with three glasses of the iced white spirit from the frosted bottle.

The burble of American musak pervading all through the east and west wings of the White House came faintly through the closed doors. On noticing it, the President's face twisted with distaste. After a moment he got up again and put on a long-playing record. Soon the musak outside was drowned by the urgent lilt of balalaika music, and his face relaxed into a smile.

The President touched the top of his head again gingerly as he settled back behind his desk to consume further helpings of vodka and caviare at a more leisurely pace. He picked up a pencil and doodled on his yellow pad of legal notepaper. He slowly wrote eight words and began decorating the first letter of each.

The knock at the door startled him. He hastily pushed the bottle, glass and plates back into his desk and brushed crumbs from the blotter and the lapels of his jacket. Straightening his tie, he went and unlocked the door.

Defense Secretary Stanley George hunched his tall thin body into the room, a wan smile invading his ascetic features.

'You wanted to see me, Mr President?' he asked, pretending he hadn't noticed that the door had been unprecedentedly locked. As the President sat down behind his desk the Defense Secretary's sharp eyes noticed three tiny black globules of caviare on the President's yellow note-pad.

'Yes, sit down, Stan. I wanted to ask you something. What do you think about me having a summit meeting with the Soviet First Secretary?'

George's eyebrows moved up towards his white hairline in surprise. 'But you visited Moscow officially for talks with the entire Soviet leadership only nine months ago, Mr President. And after this recent, um, unfortunate affair the international atmosphere is, ahem, to say the least, strained.'

'But we could put it right, Leonid Andreyevich and I.'

George's eyebrows went up again at the unprecedentedly familiar use of the First Secretary's patronymic. His ear, too, could not mistake the Slavonic flavour of the music coming from the newly installed hi-fi.

'I think we got a lot in common,' the President went on. 'I really begin to feel differently about him. He really isn't such a bad guy at all. I feel there's a lot of me in Leonid Andreyevich and perhaps even vice versa.'

He fingered the little hairpiece glued to his scalp. It was itching a lot today. 'Damn this cut,' he said absently.

'I beg your pardon, Mr President?' said the Defense Secretary.

'Nothing,' said the President.

The Defense Secretary began composing in his mind a confidential report in which he would suggest the President might have been deeply affected mentally by his experience, that he showed every sign of having gone soft on Communism.

'What about a trip to Eastern Europe then, Stan?'

'I don't think it's advisable right now.'

'Not even a little trip to Warsaw, Poland – great vodka there – or Bucharest, Romania?' said the President plaintively.

'I wouldn't think so, Mr President. Even if the State Department concurred, which I would doubt, it would take them at least three months to prepare the visit.'

'Goddamn this red tape,' exploded the President. He got up from his desk to go and look morosely out of the window into the Rose Garden.

The Defense Secretary took the opportunity to try to decipher the upside-down doodle on the pad where the caviare lay. He thought he had it once, but he knew he must be wrong. The President of the United States in office could never have written on his desk pad, 'Happiness is not having a country to govern'.

'We're all prisoners of our jobs, Stan,' the President said quietly.

'I beg your pardon, sir,' said George, mentally writing 'recommend full psychiatric analysis' into his forthcoming report.

'Forget it, Stan,' said the President rising abruptly and escorting the Defense Secretary to the door. He patted the thin man on the shoulder and ushered him out.

The President stepped halfway through the door and glared at the Pentagon general sitting in the hall with the black briefcase on his knee. He glared too at the bare-headed girl with the strange eyes who sat beside him. The President's gaze lingered briefly on the smooth contours of her head. Then something else caught his eye.

Further long the corridor, skulking half out of a recess, he glimpsed the man with his defibrillator. The man tried to flash a smile of welcome but the President pretended not to notice. He shuddered, turned back into his office and shut the door quickly.

He leaned his head back against it and closed his eyes. As he stood there his lips moved and one almost inaudible word escaped.

'Helga.'

The curtains at the open windows blew inward in the autumn breeze as though waving mockingly at him. The President opened his eyes, walked to the desk and lifted a telephone. 'I want to make a maximum-security international call from the basement dome in five minutes,' he said. 'And tell Gerrard Conroy's deputy I want to see him,' he added and hung up. The President, suddenly feeling much better, began walking around the office with his hands in his pockets whistling 'Midnight in Moscow'.

Helga Mikunov pushed Groot unceremoniously before her down the flight of stone steps to the experimental chamber containing the laboratory benches, the draught-simulator tunnels, the giant refrigerators and the dehydrating drums. At the foot of the steps she stopped and picked up a clipboard and ballpoint pen. She thrust the pen into one of Groot's manacled hands and motioned him to sign. He read the brief, cyclostyled form: 'I hereby agree to submit myself for experiments in connection with research into the causes of the Uncommon Cold in return for monetary fees and hereby absolve the authorities from any consequences to my health and well-being whatever they may be. Signed . . .'

'Why do I have to sign this?' he asked.

'So there will be no questions asked about your body.' Her dark eyes looking through him were distant and cold.

'Then I'll be damned if I'll sign,' said Groot, snuffling.

'Suit yourself. We will forge it anyway,' she said and pushed him towards the door of the nearest draught-simulator tunnel.

'Undress!' The one-word order rang echoing through the deserted experimental chamber.

Groot looked round inanely at Helga with his charred eyebrows raised. He was on the verge of another series of sneeze explosions.

'Undress!' she repeated tonelessly. She pressed a switch which set the wind moaning eerily in the draught-simulator tunnel.

'What, with handcuffs on?' said Groot incredulously.

Without speaking Helga Mikunov walked up to him and began unbuttoning his shirt. He tried to back away and the shirt ripped. She tugged hard with surprising strength and tore the shirt from his back, tossing it on the floor. Quickly and efficiently with deft fingers she unfastened and removed his trousers, socks, and underpants before tearing his undervest bodily from him to get round the handcuffs.

Thirty seconds later he stood naked and bemused before her. But her gaze went through him as if he was of no substance whatsoever.

'Go now into the tunnel,' she said, lifting an imperious arm to point.

Groot tried to look into the mysterious eyes, now sea-green, that shimmered above magnificently broad, dramatic cheekbones. For a moment he again felt he saw a flicker of some expression significant to him. But it was gone in a moment and the eyes seemed to bore again into his soul with a hot, mesmeric fire.

Feeling light-headed and in the grip of an irresistible and inexplicable force, Groot turned and walked obediently into the icy blast of the draught-simulator tunnel.

Helga watched him go, staring at his broad, naked shoulders. All the time her eyes remained soulless, as bright and hard as diamonds. Without any sign of emotion whatsoever, she reached out and pulled a lever which opened the walk-in refrigerator at the end of the tunnel into which Groot, snuffling and sneezing, would pass to his death.

'Atishoo! Atishoooo! Aaaatiishououo!'

Groot's progress along the tunnel was traced by his echoing sneezes. Helga followed, parallel with him, still staring intently at his shoulders and the back of his neck. And as she continued to watch him the hard expression in her eyes gradually softened.

Groot emerged from the tunnel as though walking in a dream. He began to cross the thirty feet of open floor to the door of the refrigerator vault.

Helga stood still suddenly. Her demeanour had changed and her gaze ran down his smoothly muscled back and over his fuzz-covered thighs with a new urgency. She looked again too at the thick blond hair curling down onto his neck.

Abruptly her wide sensual lips parted and she sucked in a long agitated breath. Her eyes smouldered and her nostrils flared. An electric shudder passed up the entire length of her spine from her coccyx to the nape of her neck.

Groot reached the threshold of the refrigerator, paused, squared his shoulders then stepped in. The door, operated by a photoelectric cell connected to the two-hour clock on the outside wall, began to swing closed behind him.

'GILBERT!'

Helga Mikunov called his name with a desperate intensity. At the same time she dashed with outstretched arms towards the refrigerator. Groot had disappeared into the dark interior and the door was almost closed.

She reached out quickly and got her hands round the thick metal door, halting its smooth hydraulic movement. With a lithe wriggle of her hips she slipped quickly through. The door closed with a final immutable sigh imprisoning them both in the cold gloom that was lit by a single dull red globe in the roof.

Groot, who had not heard her cry, turned in astonishment.

'Helga!'

'Gilbert!'

Their breath steamed in clouds in the cold frosted air.

She moved to him, reached out her arms and pulled him against her.

'I could not resist you, Gilbert,' she said throatily, beginning at once to shiver herself. 'I had to follow you! I ... watched you ... you're so young ... alive ... so virile ... After all those terrible old pot-bellied ...' she shuddered violently. 'You've broken the spell.'

Groot looked at her, astonished for the moment. 'Great!' he said at last, holding back a threatened sneeze. 'But can we possibly survive for two hours in here?'

'Nobody ever has before.'

'We must try.'

'Yes, of course,' she said, her mouth close against his ear. Outside, the hand of the two-hour clock clicked to the one minute mark.

'What can we do to keep warm?' asked Groot.

Helga replied, not in words, but with an urgent single movement of her lower body.

The First Secretary of the Soviet Communist Party sat, chin in hand, staring disconsolately out into Red Square. A half-eaten hamburger swimming in tomato ketchup lay at his elbow and he occasionally sipped absently from a bottle of Coca-Cola with a straw in it. Hot American jazz music blared from a portable radio on the desk.

When the knock came at the door he just had time to scramble the remains of the food and drink into the middle drawer of his desk before the Premier entered.

'You wanted to see me, comrade?'

'Yes. What's your reaction to my having a summit meeting with the American President?'

'Hardly wise, Comrade First Secretary,' replied the Premier uneasily. 'Especially at this sensitive time...'

'But, you know, I have been having second thoughts about him. I think maybe he's not such a bad sort of man. I sense he's got something essentially Russian in his make-up. I feel drawn to try to reconcile our differences through personal contact...'

'I'm afraid after recent events the entire Politburo would be against it, to say nothing of the Central Committee, comrade.'

The First Secretary's brow furrowed in thought.

'Would you mind,' said the Premier hesitantly, 'if I turned this down?' He moved over to the radio and switched off the Voice of America broadcast of Dixieland jazz.

The First Secretary didn't reply. He gently stroked the top of his head with the fingers of his right hand. He began to scratch it then stopped. It was itching furiously today.

'Never mind, comrade,' said the First Secretary with an obviously unhappy sigh. 'I just thought I'd ask your opinion.'

The Premier retreated, beginning, as he went through the door, to compile a secret report in his mind on the oddities of the First Secretary's behaviour following his sojourn in the West. He decided he must call a meeting immediately and start plotting secretly to remove him from office.

As he passed down the corridor the Premier nodded formally but with ill-concealed unease to the girl with a shaven head who was sitting wide-eyed beside the Soviet general who clutched the black attaché case on his lap.

When the door closed the First Secretary got out the hamburger and Coke again and chewed and swigged with renewed relish. When he had finished he brushed the crumbs from his lips with the back of his hand. He stared for a moment at the marble bust of Marx and the portraits of Lenin and Stalin on the wall. Then he shrugged and picked up one of the bank of telephones on his desk. 'I want to make a maximum-security international call from the dome in the Kremlin basement in five minutes' time,' he said firmly. 'And tell Undrupuv I want to see him urgently!'

Dr Dagmar Froggerty, MD PhD, swooshed a thick slice of oatmeal bread through the remains of the half-pound of cream cheese that still clung to the edges of the plate and pushed it in his mouth. As he munched he looked at his watch. 'Where is Helga all this time?' he muttered to himself through the mouthful of food. 'It's almost two hours since they went down.'

He wiped his fleshy lips with a napkin and carefully replaced the napkin, plate and a salt cellar in the drawer in his desk. His jowls continued to vibrate as he finished masticating.

'Helga!'

He opened the door of his study and called into the corridor. When there was no reply he hurried out.

The experimental chamber was deserted as he waddled rapidly down the flight of stone steps but the wind was still moaning eerily in the simulated-draught tunnel. He hurried round it to the Number Three Refrigeration Vault and gazed at the clock beside the door. The hand clicked into the fifty-ninth minute of the second hour as he watched. He looked round and nodded with satisfaction when he saw the rumpled heap of Groot's clothes lying at the entrance to the draught tunnel.

'Helga!'

He called again, but only the echo of his voice came back to him from the three giant drum dehydrators that looked even more like launderette spin driers with their massive, round glass doors standing open. While he waited he leaned into the nearest one and peered at the rows of virus culture slides clamped around the inside of the drum. The drum itself was almost as big as a water-mill wheel and he became engrossed in his inspection of the slides.

Then a sudden click behind him made Froggerty turn quickly. The single hand on the refrigerator clock had moved onto the two hour mark and broken the photoelectric cell circuit. The door of the refrigerator had swung open two feet and Froggerty hurried eagerly towards it.

The shaft of yellow light that fell through the open door into the red dimness of Number Three Refrigeration Vault startled Groot and Helga as they shivered together as one body in a tightly locked embrace.

'You were magnificent, Gilbert,' whispered Helga shudderingly in his ear. Then hearing footsteps outside, she disentangled herself hurriedly from him, pulled on some clothing and went quickly towards the door.

Fingers like bunches of fat white bananas appeared around its side, then Froggerty hauled the refrigerator door back.

'Helga! For God's sake, what happened? Are you all right? Is Groot dead?'

He rushed towards her and began chafing her hands and wrists. But she pushed him back clear of the door.

'Helga!' His voice shook with fury as he saw over her shoulder the shuddering figure of Groot emerging from the dark interior. The naked journalist was blue with cold but palpably alive.

'Hear this, Helga,' he said, quietly, employing his hollow, hypnotic voice, 'hear . . . this. Tell . . . me . . . what . . . happened.'

Helga stared obediently into his oyster eyes. 'I was locked inside too. It was a mistake . . .' Her voice had again taken on the faraway, submissive tone that Groot had noticed earlier in the upstairs study.

'Never mind,' snapped Froggerty. 'We must finish him now. For the sake of world peace.'

He stepped quickly up to one of the laboratory benches and picked up a phial of liquid and a hypodermic. 'You did not obey my orders upstairs, Helga. We must renew his sensation-depressant,' he said, half to himself, jabbing the point of the needle into the phial and drawing up the serum into the hypodermic barrel. He leaned over and pressed a switch at the back of the bench. A motor whirred into life and as he came back towards Helga the drum of the nearest dehydrator began to spin with a quiet hum.

'Hear this, Helga,' he said gazing deep into her eyes. 'Inject Groot and escort him to that dehydrator.'

She took the hypodermic without shifting her eyes from his. Then she turned and went quietly towards the blue, shuddering figure.

Groot watched uncomprehendingly. His shoulders sagged from his great survival effort.

With her back to Froggerty, Helga took Groot's trembling right arm in hers and pulled it onto the hypodermic. She pressed the plunger, held it down, then tossed the empty syringe aside.

Holding the bemused Groot by his left arm, she turned and walked him slowly back towards Froggerty and the door of the dehydrator that stood wide open behind him.

Froggerty watched them come towards him with intent eyes. The black specks of his pupils had widened out to eclipse the oyster whites. Helga Mikunov stared straight ahead as she moved, her head tilted upwards. Her magnificent cheekbones were highlighted with shadows under the directly overhead neon lights. The exhausted Groot moved where he was led in a trancelike daze.

Froggerty stepped aside as they neared him, allowing them a clear passage to the open door of the moving dehydration machine. The drum had gathered speed now to become a rotating blur, and was emitting a high-pitched whine as well as throwing out waves of fierce heat.

As they drew abreast of him, Froggerty noticed with a start that yellow serum was running down the inside of Groot's right forearm and dripping onto the floor.

'Helga, you haven't injected him properly!'

Helga stopped and turned slowly towards Froggerty. Her wide dark eyes locked into the gaze of the scientist.

'Yes, Dr Froggerty,' she said in a sibilant whisper. 'I have injected him wrongly – In fact I have not injected him at all. The needle did not puncture the skin. Groot's right. You're a dangerous *no-sex maniac* of the worst kind.'

The fat man's eyes widened in fear for an instant. Then they narrowed again. 'Hear this, Helga,' he said hollowly. 'You will obey my instructions. Otherwise you endanger the peace and freedom of the world. Inject him now!'

Their eyes remained locked and neither moved. The silence stretched to half a minute. Then Helga suddenly breathed deeply: in response, her breasts heaved to strain tight against the thin stuff of her black shirt.

Froggerty's gaze flickered uneasily downward away from hers for a tenth of a millisecond. In that instant Helga lunged towards him and grabbed his left arm, calling to Groot to grab the other. Groot moved quickly to his other side and grasped his right arm. Together they rushed him struggling towards the open door of the dehydrator. He let out a cry of pain as his knees struck the rim of the door. Without pause they tumbled him over the edge like a soggy sack of refuse. The drum, revolving at one hundred miles per hour, snatched at the ponderous body and sucked it rapidly inside.

A brief screech like the sudden application of a car's brakes on a wet road rang for a moment above the high-pitched whine of the spinning drum.

Then he was gone.

Groot fell back in an exhausted shivering heap on the stone floor. Helga heaved on the heavy door and closed it. She stood back gasping for breath, staring in through the circular window as the drum continued to revolve at high speed.

Dr Dagmar Froggerty, already fast dehydrating along with twenty-five million uncommon cold viruses of a particularly virulent strain, had become nothing more than a white circular blur through the glass.

'Hello. Is that you, Leonid? This is the President of the United States of America ... Great, thank you. How are you, Leonid? ... No, no, this is my call to you ... Oh ... really, you were calling me too? ... Well, it doesn't matter whose call it is now that we're connected. Great to hear you again ...'

The President glanced nervously over his shoulder although he was completely alone in the maximum security dome where SAGNASCRAP had conducted its historic meetings. Even the uniformed colonels on duty outside were standing with their backs to the glass. A silent dog-whistle, relic of Conroy's reign, was mounted on the music-stand at his elbow. At the President's insistence, the agent working it was standing outside, pumping his bellows, and a rubber tube leading to the stand had been pushed through a sealed hole drilled in the glass.

'Look, Leonid, I've been thinking. I think you're a pretty level guy. I've been wrong about you. And I wonder whether you feel the same way as I do after our recent experience ... I sum it up this way, Leonid, if you agree.' The President paused and read from the top sheet of his yellow note-pad. '"Happiness," I've come to believe Leonid, "is not having a country to govern." How does that grab you? ... You agree? Say, that's great ... Sure you can call me Squeaky. But, hey, wait a minute! How did you know that? I never told anybody that ... You don't know, it just kind of popped into your head? Strange ...

'Look, things are not good, Leonid. My country is full of crazy, shaven-headed women. You've got a humiliating Playbaby Club in Red Square, right? ... So look I got an idea. You and I belong together, don't we? I don't know why I say that but we got something in common. I feel it very strongly ... You feel it too? That's great, Leonid ...' The President grinned delightedly.

'Look this is my idea, Leon, can you get Undrupuv to get hold of Helga? ... You had exactly the same idea? Great! Right. I've talked to Conroy's deputy. He advises me the best place would be Vila ... Where is that? That's a capitalist tax-haven island in the New Hebrides in the Pacific ... right ... Now look, you get Undrupuv to organise Helga. That would be great. And look, to finance us, I got another great idea ... Joint memoirs ... Yeah, joint memoirs, our joint autobiography ... No, hell, I can't write either, but I thought we'd get Conroy's deputy to get us this journalist fellow Groot to ghost them for us . . . Right, there's no tax at all on Vila . . . the book would be a worldwide bestseller for sure . . . enough money to fund us for the rest of our lives . . . Yeah, I think we got a great and peaceful future together . . . Okay, look, Leonid Andreyevich, I'm very glad you love the idea . . . And I guess I will be able to get some duck-shooting there, huh? Hey, what am I saying? I've never shot duck in my life . . . What's that? No, I don't know if there's a ten-pin bowling alley . . . but we can build one. I didn't know they played that in Moscow . . . But don't forget one thing above all other, huh? . . . The caviare and vodka, of course, Leonid . . . Bring lots – sure, at least a dozen crates . . . You want what? What? . . . A gross of Cokes and hamburgers? . . . I'll get ya a shipful . . . Okay, Leon, whatever you say, baby . . . Seeya in Vila. 'Bye Leo.'

In the book-lined study of the Uncommon Cold Research Station in Berkshire, England, Gilbert Groot huddled shivering by the roaring fire wrapped in a blanket. He sipped a tumbler of hot milk laced strongly with whisky. Helga Mikunov, also wrapped in a blanket, sipped a similar glass of hot milk and whisky on the other side of the hearth.

When his shivering quietened enough Groot pulled a typewriter towards him on the low coffee-table and inserted a blank sheet of paper. He looked at his watch.

'I'll just catch the last edition of the Fleet Street papers,' he said.

Helga Mikunov smiled a smile of serene indulgence in his direction as he began to clatter the keys of the typewriter.

'Tonight I can reveal the truth behind the world-shattering events of the past few days,' he began, typing rapidly with two fingers, 'From the unlikely setting of the Uncommon Cold Research Station in the heart of rural Berkshire, a fiendish, crazed, psychiatric sexologist planned to gather into his hands more power than any other man in history. But with the assistance of his chief assistant, the legendary beauty Helga Mikunov, I managed against all the odds . . .'

The simultaneous ringing of two phones, one on the desk, the other on the coffee-table, interrupted his flow of prose. He picked up the receiver nearest him while Helga answered the other.

'The Kremlin, Undrupuv for you,' said Groot, holding the receiver towards Helga.

'The White House – for you,' said Helga, handing her receiver to him.

They spoke briefly into their respective telephones. Then they hung up simultaneously and turned to one another.

'Have you ever heard of Vila?' they both asked in unison.

Chapter Twenty-Five

Gilbert Groot sat in the shade of the veranda in his shirt sleeves tapping out the last of an historic series of world scoops that would ensure him a permanent place on the roll of honour when the definitive history of international journalism came to be written.

He paused to listen to the voice of a BBC World Service news announcer coming from a short-wave radio in the cool, richly furnished interior of the rented house ... 'still no news of the whereabouts either of the American President or the Soviet Communist Party's First Secretary. Both disappeared again yesterday only two days after being repatriated from the clutches of a new-style guerrilla organisation which pushed the world to the brink of war ...'

Groot looked towards the table in the tree-shaded garden where the President and the First Secretary sat relaxedly sipping iced vodka and Coca-Cola respectively. They were smiling warmly at each other as they talked and read to each other from brochures about Vila, their new home. From time to time, snatches of their conversation drifted to Groot across the shadow-dappled grass.

'We're well out of it all here, Leon,' the President was saying, 'one thousand four hundred miles from Sydney, Australia, eleven thousand miles from Great Britain, five hundred miles from Fiji – and only three thousand people living here ... and when we get these memoirs done, no income tax, no profits tax, no capital gains tax, no death duties...'

Groot heard the First Secretary laugh. He watched as they leaned towards each other and shook hands warmly for the twentieth time congratulating themselves on the wisdom of their action.

Groot pulled the cable form out of his typewriter. As he read it over to himself he realised belatedly that his inbred gossip-column style still had a tendency to swamp whatever subject he was writing about.

'East–West Leaders "Elope" to Secret Hideaway – by Gilbert Groot,' he had written. 'America's President and the Soviet Communist Party First Secretary, I can reveal, are sipping iced drinks together today at a luxury secret home somewhere in the tropics. In the drowsy, sundrenched garden, they often clasp one another warmly by the hand. Having spent several hours with them as their private guest, I can exclusively predict they will remain something more than "just good friends" for a long time to come... They flew secretly to this location – which I'm sworn not to reveal – from their respective homes in Moscow and Washington and in some ways they are the world's most unlikely runaway twosome. Even they cannot at present offer a satisfactory explanation for the sudden, overwhelming sense of friendship they feel. If you ask them what they see in one another, they simply scratch their heads and smile mysteriously. They have invited me to ghost a book of their joint memoirs which is bound to become a worldwide bestseller... These full and frank revelations will show dramatically that even sworn enemies can overcome their hostility to one another – if they are given the right opportunity to change their minds...'

Groot glanced up as the shadow of the President fell across the typewriter.

'You're sure everything's all right with Helga?' the President asked, his face clouded with anxiety.

'Yes, quite sure,' said Groot. 'She had to stay behind at the airport because she was having a bit of difficulty at the customs. She urged me to take a taxi ahead of her so you wouldn't worry. I shouldn't tell you, Mr President, but it's probably the gifts she's got for you both.'

'Really?' said the President, looking pleased. He glanced furtively over his shoulder at the First Secretary to make sure he could not hear. 'Who do you think she's gonna choose outta the two of us, Gil?'

'I've really no idea,' replied Groot innocently.

'Okay, forget I asked.' The President patted Groot's shoulder and turned to go back to the table in the garden. Then he stopped. 'Oh, Gil, you know you can drop that Mr President stuff now if you like. We've both resigned. We sent telegrams an hour ago.'

'If you don't mind, Mr President, I'll stick to the old form – at least until we've done the memoirs. It seems right and dignified somehow.'

'Okay,' said the President genially and went back towards the garden with a wave. On the grass, he stopped and turned back once more. 'He's a great guy this Leonid, you know, Gil. I like him a helluva lot.' He paused, searching for some clearer expression of his feelings. 'Above all, I like his brain.'

A swirl of dust moved along the road momentarily blotting out the distant view of the sparkling blue sea.

'Looks like a taxi coming,' called Groot.

The President and the First Secretary stood up and shaded their eyes. The taxi turned through the avenue of palm trees into the drive and came slowly up to the front of the house. When it stopped the driver got out and opened the passenger door.

After a slight delay, Helga Mikunov stepped out.

She wore figure-hugging white silk sheath pants, a white silk shirt stretched tight over her proud breasts and plunging coolly open to her waist in a narrow revealing V. Beneath a large sun-hat she shaded her eyes to gaze round the garden. When she spotted the two former world leaders on the lawn she waved, then started towards them, her long, silk-clad legs flashing in the tropical sunshine.

From a white-gloved hand she dangled two small parcels on coloured string.

The President and the First Secretary watched transfixed. They were standing in the shade of the trees waiting with bated breath as she swayed towards them.

Unconsciously they moved a foot or two further apart so that they would be in no doubt upon which of them she was bestowing her final choice.

Her sensual lips were parted in a wide smile of pleasure as she drew near and the President felt his chest constrict so tightly that he almost choked. Beside him, the First Secretary was clenching and unclenching his large peasant hands convulsively.

Helga walked right up to them, then stopped. She put the gifts on the table and held out both her white-gloved hands to them simultaneously, her right to the President, her left to the First Secretary.

'How lovely to see you both,' she said huskily, holding both their hands with an equal pressure.

They grinned fixedly back at her, caught fast in an agony of suspense. Still smiling, she stepped forward and kissed them lightly in turn upon the cheek – in both instances, small, chaste kisses of sisterly affection.

'I have presents for you both,' she said, turning to pick up the gifts.

They eagerly tore off the wrappings then blushed with embarrassment. She smiled fondly at the sight of the two ex-Superpower leaders clutching the little silver nymphette statues in their hands. Both ornaments rejoiced significantly in luxuriant manes of normal, ultra-feminine hair.

'You're both better now,' she said softly. 'I'm very pleased with you.'

They smiled shyly and nodded. Then, still watching her face expectantly, they put their presents aside.

'Are you going to stay with us, Helga?' asked the President in a tense voice.

Helga looked steadily at both of them for a long moment. Then she shook her head slowly, a sad smile turning down the corners of her mouth. 'I'm sorry. I was grievously deceived by the previous leader of the

Organisation. But I have learned much. As its new leader I must continue to strive to achieve its high aims of peace and freedom for all mankind...' She paused and looked at her watch. 'My work unfortunately is not yet finished. Our modern angels of mercy must continue to take their place in the world's highest counsels... It will not be easy. They need leadership and supervision.'

Groot, who had stepped down from the veranda, hovered uncertainly a few yards away on the edge of the lawn, watching and listening carefully. His face, too, betrayed signs of an anxious curiosity. On catching sight of him, Helga hurried to his side and gazed for a moment into his bespectacled eyes.

'You know, Gilbert,' she whispered, 'if my life were my own, it would be you... You are incredible... *You* are truly *numero uno*...' She took both his hands in hers for a brief moment. 'But I can't stay... So I shall ask Moira to come here soon...'

She turned on her heel and walked back to face the two ex-world leaders. Simultaneously the anguished eyes of the President and the First Secretary searched her face for signs that she might be about to change her decision.

'Why must you go?' asked the President.

'What other work must you do?' asked the First Secretary.

Helga looked quickly at her wristwatch. 'I'm sorry, I must leave you now. My plane departs in thirty minutes.'

'But where are you going?' The President and the First Secretary blurted out the tortured question in unison.

She had started to walk away without answering and they stared after her with deeply hurt expressions in their eyes. Then, seeming to sense their feelings, she stopped and looked back at them over her shoulder. For a moment the faintest of smiles played across her face.

'I face my biggest challenge of all now, gentlemen,' she said huskily.

'What? What is it? Where?' they demanded breathlessly.

Her smile became enigmatic. 'I'm going to China.'